As Garrick walked toward her, that perfect smile on his handsome face, she couldn't be stern with him. Not with her heart fluttering like a baby bird trying to fly for the first time.

Garrick reached her in seconds. If she didn't know better, she'd think he was one fine-looking cowboy. Fine-looking, yes. Cowboy, definitely no. During his short stay at Four Stones, he'd shown very little interest in ranch life.

"Good morning, Rosamond. You're the picture of beauty, as always."

She smiled. "You're not so bad yourself, cowboy."

He doffed that silly white Stetson she'd forced him to accept and gave her a sweeping bow. "My lady, at your service. Do you have steers to rope? Calves to brand? Cows to milk? I am yours to command."

His offer, delivered in the English accent she was beginning to love, brought laughter from the children nearby. At a glance, she could see they were entirely too interested in her conversation with Garrick.

"No branding today, but you can help me round up these mavericks so we can get their three-legged race started."

"I can do that." He studied the children almost like a schoolmaster, giving her heart another lurch. Where had that thought come from?

Florida author and college professor **Louise M. Gouge**
writes historical fiction for Harlequin's Love Inspired
Historical series. In addition to other awards, she has
received the prestigious Inspirational Readers' Choice
and the Laurel Wreath Awards. When she isn't writing
or teaching her classes, she and her husband, David,
enjoy visiting historical sites and museums. Please visit
her website at blog.louisemgouge.com.

Books by Louise M. Gouge

Love Inspired Historical

Four Stones Ranch

Cowboy to the Rescue
Cowboy Seeks a Bride
Cowgirl for Keeps

Ladies in Waiting

A Proper Companion
A Suitable Wife
A Lady of Quality

Love Thine Enemy
The Captain's Lady
At the Captain's Command

Visit the Author Profile page at Harlequin.com for more titles

LOUISE M. GOUGE

Cowgirl for Keeps

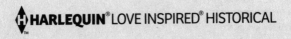

HARLEQUIN® LOVE INSPIRED® HISTORICAL

PLEASE RECYCLE · THIS PRODUCT IS RECYCLABLE ·

Recycling programs
for this product may
not exist in your area.

™ LOVE INSPIRED BOOKS

ISBN-13: 978-0-373-28319-4

Cowgirl for Keeps

www.Harlequin.com

Printed in U.S.A.

Delight thyself also in the Lord,
and He shall give thee the desires of thine heart.
—*Psalms* 37:4

This book is dedicated to the intrepid pioneers who settled the San Luis Valley of Colorado in the mid- to late 1800s. They could not have found a more beautiful place to make their homes than in this vast 7500-foot-high valley situated between the majestic Sangre de Cristo and San Juan Mountain ranges. It has been many years since I lived in the San Luis Valley, so my thanks go to Pam Williams of Hooper, Colorado, for her extensive on-site research on my behalf. With their permission, I named two of my characters after her and her husband, Charlie. These dear old friends are every bit as kind and wise as their namesakes. I also want to thank my dear husband of fifty years, David Gouge, for his loving support as I pursue my dream of writing love stories to honor the Lord.

Chapter One

Denver, Colorado
May 1883

"I tell you, Percy, my uncle's American enterprise will be a disaster. Look at these ragtag masses." Garrick Wakefield waved a dismissive hand toward the crowds milling about the Denver train station. His gesture stirred up the stench of burning coal and unwashed bodies. "It's far worse than I expected."

Most travelers on the platform beneath them were clearly lower class. Unkempt children dashed about with no parental restraint. Cowboys—he shuddered at the term—wore guns strapped to their dusty, wrinkled trousers. Beggars sat against the depot's brick walls, their hands lifted in supplication to all passersby. In grating American accents, hawkers advertised their wares. How Garrick longed for a pastoral English countryside.

"Tut, tut, old man. It's not so bad." Percy, ever the optimist, could afford to overlook the chaos. A cousin from Garrick's mother's family, with an unentailed inheritance to spend as he wished, Percy didn't face a future dependent upon another man's whimsy. "I find this country delightful."

"Indeed? How so?" Garrick spied a mother on the lower platform struggling with tattered baggage and several children. Compassion welled up inside him. Where was the woman's husband? If he could get through the tangled crowd, he'd offer to help. Why didn't one of those cowboys or another closer man lend a hand? Their neglect validated Garrick's disdain for the lot of them. If she came closer, he'd step down and offer assistance.

"Look at the beautiful scenery." Percy indicated the mountains to the west. "Every bit as majestic as the Scottish Highlands, what?" His eyes brightened. "Can you not feel the call to climb them?"

"I'll grant you that. But remember the endless rivers and plains we crossed to get here." At least they'd traveled by train, not in oxen-drawn covered wagons such as those they'd passed along the way. "Too much wasteland."

A conductor called "All aboard," and the crowd moved toward the train's open doors, where uniformed porters assisted passengers up the steps. A quick glance down the length of the platform assured Garrick that his and Percy's valets were seeing to their trunks.

"These Americans have no manners, no refinement. If Uncle could see them, he'd change his mind about this business venture." After a lifetime of prejudice against all things American, Lord Westbourne had met one single gentleman rancher and revised his opinion of the entire country. He'd sent Garrick to build a hotel, not in Boston or New York or even this growing city of Denver, but in some village in southern Colorado, barely a smudge on the map.

"Come now. Not all Americans are the same." Percy

elbowed Garrick and nodded toward two ladies rising from their seats on the lower platform.

After taking a few steps, the stylishly dressed young misses turned to glance toward Garrick and Percy before moving toward the train. Something struck Garrick's midsection, and he looked down to see if Percy had hit him. No, the shock was entirely internal and caused by the exquisite girl in the lavender traveling suit and matching hat. Her stunningly beautiful countenance bespoke an English heritage: a porcelain complexion framed by shiny dark brown hair upswept in an attractive coiffure. Her elegant posture and carriage suggested she might very well be used to gracing London's finest drawing rooms. If propriety didn't prohibit his addressing her, he'd step forward straightaway and introduce himself.

"Did you see her?" Percy sounded breathless. "Have you ever seen a more beautiful lady? Why, a man could be tempted to propose on the spot based upon her looks alone."

Garrick huffed out a sigh. Of course Percy was joking, but with fortune enough to last beyond a lifetime, he could well afford to consider marriage. Conversely, Garrick had lost all such expectations at the age of nineteen when his childless widowed uncle had remarried. His young bride had borne him three healthy sons in his old age. Yet hadn't Garrick himself encouraged Uncle to remarry in his loneliness? That was as it should be.

However, at the age of twenty-five, instead of anticipating an inheritance of title, wealth and lands, Garrick had been forced to revise his expectations and work for his living. He wouldn't mind so much if he didn't also have to provide for Helena's dowry. His younger sister must make a good match even if Garrick never could.

"Yes, she's quite lovely." A melancholy twinge stung inside his chest. Though it would be ill-advised, Percy could pursue the young beauty if he liked. Garrick could only admire her from afar. Or he could redirect his cousin's attention. "Her companion is rather pleasant looking. Perhaps her ginger hair denotes an Irish heritage."

"It's the redhead I admire, cousin." Percy laughed in his merry way. "As it appears we'll be on the same train, it's a shame we've no one to introduce us. What a jolly chat we could have with them as we travel."

Profound relief flooded Garrick's chest. Which was ridiculous, of course. Even though they fancied different girls, as Percy said, they had no proper way to meet them. Nor would it be wise to do so.

A piercing whistle cut short his thoughts as a westbound train approached on the second track. Garrick glanced toward it and saw a small child, one belonging to the harried young mother, toddle after a red ball between the tracks. Did no one closer see? Driven by horror, Garrick plunged down the steps and through the crowd, using his walking cane to move people aside. Others now saw the danger and cried out.

Garrick dashed onto the track and snatched the child back moments before the great black engine chugged into the station, steam blasting from its undercarriage. He restored the toddler to his hysterical mother. Beside her, a teary-eyed lad of perhaps fourteen years held a small girl.

"Thank you, sir. I didn't see Jack wander off." He stuck out a grimy hand. "I'm Adam Starling."

"How do you do, Adam?" Moved more than he cared to admit, Garrick shook the lad's hand. Clearly he endeavored to be the man of the family. Garrick knew very well the problems faced by an eldest son. As others congratulated him, he brushed past them. His train would depart momentarily, and he must drag Percy from his stupor induced by watching the scene. Poor chap. He always hesitated in times of crisis. Perhaps on this trip he'd learn to be a bit more aggressive.

"We should board." Garrick nudged his cousin's arm.

"I say, old man, brilliantly done." Percy walked beside him toward the first-class coach. "Nothing short of heroic."

"Nonsense." Garrick hated such praise. If he were a true hero, he'd have saved another Jack five years ago. The hapless village boy had sunk beneath the black surface of Uncle's lake before Garrick could reach him. His lifeless body was found in a marsh days later and returned to his widowed mother. If only Garrick could have reached him.

Remorse wouldn't restore life to that Jack, but it did spur him to help the less fortunate whenever possible. Besides, if he craved admiration for today's actions, it was from the beautiful young lady in lavender, who'd boarded the train before he even noticed the child's dire circumstances. Too bad she hadn't observed the drama.

A foolish thought, but a momentary diversion from the unwelcome duties that lay ahead. *Lord, help me* had been his cry to the Almighty since losing all of his expectations, and would continue to be until his dying day.

Rosamond Northam waited until she and Beryl Eberly sat down in the first-class coach before venting her indignation. Even when she did, the lessons learned at Boston's Fairfield Young Ladies' Academy didn't fail her.

"Gracious, what an arrogant man." She spoke in a soft tone, holding back harsher words she'd have used three years ago. Being back home in Colorado, back among her own people, would challenge every lesson she'd learned, especially when a foreigner—an Englishman at that—criticized her beloved homeland, particularly the state of Colorado.

"His friend seemed pleasant enough." Beryl spoke wistfully and stared out the window as if searching for the men. "Dignified, too."

"Don't look for them." Rosamond gently patted Beryl's hand, her heart twisting with concern.

"I wonder if they'll be on this train." Beryl glanced over her shoulder and gasped softly. "They're sitting back there on the other side. Do you suppose we could meet them?"

"Shh!" Rosamond sent her a scolding frown. "No, we can't meet them. Why would you want to? If anything, I'd like to show the dark-haired man just how *unrefined* we can be, as in behaving in our old cowgirl ways, talking loudly with improper grammar." She smothered an undignified giggle and risked a quick look their way. My, the dark-haired man was handsome to a fault. Too bad good manners didn't accompany that well-formed face and physique. "But someone else in this coach may be traveling to Esperanza. Our school's reputation would be ruined before we even build it if we teachers behave in an unseemly fashion."

Beryl's face lit briefly with humor. "That dandy could use a comeuppance, but I wouldn't wish to offend his friend." She settled back in the leather seat and gazed out the window again.

Rosamond's heart ached for Beryl. The middle child in a family of five girls, she'd been every bit a cowgirl like the rest of them until she had been shot during a bank robbery and almost died. Rosamond and the five

Eberly girls had grown up riding, shooting, branding—anything a cowboy did. But Rosamond's family had three grown sons and a passel of hired hands to tend to the many duties around Four Stones Ranch, so her parents agreed to her dream to build a high school for Esperanza. With the Lord's blessing, they could construct the school this summer and open it in September. Rosamond hoped Beryl's parents would let her teach rather than return her to ranching.

A well-dressed older couple took the two seats facing the girls. On the trip across the country, other such couples and matrons had offered themselves as chaperones, and these two did the same, engaging Rosamond and Beryl in conversation and keeping at bay undesirable men. The lady smelled of rosewater just like Mother, and the gentleman of cherry tobacco like Father. What pleasant reminders of home. Upon the couple's arrival, Rosamond saw Beryl relax a little. Perhaps her interest in meeting the young man was generated by a desire to feel safe. Rosamond could find no fault in that. Maybe the Lord would make a way for Beryl to meet the nicer Englishman, hopefully without his arrogant friend nearby to crush her spirits.

For her own part, at twenty-one, she'd given up on romance. None of the eligible men she'd met in Boston had found her personal ambitions compatible with their need for a docile Society wife. Nor did she wish to assume the many responsibilities of a rancher's wife. Without doubt, God called her to educate the youth of Esperanza; therefore, she'd be a spinster.

The train chugged out of the station and rumbled southward along the Front Range of the Rocky Mountains, where the morning sun illuminated snowy peaks. Rosamond drank in the beloved sights of her home state.

Later they passed Pikes Peak, and in time her beloved Sangre de Cristo Range came into view. Her heart skipped. She would arrive home in just one more day.

After a night in a Walsenburg hotel, Rosamond and Beryl boarded the westbound train for their last day of travel. Rosamond sat on the aisle in the middle of the car and whispered to Beryl. "Don't look now, but those sissified Englishmen boarded after us." She nodded toward the closed window. "You can see their reflections."

Beryl's face brightened for the first time since they'd awakened that morning. The closer they traveled toward home, the bleaker her mood. Too bad a handsome foreigner was the one to cheer her. To Rosamond's dismay, her friend did turn. And look. And smile!

"Tst!" Rosamond kept her voice low. "Don't do that. Remember our lessons in deportment. It just isn't done."

"I know." Beryl sighed. "He started to tip his hat, but his friend stopped him."

"What?" Rosamond glanced back at the other man. He tilted his head, and surprise crossed his well-formed countenance. He seemed about to smile. With a haughty sniff and lift of her chin, she faced the front. That snob kept his friend from showing a common courtesy to a tender soul like Beryl and then attempted to flirt with *her*. The very idea!

The train moved forward, and Rosamond's heart skipped. They'd be home by midafternoon.

"Let's talk about our plans." She must divert Beryl's attention from the Englishmen. Although they'd exhausted just about every subject during their long trip, she never tired of her favorite one. "I'm thankful Father's already approved the building of the school, but I hope he'll let me supervise its construction."

"Aren't four classrooms too many?" Beryl chewed her lip, and Rosamond reminded her with a quick shake of her head to stop that bad habit. "With only the two of us teaching…"

"I'd really like more rooms, but I think four is a good start." Rosamond's heart raced. Soon she'd put her ideas to work. "We'll need to hire more teachers before you know it. Maybe we should build two stories from the outset."

Beryl nodded absently. From the way she kept turning her head to the side, Rosamond knew she wanted to look back at the blond man. If propriety didn't dictate otherwise, she'd have made sure her friend met him before the train reached Esperanza simply to annoy his companion. She quickly dismissed the thought. She'd put aside such spitefulness seven years ago when she'd become a Christian. How could she ask the Lord to bless her endeavors when her behavior didn't show His love to others? Even to rude Englishmen.

The train began to build up speed for the ascent to La Veta Pass. Rosamond always found this part of the trip exhilarating. Soon they'd be in the midst of the Sangre de Cristos. As a token of promise, fresh, crisp air seeped into the car beneath its front door and around the windows. She inhaled a long, satisfying breath and smiled in anticipation of seeing her dreams come true.

The moment the train began to accelerate, however, it slowed to a halt, the wheels squealing in protest against the iron rails.

"Wake up, Abel." A woman of perhaps thirty years, seated up front and facing the rest of the car, shook her sleeping husband. "Something's wrong." Abel slept on, clearly unconcerned, his head resting back against the front wall, arms crossed, legs stretched out and a wide-brimmed hat pulled over his face.

Beryl grasped Rosamond's arm. "Why are we stopping?"

"Shh. There, there." She patted Beryl's hand. "I'm sure it's fine. Probably something on the tracks. The men will see to it." *Lord, please let it be something as simple as that.*

Instead, gunshots erupted by the engine. Gasping, Beryl seized Rosamond's forearm in a vise grip. The coach's front door burst open, and three armed men rushed in. Dressed in rough coats and dusty trousers, with bandannas over the lower halves of their faces, they waved pistols. Outside, other men on horseback held the engineer and fireman at gunpoint. Rosamond couldn't tell how many were in the gang. She prayed no one would be injured, especially Beryl. She'd almost died in that bank robbery. Indeed, her confidence and fearlessness died that day.

"Hand over your money and gold." The leader jammed the barrel of his gun under the nose of an old man. "Gimme your valuables."

The poor man shook too violently to obey, so the outlaw shoved him down on the seat and dug into his victim's coat pocket, removing a wad of cash secured in a monogrammed money clip.

Another outlaw held out a brown canvas sack as if taking up a church offering. The third man helped himself to the sleeping man's wallet and the wife's wedding band and moved down the aisle.

At the front of the car, the sleeping husband awoke and stealthily rose up, tall and broad-shouldered, behind the last outlaw, gun in hand. Rosamond couldn't let him fight these outlaws alone. She pried Beryl's hands from her arm and bent down to her tapestry satchel. If she was careful, the outlaws would think she was retrieving valuables. Instead, she wrapped her hand around the handle of her Colt .45 revolver and tucked it into the folds of her skirt. She'd made sure it was loaded before they left the Walsenburg hotel this morning. Now, should she shoot the gun from the closest outlaw's hand or wait to see what the man up front did? With Beryl shaking and terrified, Rosamond couldn't decide.

"I say, what a thrilling adventure. A real Wild West holdup, what?" The dark-haired Englishman grinned as the outlaws came closer. "Did you plan it for our amusement?"

Rosamond watched him grip his ebony cane close to his side. With his other hand, he reached into his black frock coat, pulled out an engraved gold watch and swung it on its fob. "Do let me play. Come along, gentlemen, and take the pretty timepiece." Was he crazy or incredibly brave?

"Pip, pip, old man, such a lark." The blond Englishman laughed, but like his friend, his posture indicated he was ready for a fight. Rosamond's opinion of both men rose several notches. Dandies they were. Sissies they were not.

"What have we here?" The outlaw leader bent down and leered into Rosamond's face, his whiskey breath causing her to recoil in disgust. "A couple of pretty misses. Say, boys, what say we take them along—"

Crack! A flash of black and gold whizzed past her face as the dark-haired Englishman's cane slammed down on the outlaw's gun hand, knocking his weapon to the floor. An upward thrust of the cane bloodied the man's nose, and a third downward strike on his head sent him sprawling into the aisle. The Englishman placed one foot in the center of the man's back and held him in place.

"Easy does it." Up front, the tall man held his cocked gun at the head of the third outlaw, who dropped his revolver.

The second outlaw released the brown bag and raised his gun to shoot the Englishman. Rosamond stood and aimed her cocked Colt at his ugly face. "I wouldn't do that if I were you."

With a sneer, the outlaw turned his gun toward her, but the blond man used his cane to strike a hard blow to his forearm. Like his friend, he finished the job with two more whacks to the face and head.

The eight male passengers ordered the outlaws to the front seats and stood watch, weapons at the ready. The six ladies redistributed the valuables to their rightful owners.

"I'll check outside." The tall man exited cautiously. Several shots were fired. Then quiet came over the scene.

Soon the fireman, sooty from head to toe from his job of stoking the engine with coal, entered the coach. "Howdy, folks. I see y'all have these three taken care of. The rest of the gang lit out fast when that lawman came out. No harm's been done except to the train's schedule. We'll make it up on the down side of the pass, so y'all be sure to hang on tight." His levity stirred camaraderie amongst the travelers, strangers before, but momentarily friends. "That there lawman'll round up these three shortly and keep 'em in the freight car till we get to Alamosa."

So the tall passenger was a lawman. Maybe he was headed for Esperanza. Father had planned to hire a sheriff after the bank robbery. Rosamond hoped this man was the one. She sent up a silent prayer of thanks that none of the passengers were harmed.

Beside her, Beryl hugged her middle, the site of her wound, and whimpered softly.

Putting away her gun, Rosamond wrapped her arms around her friend. "Shh. It's all right. No one's hurt."

Beryl nodded, but her eyes glazed over as if she weren't truly aware of her surroundings.

As much as Rosamond wanted to cry, she forbade herself to let go of her emotions. Someone indeed had been hurt: her sweet, fragile friend. Maybe she'd been wrong to insist that Beryl return to Colorado.

From the way Percy chatted cheerily with the other men as they guarded the miscreants, Garrick could see he'd enjoyed the whole affair. Garrick himself found the entire incident thrilling. Not that he'd wish to repeat it, of course. Having a gun pointed at one's heart did odd things to a man's nerves, proving what he'd always believed about the American West. This was an uncivilized land and would remain so. A cultured nobleman like Uncle and his aristocratic friends wouldn't enjoy their holidays here. The hotel Garrick had been sent to build—one after the English tradition—may be all well and good out in the middle of nowhere, but how would people travel there safely? And what would they do once they arrived?

Still, the courage of the other passengers impressed him, especially the lovely brunette. He'd been appalled to see her using a weapon but was fascinated by her composure, her courage. He'd never known an English lady who possessed such poise in the face of deadly danger. Unfortunately, her friend didn't fare as well. Even now, the brunette held the trembling redhead in a comforting embrace.

Percy also noticed them. "Should I inquire as to whether they need anything?"

Garrick hesitated. If his cousin spoke to the distressed lady, friendship might follow, especially if Esperanza was her destination. Yet he couldn't deny his own interest in speaking to her brave companion. "Yes, do ask."

Percy started toward them. The brunette looked up and shook her head, fire sparking in her eyes. Percy obeyed her unspoken order. What a woman! Garrick would think twice before challenging her about anything. Ever. She reminded him of his childhood governess, a formidable woman who'd never taken any nonsense from him, and with whom he'd never won a conflict. Perhaps this was another reason not to meet this lady. Clearly, she belonged to this land. He did not.

Even that awareness didn't douse his fascination with her. Yesterday he'd tried to devise a proper way to meet her, but could not. He'd decided the matter would run the usual disappointing course of his life. As the poet wrote, they were ships passing in the night. "Only a look and a voice, then darkness again and a silence." For an American, Longfellow wrote quite eloquently on the matter. Yet here they were on the same train for a second day. Did that portend an improvement in his life journey? No, he mustn't even consider it. She was an *American*!

The lawman took charge of the three outlaws, securing them in the freight car. With the passengers seated again, the train chugged up the mountain pass toward Garrick's future, one he had no heart for, but the one Uncle had set before him. Somehow he must make a success of it, not only for Helena but for his own self-respect.

"I say," Percy whispered. "I believe the Lord has it

all planned. Despite the ladies' rebuff a moment ago, we shall marry them before the end of summer." He cocked one blond eyebrow.

"Are you mad?" Garrick whispered back. "It's one thing to admire a pretty girl, another thing entirely to marry her." As if he could ever afford to marry.

"Wait and see." Percy jostled Garrick playfully. "By the end of summer."

He shook his head. Arguments could never douse Percy's optimism. If he did meet the pretty redhead, Garrick must ensure no marriage took place. Such an alliance would never be accepted among their acquaintances in England. Thus, Garrick must forgo meeting the lovely brunette, for no future lay in America for either him or Percy.

"I've a plan." Percy spoke in a conspiratorial tone. "When we arrive in Esperanza, we'll arrange our exit in time to hand the ladies down from the train."

"But—" Garrick stopped. Although Percy was on holiday, he himself must attend to business. The manner in which he emerged from the train would either impress or disappoint Colonel Northam. He intended to make a good impression. Perhaps Uncle's business partner would approve of his showing courtesy to the young ladies. "Yes, of course."

Percy's face beamed like a schoolboy's in the thrall of his first infatuation. Garrick's stomach churned.

Rosamond hadn't meant to be rude to the Englishmen, not after they'd shown such courage. She should apologize to them. But Beryl needed help to calm down before they arrived home. This hysteria wouldn't be accepted by her stoic family, nor did strangers need to get involved.

"Shh." She wrapped a traveling blanket around Beryl's shoulders. "Everything's all right. The Lord protected us. Did you see how all the passengers made short work of those bumbling outlaws?" She laughed softly.

In fact the dark-haired Englishman had been particularly brave to entice the outlaws with his exquisite gold watch. He'd obviously planned to subdue them with that fine ebony cane with the hound-shaped gold head. That took courage. The watch, the stylish cane and his finely tailored suit marked him as a man of wealth. Why would such a man travel to Colorado? She'd probably never know.

"Cheer up." She hugged Beryl again as the air seeping into the car turned frigid. "Remember to take slow, deep breaths to calm yourself."

Inhaling, Beryl nodded. Her eyes lost focus, and she seemed dizzy. "Oh, my."

"Lean your head on my shoulder." Rosamond spoke in a soothing tone. "It's the altitude. I'm a bit dizzy myself. We'll get used to it again." After living at sea level for several years, they faced the same challenge as any newcomer to the 7,600-foot high altitude of the San Luis Valley. In time, they'd become accustomed to the thinner air.

"Rosamond, how will I keep my family from finding out?" Beryl didn't need to explain. They'd often discussed this, usually after some loud noise sent her into a fit of trembling. A textbook slamming to the floor. A plate shattered in the dining room. Sometimes even the chime of the academy's bell-tower clock.

"You must tell your mother about your fears." Like her four other daughters, Mabel Eberly was a feisty, resilient woman who'd gained her strength after moving west. Surely she'd know how to help her middle daughter.

Beryl shook her head. "I can't. She won't understand. Promise me you won't tell anyone."

With a reluctant nod, Rosamond exhaled crossly. The evil men who'd shot Beryl now languished in the Canon City prison with twenty-five to thirty-year sentences. They should count themselves blessed. If she'd died, they'd have been hanged. Rosamond prayed they'd never be set free. Not after they'd destroyed Beryl's peace and confidence.

While they ate their boxed dinners, the train descended into the San Luis Valley. Warmer air now streamed into the car as the engineer made up for lost time. Wind from the south swept across the Valley floor, sending a gauzy black curtain of smoke past the window. After a short stop in Alamosa, where the lawman turned the outlaws over to the local sheriff, the train sped over the tracks toward Esperanza.

She sometimes heard the Englishmen talking but couldn't distinguish their words over the rumble of the train. Maybe they'd like to see the sand dunes at the foot of Mount Herard. She doubted such a natural wonder existed in their country. Yet from those first snobbish words she'd heard the dark-haired man say in the Denver station, she assumed he wouldn't appreciate any of the wonders of America.

Rosamond's heart began to beat in time with the clatter of the iron wheels on the track. Her parents would be waiting at the Esperanza station, maybe one or two of her brothers, as well. She couldn't wait to see everyone, including Rand's bride of just over a year, her own former roommate.

When she and her parents had traveled to Boston for Mother's health and to enroll Rosamond in the academy, they'd become very fond of sweet Marybeth O'Brien.

Certain she was the perfect bride for Rosamond's second brother, her parents had arranged the marriage. Now they had a baby boy, cousin to her oldest brother Nate's boy and girl, darling children to carry on the Northam legacy.

Rosamond felt a familiar pang. She'd love to be a mother, but no husband would permit his wife to teach other people's children and neglect her own. Certain of her calling from the Lord, she must choose to regard her students as her intellectual offspring.

The train chugged into Esperanza and slowed to a screeching stop, puffing out great blasts of gray-white steam. At the sound, Beryl twitched nervously.

"Shall we go?" Rosamond stood and gathered her bag and parasol.

"Can we wait until the crowd disperses?" Beryl gazed up at her, eyes brimming.

Rosamond sat. "All right." But not for long. She'd already spied her younger brother, Tolley, standing with two of the Eberly sisters. My, he'd grown tall over the past two and a half years, towering over Laurie and Georgia. She couldn't wait to get back home with her beloved family and friends.

"Dear ladies, may we assist you in any way?" The blond man stopped by their seat.

Rosamond smiled. "Thank you, but we need another moment."

"Of course." The dark-haired gentleman bowed. "We'll wait outside to help you down."

"That would be very kind." What had changed his attitude?

"We'll be waiting just outside," the blond man repeated. He and his friend walked toward the front of the car.

"Everyone's gone." Rosamond stood and gripped her

tapestry bag. "We must go." She was bursting with excitement even as she ached for Beryl.

As promised, the two men awaited them. The blond man helped Beryl down, his solicitous smile warming Rosamond's heart. The dark-haired man offered her no smile, only his gloved hand. When she took it, she felt the strength that went into knocking the outlaw senseless.

"Thank you," she managed to say over an odd little lump in her throat.

"Well, now." A familiar bass voice sounded across the platform. "I see you young folks have met."

"Father!" Rosamond dropped her bag and flung herself into his outstretched arms. "Oh, it's so good to be home."

"My darling girl, you've grown even more beautiful since last fall." Father placed a kiss on her cheek and then held her at arms' length. "How was your trip?"

"See here." Mother pushed herself into the mix to embrace Rosamond, her fragrant rosewater perfume sweetening her welcome. "I want my hug before we talk about the trip."

One by one, her brothers, Nate, Rand and Tolley, greeted her with eager embraces and teasing words. The crowded platform grew chaotic as other passengers connected with loved ones and gathered luggage. Lifting a prayer for Beryl, Rosamond waved to her friend, who was whisked away by two of her four sisters.

"Colonel Northam, I presume." The dark-haired Englishman approached Father, hand extended.

"Garrick Wakefield." Father pumped the man's hand with enthusiasm. "Welcome to Esperanza. I see you've met my daughter." He brought Mother forward. "Charlotte, may I present Mr. Wakefield, Lord Westbourne's nephew and representative?"

An indescribable sensation charged through Rosamond. What on earth was happening? Had the haughty Englishmen come to see Father? To do some sort of business with him? She glanced toward her brothers, but only Tolley looked her way, edging closer and putting an arm around her waist.

"Who's the dandy?" The annoyance in his voice echoed her own feelings, and she responded with a shrug.

"Mrs. Northam." Mr. Wakefield, all deferential now, kissed Mother's hand and then brought his blond friend forward. "Mrs. Northam, Colonel Northam, may I present Percy Morrow, my cousin. He accompanied me to your beautiful country."

So now it was a beautiful country, not a wasteland? While the blond man spoke pleasantries to her parents, Rosamond rolled her eyes. Tolley snickered. How interesting that friendly Mr. Morrow was stuffy Mr. Wakefield's cousin. The two couldn't be more different.

"How did you and Rosamond meet?" Father put an arm around Mr. Wakefield's shoulder as he would Nate or Rand. The Englishman squirmed a little.

"Actually, sir—"

"Gracious, Father." She leaned into her younger brother's comforting shoulder. "I haven't met this gentleman. With no one to introduce us, propriety prevented our meeting."

Her two older brothers howled with laughter.

"My, my," Rand said. "Our little cowgirl's become all sophisticated."

"Do you suppose she's forgotten where she came from after two and a half years in that highfalutin eastern school?" Nate, the oldest, nudged Rand. "We'll have to remind her."

"Never you mind." Rosamond would enjoy their teasing much more if Mr. Wakefield weren't watching with such an interested—or should she say, an *appalled*—expression. "Just wait. You'll see I can still keep up with the likes of you."

"That's enough foolishness." Father beckoned to her and draped his arm around her shoulder. "Rosamond, may I present Mr. Garrick Wakefield. I met his uncle, Lord Westbourne, when your mother and I were in Italy last year. The earl's sent Garrick to build that hotel Esperanza's needed. Since this will be a joint business venture, you'll be working alongside Garrick to see everything's done right."

She heard Father order her brothers to collect her trunks. Heard Mother chattering about a special supper at the ranch. But Rosamond could only stare at Mr. Wakefield while he stared back at her, obviously every bit as shocked as she was over Father's unexpected announcement. Work alongside this pompous Englishman? Never in a million years. But when Father gave an order, not one of his children ever succeeded in dissuading him from his purpose.

Chapter Two

To Garrick's shock, Miss Northam's horrified expression conveyed only disdain for him. While Colonel Northam walked away to welcome the lawman who'd traveled with them, Garrick scrambled to recall any way by which he might have offended the young lady. Perhaps Percy could help him.

Percy, however, had located their valets and, with the help of the three Northam brothers, was seeing to their luggage. Each cowboy effortlessly carried a trunk to a nearby wagon, an impressive feat. Or should he refer to them as ranchers instead of cowboys, since they were sons of a landowner? In England, such an erroneous form of address could cause severe embarrassment, even censure if a person of influence took offense at the misnomer. No doubt these Americans had a similar custom, even in their uncivilized land.

Ah, that was it. In the Denver train station, Miss Northam must have overheard him disparaging her country. Even before meeting her, he'd destroyed every chance of obtaining her good opinion. And her father expected him to work alongside her, to actually consult with her? With her aloof disposition and his plans already well-formed, that would be disastrous.

Apparently unaware of his daughter's or Garrick's chagrin, Colonel Northam sent his son Nate to show the lawman around the town. Equally unaware, Mrs. Northam gave instructions as to which conveyance each person should ride in to the ranch. Rand drove the box wagon with Garrick's valet beside him and Percy's valet perched precariously on a trunk. A third brother, whose name Garrick couldn't recall, rode on horseback. Colonel and Mrs. Northam took the front seat of a surrey while Miss Northam squeezed in between Garrick and Percy in back.

Glancing around, Garrick observed the nearly empty station platform. Only the harried mother from Denver remained with her children. She and Adam appeared to be searching for someone. Garrick prayed their person would arrive soon so the poor woman could get some assistance. Again, circumstances prevented him from helping, but Adam held little Jack's hand firmly, so Garrick dismissed his fears.

They drove down the street—a lofty term for these dusty roads—with Colonel Northam pointing out various establishments: the general store, the new jail, the bank, a café. "And that's the site of the hotel." He swung out one arm in a grand gesture, as though showing off an elegant manor house.

All Garrick saw was a large, roped off plot of grassless land, large stacks of wood and what appeared to be building supplies under canvas tarpaulins. "Ah, very good, sir." At least the plot was a decent size. With no close buildings to limit expansion, perhaps they could purchase more property nearby. After all, they'd need outbuildings such as a stable and a laundry—mundane things Garrick had never thought of before Uncle handed him this assignment.

The Colonel's tour over, he turned the horses down a southbound highway and began to speak quietly to his wife.

The cozy seating arrangement would have been decidedly pleasant if not for Miss Northam's stiff posture and the firm line of her full lips. Again she reminded Garrick of his formidable governess. But should they come into conflict over the hotel, he would not defer to this American miss as he had to Miss Shaw. Perhaps, now that they'd met, he should take a reading of her amenability by engaging her in chitchat.

Percy spoke first. "I say, Miss Northam, do you suppose your friend is well?"

She scolded him with a frown and a quick shake of her head and then spoke in a bright tone. "Indeed she is. Her sisters brought her mare so they could race home. She always finds a brisk ride exhilarating."

"Ah, very good." Percy relaxed. "I enjoy a brisk ride, as well." He gazed off thoughtfully, and Garrick could well imagine he was devising a plan to see her. "Would it be impertinent of me to ask her name?"

Miss Northam hesitated before saying, "Not impertinent at all. Beryl Eberly. The Eberly family owns the ranch west of ours."

"Beryl Eberly." Percy spoke the name reverently, as Romeo might say *Juliet*. "Lovely. And just a short walk away."

Miss Northam smiled. "A short ride. An impossible walk. I'll take you there tomorrow and introduce you."

Garrick wished her smile were aimed at him, but he supposed that was too much to ask. In any event, from the way she issued orders with a mere frown, he could see Miss Northam and he were utterly incompatible.

"I shall hold you to it, Miss Northam." Percy beamed in his boyish way, in spite of his twenty-four years. How uncomplicated his life was.

"Please call me Rosamond. We're not formal out here."

Vacillating once again in his feelings toward her, Garrick wanted to ask if the invitation were open to him, as well. The words stuck in his throat. After all, in England one only used Christian names with family or very close friends, and certainly not with new acquaintances. And now that he'd considered this entire situation, he wondered whether Uncle had made a serious error in judgment. If Colonel Northam possessed sufficient wealth to enter a business arrangement such as the hotel, why hadn't his servants managed the baggage instead of his sons? Garrick would have to ascertain how much the Northams were investing in the project before he committed any of Uncle's funds. If the Colonel had taken advantage of his trusting nature, Garrick would put an end to such duplicity.

She shouldn't have promised to introduce Percy to Beryl. Shouldn't have said anything about her friend's preferences. But she needed an excuse to check on Beryl rather than waiting to see her in church on Sunday. For now, she found being seated in between the two Englishmen a grand metaphor for the tight spot Father had put her in. This evening she must speak to him privately and remind him about her plans to build a high school, plans he'd agreed to months ago. Once she began her own work, she'd be too busy to help Mr. Wakefield with the hotel.

Yet even as she tried to divert her thoughts, ideas came unbidden to her mind. The Walsenburg hotel, where the train passengers had laid over last night, was a pleasant establishment with sufficient amenities to satisfy people passing through. But she could envision something on a grander scale, such as Boston's Parker House, only with a Western theme. Miss Pam Williams's rolls were every bit as delicious as Parker House rolls. They could hire her to manage the restaurant and cook her special Western recipes for the guests.

Rosamond would find ways to make visitors at the hotel feel at home while they took one- or two-day trips to the various wonders around the San Luis Valley: the sand dunes, Raspberry Gulch, La Garita Arch, the recently discovered Indian wall paintings. They could go fishing on the Rio Grande or swimming in San Luis Lake. Memories of childhood excursions filled her mind. So many opportunities for tourists to enjoy. Maybe one of her brothers could establish a guide business to work out of the hotel.

The top story of her family's ranch house came into view, and all such plans vanished. Home! What a wonderful, beautiful place. After two and a half years away, she felt a lump rising in her throat.

Father turned the buggy down Four Stones Lane and drove to the front door, probably because of their guests. Unless the family was holding a special event, everyone around here always came to the kitchen door, the neighborly thing to do. Rand did drive the wagon around back to carry the trunks up the back stairs. Tolley had ridden ahead to alert the household, so upon the travelers' arrival, Rosamond's sisters-in-law and their sweet babies poured out of the house to greet them.

As always with her family, chaos reigned, especially when the dogs raced over from the barn to join the melee. She gave each family member an enthusiastic hug, cooing over her four-year-old niece, Lizzy, and eighteen-month-old nephew, Nate Jr., nicknamed Natty. Her newest nephew, Randy, melted her heart when he offered a smile that revealed one tiny tooth.

The two Englishmen bore up fairly well, greeting Nate's wife, Susanna, and Marybeth with impeccable manners. Mr. Wakefield—she didn't want to call him Garrick because it suggested a friendliness she didn't feel—rose slightly in her estimation when he knelt down to greet Lizzy and Natty. He seemed used to children, perhaps even liked them, if his charming smile and silly chatter were any indication. He even acknowledged Randy with a few nonsense words and a gentle touch on the baby's tiny hand.

After the chaotic introductions, Mother bustled everyone into the main parlor and gave room assignments. She sent Percy to one of the newer rooms over the ballroom, with the two valets sharing a room next to him. Mr. Wakefield—oh, bother; if she called Percy by his first name, she must do the same with Garrick—would stay in Nate's old room two doors down from hers. Like Nate, Rand now had his own home, so Tolley roomed alone.

After Rosamond greeted everyone, she dashed upstairs to her bedroom. Nothing had changed. The pink-and-blue patchwork quilt still covered her four-poster bed. Her blue velvet chair sat by the open window where white ruffled curtains fluttered in the afternoon breeze. On the bedside table, two pink roses graced her cut-glass vase, an heirloom from her late grandmother.

Joy bubbled over into laughter as she gazed out the window at Mother pushing Lizzy in a swing hanging from the branch of a cottonwood tree. For over two years, the family had prayed anxiously for Mother's health, and the Lord had answered their prayers.

In her oak wardrobe, Rosamond found a favorite yellow calico dress, left behind because it was deemed too countrified for Boston, and quickly changed from her traveling suit. Her sisters-in-law needed her in the kitchen, and helping to prepare supper was just the thing to work out the kinks from sitting many days in train cars. Going down the back stairs, she sang a cheerful version of John Howard Payne's "Home, Sweet Home." She flung open the kitchen door, finishing with a resounding last line: "Be it ever so humble, there's no place like home!"

Garrick sat at the kitchen table, his face a study in mortification that matched exactly how she felt. Had her joyful singing broken some British rule of etiquette? Too bad. If he didn't like her music, he needn't listen. She wouldn't let him ruin her happiness.

Garrick hadn't been in a kitchen since childhood when he and Helena used to pester Uncle's cook for treats. Yet here he sat while Percy and the Northam brothers chatted as if they were in the drawing room of White's Men's Club in London, where Garrick would much prefer to be rather than in this American ranch house. Instead of uniformed footmen serving him high tea or his fellow members inviting him to play a hand of whist, a pretty Mexican girl—the family cook—offered biscuits and coffee. Her smiling demeanor and shared grins with the two young Northam wives indicated a decided lack of propriety for a servant, at least by British standards. He wasn't certain Uncle ever met his cooks, for all communications with below stairs were done through the housekeeper and butler.

Still, he couldn't complain about the American informality. Here in this cozy, crowded room, he could enjoy the aromas of roast beef sizzling in the oven and bread rising on the sideboard. While the biscuits—he supposed he should call them cookies, as the locals did—managed to stave off his hunger, he could well imagine supper would be a satisfying experience.

A sudden glorious sound from the back hallway wafted closer to the kitchen door, a lovely soprano voice lifted in a spirited rendition of the usually melancholy "Home, Sweet Home." As the song ended in a majestic high note rather than descending into pathos, Miss Northam burst in, her pretty face aglow with happiness. Her eyes focused on Garrick, and her expression turned to shock and then dismay. Now his face felt like a mask reflecting the same feeling. Why did she find the sight of him so troubling? He forced a smile and stood. "Miss Northam."

Percy jumped to his feet. "Miss Northam."

The brothers remained seated.

A smile crept over her stunning face, and something struck Garrick's midsection. Must he always feel a jolt when encountering her?

"Good afternoon, *gentlemen*. Howdy, Nate, Rand, Tolley."

"Hey, now." Nate stood, urging his brothers to do the same. "We're gentlemen, too." He approached his sister and hugged her, and his wife followed suit.

Garrick felt a pang in his chest. Issues of propriety aside, the genuine affection among these Northams reminded him of sweet Helena. Somehow he must make Uncle's project work so he could provide his sister with a dowry.

"Do be seated." Miss Northam took an apron from a

hook on the wall and donned it over her pretty yellow frock. "On second thought, you men should vamoose and get your chores done so we ladies can get supper on the table."

"Look who's giving orders after being home five minutes." Rand chucked his sister under the chin and brushed his wife's cheek with a kiss on his way toward the back door.

"Say, is *vamoose* proper grammar?" Tolley grabbed a handful of cookies from the serving platter on the table as he headed after Rand. "Or did the Colonel waste his money sending you to that fancy Boston school?"

Nate followed his brothers, beckoning to Garrick and Percy. "Come on, fellas. Let's skedaddle before the hen party begins. We'll show you around the place."

"I say, that sounds capital." Percy followed them, giving Garrick no choice but to do the same.

"Not so fast." Susanna's order stopped them all, and a significant look Garrick couldn't decipher passed between her and Nate. "You can save that for tomorrow. These gentlemen are still in their nice travel clothes."

"Maybe they'd like to see the house first." Marybeth gave Rand the same look.

Now the older brothers eyed each other while Tolley huffed in annoyance, apparently eager to do those chores.

"Tomorrow. Right." Nate seemed to be smothering a grin. "Gentlemen, we'll see you at supper."

The three men made their exit without argument, so Garrick concluded that the ladies gave the orders in this family. As much as a turn around the ranch might refresh him, he wouldn't contradict either young Mrs. Northam by insisting upon going with their husbands. Percy didn't seem to mind the change of plans. But then, very few things bothered him.

Susanna, a tiny blonde with an accent he recognized as from the American South, turned her attention to Rosamond. "We can manage supper. You take our guests on a tour of the house."

"Oh, but…very well." Miss Northam removed her apron. "Come along, gentlemen. We'll start with the dining room."

She led them through the swinging door by which they'd entered earlier. The room was surprisingly large, with a mahogany table long enough to seat twelve and matching sideboard and china cabinet, the same sort of furnishings Garrick planned to order for the hotel. Such luxuries could be a sign of Northam wealth. Possibly.

"I say." Percy paused before the large glass front cabinet. "Wedgwood china, is it not?"

Miss Northam nodded. "Father gave it to Mother for their twenty-fifth wedding anniversary. It was the talk of the San Luis Valley."

"I should think so." The words, borne on a laugh, slipped out before Garrick could stop them. Miss Northam's indignant look made it clear he'd offended her…again.

At Fairfield Young Ladies' Academy, Rosamond had learned that one never made another person feel uncomfortable, even when that person was rude. After all, one couldn't truly know what someone else was thinking. This man, however, was easy to read, even without speaking a word. His obvious disdain for her beloved Valley didn't bode well for their working together. Why had he come here if he held Americans in such contempt?

She schooled her face into a tight smile. "Shall we go to the parlor?"

They followed along, with Percy making pleasant remarks about various bits of bric-a-brac or paintings, some of which Rosamond hadn't seen before. Her parents must have purchased them in Italy when they'd traveled there last year for Mother's health.

Some new furnishings also graced the parlor—chairs, side tables, figurines. It still felt like home to Rosamond. They passed through to the ballroom, which Nate had built five years ago for the twenty-fifth wedding-anniversary party. Mother loved to entertain, and many times the community gathered here for special events. Although not used daily, the room was spotless, probably due to the efforts of Consuela, the new housemaid. Mother had written about the young Mexican girl they'd employed to help Rita manage the house. Too bad no one had written to Rosamond about the hotel.

"What a charming ballroom." Garrick's expression appeared to reflect true admiration. "One would hardly expect…I mean…" He ran his hand over the carved mahogany balustrade beside the three steps descending into the room.

Rosamond withheld a laugh. Was he truly arrogant or merely socially awkward? "Why, thank you, Mr. Wakefield."

He gave her a sheepish grin. "I heard you say first names are the custom here. Please call me Garrick."

"I will." She accepted his olive branch. "Please call me Rosamond."

"A lovely name, to be sure." His gentle tone surprised her. Was he trying to make amends? Or was she being too hard on him? "A family name?"

"No. I was named for Rosamond Oliver in Charlotte Brontë's *Jane Eyre*, Mother's favorite novel."

The pleasantries seemed to break the tension between

them. Along with Percy, they spent the next half hour exploring the rest of the house, including Father's office and library. He'd added many books while Rosamond had been away. "Feel free to borrow any of these to read at your leisure."

"Ah, American authors." Percy studied the names on the book spines. "Mark Twain, Nathaniel Hawthorne, Louisa May Alcott. I shall be delighted to read them."

"And you, Garrick?" For a moment, Rosamond's heart hitched with an odd sort of hope. How she wanted to hear he enjoyed reading as much as she did. But why? He wasn't a potential suitor. Gracious, no, not when they seemed only to tolerate each other.

"Yes, of course." He also perused the books. "One cannot graduate from Oxford without obtaining a great appreciation for fine literature."

So much for her hopes of common interests. Oxford, indeed. She doubted his education was any better than her own.

And she was expected to consult with this arrogant man? It wouldn't work. After supper tonight, she'd make Father understand that simple fact.

Garrick attempted to follow the conversation over supper, tried to speak when appropriate. But with ten adults around the table, some not schooled in the proper way to converse at mealtime, he didn't have to try hard. The playful banter among the brothers and Rosamond helped them reclaim the years of separation. Unlike English customs, they found talking across the table acceptable instead of only conversing with the persons to one's right and left.

Further, no one here dressed for dinner. Although the brothers washed hands and faces after their chores, they'd come to the table in their work clothes, dusty trousers and all. Nor did footmen serve the meal. Instead, the cook and the young ladies carried steaming bowls and platters to the table. Everyone passed the food around and served themselves. At least Garrick's and Percy's valets possessed the good sense to decline Mrs. Northam's invitation to eat with the family, insisting upon eating in the kitchen with the cook. Perhaps Rita, the senior servant despite being quite young, could explain to Roberts and Richards how she ran the household so they wouldn't get underfoot while tending to their own duties.

To Garrick's relief, after supper the two older sons and their families departed for their nearby homes, leaving behind a measure of peace, as well as a minor concern. Guests in an English house were expected to participate in the evening's entertainment: reporting the latest news, joining a game of whist, offering to read a favorite passage from a book. What did one do to amuse Americans in the evening? Travel weary though he was, he must somehow participate in whatever activities they offered or risk offending his host.

Colonel Northam soon put that concern to rest while igniting another. Like the military officer he'd been, he ordered Tolley to entertain Percy and sent Garrick and Rosamond to his office. Considering the young lady's obvious dislike, Garrick steeled himself for an uncomfortable interview.

"Have a seat." The Colonel waved them to leather chairs in front of his desk. Mrs. Northam sat beside her husband. "I know you're both tired, so I won't keep you long. Just want to give you some marching orders so you can get started on Monday. That's the day I'm leaving on business, so it's on your shoulders now."

"Father, this hotel business is a complete surprise

to me." Rosamond fidgeted. "You said in your letters I could build my high school this summer."

A high school? Garrick sat up straighter and eyed the pretty lady beside him. Obviously, she had a concern for the education and welfare of the lower classes, just as her namesake in *Jane Eyre* did. His esteem for her rose.

"No reason you can't do both." The Colonel's affection for his daughter resonated in his paternal tone and warm gaze. "Plenty of workers around now that this leg of the railroad's finished."

"Yes, but—" Her voice was tight, and her smile a grimace. "Surely Mr. Wakefield has made his plans. Why would he need my help?"

The Colonel chuckled indulgently. "The hotel needs a woman's touch, and your mother has enough to do. That leaves you. Why did I send you to boarding school if you aren't going to use what you learned? Not only that—" he held up a letter, and Garrick could see the elegant *W* of Uncle's seal on the stationery "—Lord Westbourne likes the idea just fine. He has complete trust in you and Garrick to create a fine establishment for European and American tourists alike."

"Well, then." Miss Northam clearly didn't care for the project any more than Garrick, but she at least had her school. Garrick's future, and Helena's, depended entirely upon this man's good opinion and cooperation. "With your approval, sir, we can begin tomorrow." Against his usual reserved behavior toward young ladies, he offered what he hoped was a charming smile to Rosamond. "Shall we?"

She returned one of her prim looks. "I believe Father said Monday. Tomorrow I'll help my brothers with cattle branding. Then I'll take Percy to meet Beryl. And of course the day after, we'll go to church. Do you attend church, Mr. Wake—Garrick?"

"Rosamond!" Mrs. Northam's soft voice resounded with shock. "Of course he goes to church."

Colonel Northam laughed out loud. "At least he will while he's in this house, won't you, my boy?"

Heat rushed up Garrick's neck. Did they mean to insult him, or was this just banter, like the dinner table conversation? He'd choose to believe the latter. "I try never to miss church, sir. Nothing sets the tone of a man's week like an hour of worship and a stirring sermon."

"Well spoken. You'll be glad to know our Reverend Thomas always delivers a thought-provoking message." The Colonel stood and reached over the desk. Garrick rose and shook his hand. "Now you get a good night of sleep. If you're interested in watching the cattle branding tomorrow, you're welcome to come on out. If not, please feel free to use my library." He indicated the shelves Garrick had perused earlier. "Good night."

With this clear dismissal, Garrick took his leave of these people who held his future. As he trudged up the elegant front staircase and down the long hallway, he could hear laughter coming from Percy's room. Through the partially open door, he saw Tolley was paying Percy a visit, as ordered by his father. Apparently the two got along well. Garrick was happy for his cousin. As long as he enjoyed himself, he'd stay in Colorado, where Garrick would need him now more than ever, should things become impossible for him to bear.

"Now, Rosamond." Father gave her a rare stern look. "I understand your concerns, but working on both projects will prepare you for your many and varied headmistress duties."

"Yes, Father." How could she argue against his faith in her? Didn't she believe just as strongly in her own ability to manage the school and at the same time teach both boys and girls just a few years younger than herself?

"You can always ask me for ideas." Mother came around the desk to sit in the chair Garrick had vacated. She grasped Rosamond's hand. "As a girl, I spent many happy days visiting my grandfather's hotel in Philadelphia. And, of course, the hotels in Italy cannot be surpassed. I can describe them to you in detail, and I'll help in any other way you ask."

"Now, Charlotte, I won't have you overdoing. You manage the house. That's enough." Father's eyes filled with concern. "In fact, you need more help, and I don't mean Rosamond. She'll be busy. I'm going to hire more help for the gardening and other such things."

"Oh, Frank, don't coddle me." Mother gave him an intimate smile, one that made Rosamond ache for the kind of love her parents shared. "I'm fine. Now, enough about me. Let's hear about Rosamond's trip home."

Taking the hint, Rosamond launched into a description of her last days at the academy, the graduation ceremony during which both she and Beryl had received academic awards and their lengthy train travels. They'd already heard about the attempted robbery from Sheriff Lawson, so she brushed past the event. When she almost fell asleep in the middle of her own narrative, her parents ushered her upstairs to the comforting warmth of her bedroom.

Despite her exhaustion, she knelt beside her window as she had as a child to view the sparkling diamonds sprinkled across the velvet black sky. In Boston, with its many streetlamps and lighted buildings, she'd missed the stark beauty of Colorado's nighttime skies. She'd also missed this window spot, where she'd learned to pray and to leave every concern in the Lord's hands. Tonight she prayed for Beryl, anticipating their reunion tomorrow. She prayed for her school and her future students and, finally, for willingness to obey Father in helping the Englishman build the hotel.

When she awoke the next day, the sun already shone on the alfalfa field outside her window. In the bright midmorning light, everything seemed possible, even working alongside Garrick. A joyful, giddy feeling swept through her as she dug around in her wardrobe for her split skirt, plaid shirtwaist and riding boots. After donning her comfortable cowgirl garb, she raced down the backstairs to the kitchen. She took care not to sing, even though a song played in her mind, lest Garrick hear her as she entered the kitchen and be offended again.

Her worries were groundless. Only Rita and one of the valets occupied the room. Curiously, the valet had rolled up his sleeves and plunged his hands in the soapy dishpan up to his elbows.

"What would you like for breakfast, Senorita Rosamond?" Rita was preparing sandwiches for the men who were branding the cattle, but she took a moment to stoke the fire under the skillet and lay in some bacon. "Two slices of bacon, two sunny eggs, two biscuits, strawberry jam and coffee?"

"You remember." Rosamond wasn't surprised. A mere eighteen years old, Rita already managed the entire household. More proof that Rosamond's twenty-one years wouldn't hinder her from completing both of Father's projects.

"*Sí*, senorita. How could I forget?" She poured coffee for Rosamond and set it on the breakfast table.

"May I be of assistance, Rita?" The young valet, Roberts, dried his hands on a tea towel. "I can fix Miss Northam's breakfast while you finish those sandwiches."

Rita gave him a sweet smile, and her brown eyes sparkled. "I'd be most grateful, Senor Roberts."

"Just Roberts, miss." He winked at her and then turned a more serious face to Rosamond. "I have experience in the kitchen, as that's where I started in service as a boy. If no one minds, I'd like to help Rita. I've very little to do for Mr. Wakefield today, and I like to keep occupied."

"By all means." Rosamond sat at the table and sipped her coffee. She could easily fix her own breakfast, but watching a possible romance budding right before her eyes was more enjoyable. "Where's Richards?" Percy's valet was somewhat older, perhaps in his thirties.

Roberts arched his brown eyebrows at her question. Visiting wealthy friends in Boston, she'd noticed that servants didn't chat with the family of the house. No doubt that was also the custom in England. "He went with Mr. Morrow to watch the branding, miss."

"Hmm." Rosamond hid a grin. "To watch or to protect his employer?"

Roberts also hid a grin by laboring unnecessarily over the bacon. "I'd imagine both. Our gentlemen didn't bring what you'd call work clothes, so it'll be our job to repair any damage."

A memory popped into Rosamond's mind. Last night, Nate, Rand and Tolley traded looks suggesting they'd devised some initiation into the cowboy world for the Englishmen. She needed to eat before joining the branding, but she dearly wanted to see what mischief her brothers planned for their hapless victims.

"On second thought, I'll just take this." She picked up a beef and cheese sandwich, wrapped it in a napkin and tucked it in her pocket. With her coffee cup in hand, she headed for the door. On a hook by the back entrance hung her old hat right where she left it before going back East. Prepared to reenter her old life, she dashed out into the warm May sunshine.

And she'd try very hard not to laugh too much at whatever disaster fell upon stuffy Mr. Garrick Wakefield.

Chapter Three

Garrick, Percy and Richards perched on the fence of the labyrinthine corral to watch the Northam brothers work. Cattle branding was a messy, noisy business, but no more so than sheep shearing, which Garrick had observed every spring at Uncle's manor. As heir presumptive, he'd spent his first eighteen years learning about his future responsibilities. Even after six years of knowing he wouldn't inherit, he couldn't put aside the habit of recording new knowledge, new experiences that might be helpful in the future. Of course, he'd never need to know about cattle branding. He'd never even dressed the deer or grouse he'd shot in Uncle's park. The gamekeepers always did the dirty work.

Yet somehow, in spite of himself, he was impressed by the Northams' personal involvement in the ranch work. They employed countless cowboys, yet stayed in the thick of the branding process. Garrick never touched a sheep, although his governess let him feel the freshly sheared wool. He suspected she enjoyed the waxy lanolin balm present in the wool.

"Hey, gents." In the center of the corral, Nate raised a branding iron in the air. "Want to try it?"

"No, thank you." Garrick couldn't think of inflicting pain upon those young calves. At least sheep shearing was painless to the animals, even welcomed, for it removed their heavy winter coats.

"Yes." Percy jumped into the corral. "I'd be delighted."

"Sir?" Seated on the fence beside Garrick, Richards called out. "May I be so bold...?"

"Certainly." Percy beckoned to him. "Come along."

Richards hopped down and strode alongside Percy with a spring in his step, as though he were on his way to a picnic.

Garrick shook his head. Richards held one of the highest ranks possible for a servant. Why ever would he want to get his hands, not to mention his clothes, soiled with such menial work with dirty animals?

"Don't you want to play?" Rosamond nimbly climbed the fence and sat beside Garrick. Pulling a sandwich from her pocket, she began to eat.

In spite of her boyish attire, his midsection did its usual dance. He really mustn't allow himself to react this way. But how did one stop the involuntary feelings? How even to relate to her? He knew so little about young ladies. The aristocratic girls he'd known in his youth turned a cold shoulder to him once his newborn cousin replaced him as Uncle's heir.

"Good morning to you, too, Rosamond."

She laughed, a musical sound that reminded him of her merry song the day before. "Are you enjoying the show?" She tilted her head toward the action in the corral.

"That? Well, I must say I feel a bit sorry for those calves."

If the rolling of her eyes was any indication, he'd said the wrong thing...again.

"If we didn't brand them, they could be stolen and someone else could claim them."

"Stolen? From right here on your father's ranch?"

Another rolling of the eyes, this time accompanied by a shake of her head, as though he were a hopeless numbskull. "The ranch doesn't grow enough hay to feed all the cattle year round, so the hands drive the herd up into the hills for summer grazing. Sometimes our cattle mingle with other herds, so the brands keep everybody honest."

"Ah, I see."

She polished off the sandwich in a rather dainty manner, considering the setting and her hoydenish garb. "You'll excuse me?" She started to jump down.

"What? You?" Garrick felt an entirely different kick in his midsection—fear. For her. The actual branding wasn't the hard part of this operation. The unwilling calves struggled violently to avoid their fate. What if she were injured?

"Yes, me." She stayed on the fence. "These are my cattle and, like my brothers, I always participate in the branding."

"Don't you mean they're your father's cattle?" He'd say anything, no matter how annoying, to keep her from danger.

She huffed out a sigh. "Yes, my father's, my mother's, Nate's, Rand's, Tolley's and mine. We're all owners of the Four Stones Ranch."

"Indeed." Garrick eyed her doubtfully. "Are you saying your oldest brother won't inherit everything?" Even for Americans, this idea was truly novel.

She gave him an indulgent smile. "That's what I'm saying. Now, if you'll excuse me."

He still couldn't let her go. "So the four stones in the ranch's name are—"

"My brothers and I."

Before he could climb down to assist her, she jumped to the ground and seemed no worse for the experience.

"Come on, Garrick." She beckoned with a charming wave of her hand, and her invitation held a challenge he couldn't refuse.

"Very well." He jumped down beside her, and pain shot through his feet. Perhaps he should purchase a pair of those cowboy boots. If nothing else, his experiences on this ranch were sure to give him some much-needed exercise.

The way Garrick and Percy plunged into the branding impressed Rosamond. As with the train robbers, they proved themselves courageous in a new and dangerous situation. After an hour or so, however, she couldn't understand why her brothers hadn't pulled a prank on their guests. Then it happened. While helping Tolley hog-tie a reluctant calf, Garrick fell into a pile of cow droppings. Even though he laughed, his disgust was obvious when he excused himself and headed back toward the house. Rosamond felt a little sorry for him, but she felt sorrier for Roberts, who must restore those filthy trousers and shirt. She'd cleaned up similar messes all her life. Obviously, Garrick hadn't.

However, she discovered herself a bit rusty at branding. The indolent years in Boston and her need to get used to the altitude took their toll. When she tried to pick up the heavy iron, she needed Tolley's help so she wouldn't cause her calf extra pain if she misapplied the white-hot brand. Winded far too soon, she begged off before the task was finished. Her ever-indulgent brothers praised her efforts and sent her back to the house.

"I say." Percy fell in beside her. "What an exhilarating experience."

"I'm glad you enjoyed it." She couldn't say the same about Garrick, so best not to mention him. "Richards seems to be enjoying himself, too."

"Odd, that." Percy laughed, clearly not troubled by his valet's request to continue working with the hands. "By the by, are we still going to the Eberly ranch today?"

"Yes. After dinner." She hoped no one would ask why she must see Beryl when they'd just spent almost two years together at school, not to mention the long trip home. "We'll go as soon as we clean up. Oh. Do you need your valet?"

Percy, who always seemed cheerful, laughed again. "Not at all. Of course, I want to present myself well, but I'll make quick work of it." He leaned close as they walked across the barnyard, as though he thought someone else might hear him. "Unlike my cousin, I didn't always have servants, so I learned to take care of myself."

Rosamond laughed with him. "Oh, you poor thing." So she'd been right about Garrick. That explained much about his behavior. She thanked the Lord she'd been taught self-sufficiency like her brothers. At least in most ways. Even out here, she must mind the proprieties that protected her reputation, even if it meant she must include Garrick in this afternoon's jaunt.

"Do you suppose Garrick would like to go along?"

Percy gave her a sly look. "You enjoy his company?"

"No. I mean…oh, dear." She huffed out a sigh. "Although it's just a short ride, we'll need a chaperone. People are particular about such things out here."

He stopped, and his blond eyebrows shot up. "Oh, my. I wouldn't think of doing it any other way."

With that settled, Rosamond sent him on to the house

while she went to the barn to see which horses were available. Pete, one of the older cowboys who no longer took part in branding, hurried over to greet her. After they'd exchanged pleasantries, he volunteered to saddle three horses for her by one o'clock.

Maybe she should have asked Pete to go with her. Now she'd committed herself to an afternoon with Garrick. Oddly, the thought didn't depress her as much as it should have.

"Very good work, Roberts." Garrick studied his reflection in the wardrobe mirror. "You've managed wonders. A cold but cleansing bath and perfectly pressed clothes." In the mirror, he checked the back of his fresh ensemble as he tried to dismiss the incident from his mind. At Eton, he'd never have lived down such a humiliating ordeal, even years later. One hapless chap whose family didn't come up to snuff in Society's view still received the scorn of former classmates over a similar event. When Garrick lost his position as Uncle's heir, he'd fallen into that same category in some people's opinion.

He knew Tolley had deliberately tripped him, but accusations would be fruitless. All the Northam brothers found the accident amusing. Perhaps he'd passed some sort of cowboy initiation when he stifled his chagrin and laughed with them. He prayed no more such incidents occurred. After checking his hair in the mirror, he sniffed his hands for the second time. "I can't detect a single bit of cow odor. Well done."

"Thank you, sir."

Roberts maintained his usual blank facade, although Garrick had seen him smile at the attractive young Mexican cook. If romance was budding, Garrick must nip it lest Roberts decide to stay in Colorado. Nor would Rita fit in as a servant in England, not even in the most liberal households. More important, Garrick couldn't afford to find a new valet. Roberts, being young and newly elevated to his position last year, settled for lower wages than a more experienced gentleman's gentleman demanded. Further, Garrick had trained him to anticipate his needs. The loss would be dreadful.

Percy knocked as he entered. "Ready to go?"

"Your riding gloves, sir." Roberts handed Garrick the tan leather accessory.

"Thank you." Garrick was tempted to tell his man to spend the afternoon washing his trousers and shirt, but that would be an insult. Roberts knew what his duties were. Garrick could only hope the washing area was nowhere near the kitchen and pretty little Rita.

After searching for their horses at the front of the house, he and Percy found Rosamond by the back entrance with three saddled beasts. Why did they use the servants' entrance when the house's facade was quite lovely, albeit quaint? These Americans. At least the family employed a groom to see to the horses. Despite the saddle's oddly shaped pommel, he soon found his seat and easily kept up with Rosamond as they rode across fields, paths and gullies.

They slowed to a walk and turned down a lane to a ranch similar to Four Stones, with an attractive two-story white house and numerous outbuildings, including a giant red barn.

"I say, Rosamond." Percy rode beside her. "Good idea to ride over to your neighbors' instead of walking. All those little streams and fences would be rather a challenge to cross on foot."

She laughed in her musical way, a sound Garrick

was becoming entirely too fond of. "I'm so glad you're pleased, Percy."

Garrick felt a pinch of jealousy, although he knew Percy's interest lay elsewhere. Why couldn't he and Rosamond get along as easily? He couldn't worry about that today. With Percy so keen on getting acquainted with Beryl, not to mention his silly vow to marry her before the end of summer, Garrick would have more than enough to do keeping his impulsive cousin from ruining his life. In England, with his large inheritance from his father's trade, Percy could marry any heiress, even an aristocrat, and begin to move into the higher levels of Society. Why would he waste his life on a nervous American cowgirl? Yet Percy was in no hurry to meet his future and had insisted upon coming with Garrick to America simply for a lark.

Rosamond rode to the back door and dismounted, tying her mare to the hitching rail. "I smell cinnamon. Mabel must be baking."

The men followed her up the back steps.

"You don't mean to walk right in, do you?" Garrick frowned.

She returned his look but quickly forced a smile. She must remember English customs were different. Even in Boston, she'd never entered a friend's house without knocking.

"Yes, I do. Mabel would be bothered if I knocked. She'd have to stop her work to answer." She opened the door and entered.

The two men followed hesitantly, but Rosamond hurried through the back hallway and into the large but cozy kitchen. "Hey, Mabel."

Plump, red-haired Mabel Eberly dropped her spoon

into the stewpot and turned, her merry face beaming. "Rosamond, honey, come on in." She embraced her warmly and then held her at arm's length. "My, you're even more beautiful than ever." She glanced at the Englishmen. "I know who these fine gentlemen are. Howdy, boys. Beryl told us how brave you were when those outlaws tried to rob the train. And George says you've come out here to build that hotel." She beckoned to them. "Come on in. Have a seat." She waved a hand toward the kitchen table. "Would you like some cinnamon rolls and coffee?"

Rosamond prayed they wouldn't rebuff Mabel's offer. While Garrick stood back, his handsome face crinkled in confusion or maybe consternation, Percy stepped over to Mabel.

"Rosamond, would you please present me to this charming lady?"

His formality tickled Rosamond, but she did the honors in all seriousness.

"Mabel, this is Percy Morrow. Percy, remember, first names out here."

Percy kissed her hand, and Mabel's sweet face turned even redder than usual. "Oh, go on, now."

Rosamond summoned Garrick with a whip of her hand and a glare Mabel couldn't see. "This is Garrick Wakefield."

He must have realized the importance of compliance, because he followed Percy's example.

"What fine manners. Now sit down." Mabel ushered them to the table and served coffee and a plateful of fresh cinnamon buns. Her merry manner seemed to set the men at ease, for they didn't hesitate to eat.

Seated by the door, Rosamond heard a soft *tst*. While Mabel plied the men with rolls in exchange for their life stories, Beryl peeked in and beckoned to Rosamond. In the hallway, Beryl embraced her fiercely.

"Rosamond, save me. Get me away from here."

"What's wrong?" Rosamond knew the answer. She'd happily donned her comfortable ranch clothes, but Beryl wore one of her Boston dresses. Underneath, Rosamond felt her tightly laced corset.

"It's my sisters," Beryl whispered anxiously and glanced toward the back door as if fearing they'd enter. "They expected me to jump right into work." She bit her lip and stared at her hands. "I'm willing to do my share, but I can't bear to get all freckled and rough-skinned again." A tear slid down her ivory cheek. "I'm terrible, aren't I?"

"Nonsense." Rosamond hugged her. "You'll get used to home life again." She didn't believe that herself. Beryl's fears ran deeper than how her complexion looked. Rosamond thought of one way to help her. "Come meet those Englishmen."

Beryl's blue eyes widened. "Not like this." She swiped away tears.

"Go freshen up." Rosamond forced a cheerful laugh. "Your ma is feeding them her cinnamon rolls, but they can only eat so much." She smirked. "The blond gentleman wants to meet you."

Beryl's eyes rounded in wonder. "Truly?"

"Truly. Now hurry."

While her friend complied, Rosamond returned to the kitchen. The two men stood, as they had last evening. Their refined manners pleased her. Not every man understood the importance of such a gallant gesture.

"Beryl wasn't expecting company." She sat in the chair Garrick held for her, another chivalrous move on his part. Her opinion of him rose a little. "She'll join us soon."

"Capital." Percy's blue eyes brightened just as Beryl's had.

Garrick, however, frowned as he reclaimed his chair. Rosamond's opinion of him plummeted. How could he dislike sweet Beryl when he didn't even know her?

"So, you boys are planning to build that hotel." Mabel poured coffee for Rosamond.

"Not I, madam." Percy chuckled. "I accompanied Garrick so I could see the famous—or should I say, infamous—American West." He leaned toward Mabel with a playful smirk. "I believe the train robbery was staged entirely for our amusement, what?"

Mabel slapped his shoulder and howled with laughter. "You'll do fine out here, boy. You'll do fine."

He grinned despite his coffee sloshing onto the tablecloth. Again, Garrick's frown revealed an opposite reaction, disapproval of the kind lady who was showing him such generous hospitality. Before Rosamond could frown back at him, Beryl entered.

The men stood, and Percy stepped forward and bowed over her hand. "Miss Eberly, I presume?"

Beryl received him with the grace she'd learned at the academy. "How do you do, sir? You must forgive me for not knowing your name. We should have introduced ourselves after the train robbery, but—" Confusion clouded her face, and Rosamond gasped softly. Her friend almost revealed her hysteria to her mother.

"Ah, but with no one to properly introduce us..." Percy touched her elbow and drew her to the table as if he were the host. "Please permit the informality. I am Percy Morrow, and this is my cousin, Garrick Wakefield."

Garrick gave a sober bow while Percy continued to fuss over Beryl. "Your mother's cinnamon rolls are delicious beyond description. Do have one."

Rosamond's eyes stung. Percy had just rescued Beryl. What a good man, exactly what her friend needed.

Beryl regained her composure, and she and Percy began to chat. Mabel eyed Rosamond and lifted one eyebrow. Rosamond returned a tiny nod, bringing a pleased smile from her hostess.

Boisterous laughter sounded in the hallway as Beryl's father and her three unmarried sisters entered. She sent Rosamond a panicked look.

"Oh, good." Rosamond knew of only one way to manage this situation: head-on. "You gentlemen will get to meet more Eberlys." These next few minutes might be awkward.

Garrick stood beside Percy while bedlam descended upon the kitchen as a ruddy, middle-aged man and three attractive young ladies in Western garb entered. Unlike quiet, well-mannered Beryl, the girls jostled each other and more yelled than talked.

"Mabel, honey," the man said, "we could smell your baking clear out in the barn." He blinked. "Well, I'll be a skinned jackrabbit. I didn't know we had company."

Garrick shuddered inwardly at the picture the man's metaphor produced.

"You didn't notice their horses? Honey, you need spectacles." With no attempt at formality, Mabel pointed at Percy and Garrick and announced their names. "Boys, this here's my George, and these are three more of our girls, Laurie, Georgia and Grace. Grace is the deputy sheriff. She's been keeping the peace in town since a bank robbery a few years ago. I'm glad we got us a fulltime sheriff now so she can help out around here a bit more. Maisie, she's our oldest daughter, is married to the town doctor. You'll meet them at church tomorrow."

While she chattered on about her family, Garrick tried

to grasp the idea of a female law officer. Granted, at nearly six feet tall and wearing a gun at her side, Grace seemed capable of managing wrongdoers. Even ladylike Rosamond had helped defeat the train robbers. Perhaps these Western women needed to be as tough as the men. Except Beryl, whose cheerful chat with Percy ended the moment her sisters entered the room. Curious. Yet no matter what he saw here, he must try not to judge any of them by proper British standards.

"I don't know, Ma." Grace grabbed a roll from the platter. "Sheriff Lawson said this mornin' he's countin' on me to help him." She took a bite but kept talking. "Beryl's home now. She can help you."

Beryl began to tremble.

"Oh, dear." Rosamond put an arm around her friend. "I'm counting on Beryl to help me plan our new high school." She smiled at the two younger sisters. "I hope you'll be enrolling in our classes."

Warmth swept through Garrick's chest. He didn't understand the situation, but Rosamond's care for her friend suggested an admirable depth of character. Perhaps working with her on the hotel project wouldn't be so difficult, after all.

"In fact," Rosamond said, "we've a lot to plan and need to start right away. Mabel, will you let Beryl spend a few weeks with us, starting tomorrow after church?"

Garrick's warm feelings sank to his stomach like a cold lead weight. With Percy and Beryl in the same house, how could he prevent their forming an attachment?

From the enthusiasm on Percy's face, Garrick feared it was already too late.

Rosamond had tried to outwit Mother's maneuvering, but here she sat beside Garrick in the church pew. This afternoon she must persuade Mother to stop her match-making. After Garrick's obvious disapproval of Beryl and Percy's developing romance, she couldn't even like Garrick, much less love him.

Of course Reverend Thomas gave a sermon on loving one's neighbor. She'd learned long ago the pastor always preached what she needed to hear, as though the Lord whispered in his ear that Miss Rosamond Northam wasn't listening to Him, so His servant must speak to her in an audible voice she couldn't miss. How silly. She hadn't spoken to Reverend Thomas since returning from Boston, so he knew nothing of her spiritual disposition. Still, she paid attention.

Despite the conviction churning within, she enjoyed being back in her home church. Would Garrick turn up his nose at their simple service? Oh, dear. There she went again, judging him. *Lord, help me to love him with Your love.*

Across the sanctuary, Beryl sat with her family. Occasionally, she smiled hopefully at Rosamond, which must mean her folks had given permission for her move to Four Stones. Last night, Mother had welcomed the prospect, for she always thrived with a houseful of guests.

Rosamond hoped none of Beryl's sisters objected. Beryl wanted to please everyone. A complaint from a beloved sister might make her stay home, whatever the cost emotionally. Yesterday as they toured the Eberly ranch with the Englishmen, Laurie and Georgia had teased Beryl about her parasol. Though she laughed, Rosamond could see they'd hurt her feelings.

As the final hymn ended, Mother gave Garrick a smile. "Rosamond will introduce you and Percy to Reverend Thomas while Mabel and I count the offering."

Rosamond smiled, despite her annoyance. "Certainly.

Come along, gentlemen." Maybe she could leave them with Reverend Thomas and find Beryl. Or leave Garrick with the pastor and take Percy to find Beryl. Rosamond didn't care for Mother's matchmaking on her behalf, but she certainly enjoyed doing it for her friend.

Garrick approved the way Reverend Thomas conducted the service. His sermon revealed an intelligent theological mind. The service was simple, the music a pleasant surprise. The gray-haired organist played the pump organ with a dexterity that belied her age. Most of the congregants sang heartily, and most sang in tune. After the closing hymn, Garrick felt his spiritual cup full to overflowing.

Mrs. Northam needn't have assigned Rosamond the task of introductions, for the minister stood at the door to speak to each parishioner. Yet after hearing a fine message on loving one's neighbor, Garrick looked forward to Rosamond's company. Her rose-scented perfume only added to the pleasure.

Each churchgoer lining the aisle received a warm, personal greeting from the minister. In return, some complimented the sermon while others shared news. Garrick planned his own remarks with care.

"Rosamond!" The minister greeted her with a warm smile. "Look at you. All grown up."

She beamed like a child praised by a parent, although the young minister was perhaps twenty-eight and no more than thirty.

"Reverend Thomas, your sermon was just what I needed today." She glanced at Garrick.

His heart sank. Did she have so much trouble viewing him with Christian charity?

"Permit me to present Garrick Wakefield and Percy Morrow."

As she made the introduction, Garrick realized his mistake. She'd looked at him only to bring him into the conversation. He must cease thinking she bore some antagonism toward him.

After the presentations had been made and hands shaken, Percy added his compliment. Garrick then took his turn.

"Your quotation from Spurgeon's sermon was most appropriate, sir." He saw Rosamond's eyebrows arch. Had his remark sounded arrogant? "When I was a lad, I had the pleasure of hearing Spurgeon speak at Metropolitan Tabernacle. His message 'Pray without ceasing' entirely changed my prayer life. In fact, my life in general."

"Ah, you know Spurgeon's work?" The minister spoke in an amiable Southern drawl.

"Indeed. I have a volume of his sermons that provides excellent reading."

"An entire volume?" If a minister could be accused of envy, Reverend Thomas's eyes took on just such a longing. "I have only a few pamphlets and quotations."

"You must borrow mine." He'd make it a gift and purchase another copy when he returned to London. "I'll bring it tomorrow." He glanced at Rosamond, whose half smile and warm gaze indicated approval of...something he'd done? "Would tomorrow afternoon be acceptable?"

"Yes." She looked behind them. "We should move on."

"Of course." He turned back to the minister. "Could we meet for Scripture study?"

Reverend Thomas smiled. "Entirely possible. We can begin tomorrow, if you like."

"Excellent." Glancing around for Percy's agreement,

he saw his cousin and Rosamond crossing the church-yard toward the Eberly girls.

Beryl gazed up at Percy from beneath her lace para-sol. The two younger ones chatted merrily. Grace stood watching, arms crossed, gun hanging at her side, and a critical gleam emanating from those intense blue eyes. Perhaps she agreed with Garrick that Percy and Beryl shouldn't form an unsuitable attachment.

He took a step in that direction only to be intercepted by Rand and Tolley Northam. Tolley gave him a curt nod, and his lips formed a thin line.

Rand shook his hand. "Did you enjoy the service?"

"Indeed, I did." He wanted to move on but didn't want to offend this man. Tolley already found him lacking in some way. For his own part, Garrick must apply today's sermon and forgive Tolley for tripping him during yes-terday's branding. It hadn't been an accident or prank, but a malicious act.

"I told my Sunday school class about you and Percy," Rand said. "They'd enjoy hearing from you. Would you address them next Sunday morning? We meet an hour before the church service, and we can invite Nate's class to join us."

The unexpected request astonished him. "It would be a privilege, sir." How remarkable that the older two brothers taught Sunday school. Speaking to the lads was an honor he wouldn't decline.

"Yeah," Tolley said. "They'll get a real hoot out of the funny way you talk."

Rand chuckled, giving Garrick pause. Was his in-vitation meant to be an insult rather than an honor? A knot formed in his chest. Whatever they threw at him, he must answer without offending or he'd risk losing Colonel Northam's good opinion.

Rand elbowed his brother. "You'd be surprised, kid. Some of these boys hanker to see the world beyond the San Luis Valley. They may never travel abroad, so this'll be a real treat."

Garrick's knot eased. Tolley, however, snorted and walked away. His brother's use of "kid" made him flinch. Oddly, Garrick felt a measure of empathy, having endured his own share of set downs. At the birth of Viscount Eddington, Uncle's first son, Garrick was demoted in Society's view. No longer heir presumptive to an earldom, thus no longer sought after for future favors, either social or political. Of course, Tolley probably wouldn't understand how crushing that had been. As one of four heirs to his father's wealth, he had a secure future, even if his inheritance was part of a dusty cattle ranch in this remote mountain valley.

Garrick must find a way to befriend him, even though Tolley seemed determined to dislike him. Even though a veiled threat shaded every look the younger man sent his way.

Chapter Four

Rosamond spent the early part of Sunday afternoon making space for Beryl's clothes in her wardrobe.

As she worked, she searched for reasons to like Garrick. He'd given his valet the day off but seemed displeased when Roberts and Richards attended a different church with Rita and Consuela. Of course before Roberts left, he made sure Garrick was properly dressed. She wouldn't let those small matters count for anything. Not much, anyway.

With her room in order, she searched for Percy and found him relaxing in a rocking chair on the front porch. Garrick sat on the porch swing.

"Are you ready?" Why did she sound so giddy? "Beryl's waiting for us."

Percy nodded. "I'll be delighted to see her again." Such a sweet remark, especially since he'd talked with Beryl just a few hours ago.

Was that frown Garrick wore his favorite expression? As they walked around the house toward the barn, Rosamond chided herself. She must stop these unkind thoughts about him.

"We'll take a wagon for Beryl's trunk," she said, "but if you feel like riding, we can saddle horses, too."

Garrick stopped. "Do you mean…?" He clamped his mouth shut and resumed walking.

Rosamond could guess what he'd started to say. "Yep." Her teachers at the academy would have apoplexy over her quick return to Western slang. Yet something about Garrick made her want to do just that. Right away, her conscience smote her. Deliberately irritating a person wasn't the way to show God's love. "The cowhands are off today, so it's up to us to hitch the team to the wagon and saddle the horses."

"Brilliant." His tone suggested something entirely different.

"Capital." Percy picked up his pace. "It's been a while since I saddled a horse. I relish the challenge."

In spite of one reluctant student and another entirely too enthusiastic helper, Rosamond managed the affair without a catastrophe. Soon she was driving the wagon up the lane, while the men rode along beside her. She occasionally glanced at Garrick and noticed him gazing at the distant mountains or watching migrating geese flying above them. Judging from his placid facade, he seemed to be enjoying himself for the moment.

Despite their disappointment over Beryl leaving them, her sisters helped load the wagon. Even Garrick pitched in with heavier items, impressing Rosamond with his strength. With servants to do everything for him, how could he be so strong?

Soon they were traveling back to Four Stones. Beryl sat beside Rosamond on the driver's bench, but she'd tied her mare to the wagon…a good sign. Her willingness to ride might be the first step toward restoring her courage.

Riding close to the wagon, Percy chatted with Beryl

over the clatter of the wheels. A stranger looking on
might assume they'd known each other all their lives.
So far, Rosamond hadn't heard a word of disagreement
between them. They liked the same books, the same
music, the same pastimes. What an agreeable marriage
they could have. Too bad Garrick couldn't hide his disapproval. Did he hold some power over his cousin to
prevent this romance?

The valets returned to Four Stones in time to help
Garrick and Percy move the trunk and luggage to the
bedroom. Consuela helped Beryl unpack, and Rita
planned a hearty meal for everyone rather than taking
the evening off. All four servants appeared to be ener-
gized by a jolly mood, and a hint of romance sparked
between Rita and Roberts. Percy and Beryl still had eyes
only for each other. Rosamond couldn't help but long for
a romance, too, but with so much work for her school
and the hotel, she'd have no time for such an indulgence.
Or so she tried to convince herself.

"That will do, Roberts." In the mirror, Garrick admired his cravat, which his man had tied with expert
precision. Yet for some reason, he felt irritated at being
fussed over despite having been dressed by a valet since
leaving the nursery.

"Very good, sir." Roberts never revealed emotion
while doing his job, although yesterday Garrick had
seen him smile constantly as he talked with Rita in the
kitchen.

When everyone left for church yesterday morning,
he'd not been pleased to see the valets and the female
servants going south while the Northam family traveled north. But, after all, it was the servants' day off.
He couldn't insist that Roberts attend the same church.

"Your portfolio, sir." Roberts handed the folder to Garrick.

"Thank you." He unfastened the clasp and thumbed through the architectural drafts to refresh his memory. All was in order. "I won't need you until after dinner. This afternoon I'm meeting the minister in town, so I'll require something appropriate for the occasion."

"Yes, sir." Roberts coughed softly into his fist, as he did when he wished to speak.

"Yes?"

"Would it be permissible for me to assist Mrs. Northam in her garden this morning?"

Pleased by his valet's thoughtfulness, Garrick nodded. "That's fine."

The smile that spread across Roberts's face extinguished that pleasure. Rita would no doubt be working with them.

Garrick had no time to ponder the matter. He must meet Rosamond in Colonel Northam's office in a few minutes. That thought instantly improved his disposition. Despite her coolness toward him, he'd missed her at breakfast. Or maybe he simply wanted to decipher that coolness and possibly overcome it. He wouldn't succeed with the hotel unless he gained her favor.

As he walked down the hallway to the front staircase, he heard girlish giggles coming through the closed door of her bedroom. Giggles just like his sister's. How would Rosamond and Helena get on? Would they like each other? But they'd never meet, so he shrugged off the thought. Another thought took its place. Rosamond and Beryl were obviously in the midst of a hen party. Would Rosamond even bother to keep their nine o'clock appointment?

Thou shalt love thy neighbor as thyself. Reverend

Thomas, referencing Spurgeon's sermon, reminded the congregation that this Scripture verse was a command from the Lord. Garrick must demonstrate God's love to the young lady by thinking well of her rather than assuming some fault on her part. After all, her care for her friend indicated a nurturing spirit, as did her desire to establish an upper school in this wilderness. In any event, he must work with her, so he'd do well to develop a positive outlook.

As instructed, he made the Colonel's office his own, spreading out his carefully made plans on the large exquisite oak desk. He'd worked with an architect in London before coming to America and knew exactly what to build. Uncle insisted he spare no expense, but of course Garrick wouldn't misuse his generosity.

"Good morning." Rosamond entered the room carrying a tray laden with beverages and fruit tarts.

Garrick's heart seemed to stop. Her gown was the color of daffodils, a shade of yellow few ladies wore well, yet it warmed her complexion to a lovely glow. How beautiful she was, especially when she smiled. Even her eyes shone with enthusiasm, a good sign this meeting would go well.

His heart hammering with this unexpected admiration for her, he stood and walked around the desk. "Permit me?" He took the tray and set it on a side table. Should he compliment her? Tell her she was beautiful? No, of course not. This was a business meeting, not a party. "I don't suppose this is tea?" Oh, bother. That surely sounded like a complaint.

She laughed. He sighed with relief.

"If you recall—" she poured steaming black coffee from the elegant porcelain pot into matching cups

"—our two countries don't share a good history in regards to tea."

"No, but—" the twinkle in her eyes alerted him that she meant the remark to be humorous "—if I'm not mistaken, the relationship between our governments has changed considerably since 1773. After the passing of more than a century, surely we've managed to persuade you as to the superiority of tea over coffee."

She handed him a cup, leaving him to add his own cream and sugar. He added considerable amounts of both to minimize the brew's bitter taste.

"I'll admit an occasional cup of tea makes a nice change. Many Americans prefer it." She took a sip and eyed him over the porcelain rim. "In my opinion, nothing beats coffee to help get the day going."

"Ah, well. To each his own. Or her own." This was hardly a matter to argue over. "I brought some gifts for your parents but haven't yet presented them. Among them is a tin of Earl Grey tea, which has become a favorite among—" he started to say "the British aristocracy," but an inner voice stopped him "—many of my friends."

"I heard of Earl Grey tea at finishing school." She appeared to pucker away a smile. "You know the earl, of course?"

"Of course." The words were out before he could stop them. She'd baited him, and he'd bitten. Now he must try to fix the damage. "Not well, though. And he's the third Lord Grey. The tea is named for the second Lord Grey."

"Be sure to tell Mother when you give her the tea." She stepped behind the desk and began to study the drafts. "She always enjoys little tidbits of history like that." She spoke absently, as if finished with the topic. Or perhaps the drawings distracted her. "So you think the Palladian style is appropriate for our hotel?" Disapproval colored her words.

While impressed by her knowledge of the architectural style, Garrick suddenly felt defensive. She'd learned of the hotel only three days ago, yet she would criticize his many months of hard work? Disparage a building design by London's finest architects?

"Of course. What could draw travelers from Europe to this wilderness better than a hotel built in the grand style to which they're accustomed?" *Bother!* That definitely sounded arrogant. He was tempted to bite his tongue. No matter what she said, he must be a gentleman.

She eyed him and smirked. "Oh, maybe something different. Something more in keeping with the *wilderness* they've come to see."

The steel-like tone in her voice set his nerves on edge and fortified his defenses. Was this a trick? A test? Or did she actually mean to sabotage the one project upon which his entire future rested?

The steely glint in Garrick's eyes signaled war, and she would gladly cross swords with him. These past few days, she'd come up with her own plans for the hotel. Some of the girls at the academy swooned over all things English, but no Englishman was going to try to reconquer her part of America while she could prevent it.

Love thy neighbor as thyself. The inner voice was soft but persistent. She knew the imprudence of failing to listen to it.

With a sigh, she dropped down into Father's chair. "I can see you've been working for some time on these plans. Why don't you show me what you've done?"

He tilted his head as if uncertain he'd heard her correctly. She swallowed a laugh. Apparently he'd expected a conflict as much as she.

"Well, um…" He came around the desk to stand beside her and shuffled through the papers as if looking for something. As he bent over her shoulder, the scent of bergamot filled her senses in a very pleasant way. Bergamot, the essence that flavored Earl Grey tea. Maybe she'd like the beverage more than expected. "It's true that I've envisioned a grand hotel in the European tradition, but when you hear everything, I believe you'll approve." At last he pulled out a crisp white page. "Here is a list of my plans."

She didn't correct his word *plans*, but in her mind, she translated it to *ideas*.

"Lord Westbourne has been very generous with the funds allotted for the project because he hopes the hotel will draw the most august guests from among Europe's aristocracy and nobility, perhaps even royalty."

"Hmm." Rosamond wouldn't let herself say more. He didn't know how much she disdained those very people. If they'd had their way in the past century, the United States wouldn't even exist, would still be colonies enslaved to the whims of a ruthless monarch and the unfeeling nobility in the House of Lords. And now that America was a prosperous country, many titled men came over here to marry heiresses, wealthy girls who coveted those titles and forgot what this country was all about. Rosamond didn't care about drawing European aristocrats to the hotel. Wealthy Americans from the East would come by the droves to experience what the Wild West offered.

"If you will notice—" his voice filled with enthusiasm, Garrick pointed to names at the bottom of the draft "—the hotel was designed by Messrs. Henman and Harrison, the architectural firm that designed the National Penny Bank in London. I've contacted Messrs. Aitohison and Walker, who built that very bank just three years ago. They await my wire and, upon receiving it, will send a team to execute the construction of the building."

Rosamond looked up at him. "Anything else?" She might as well hear everything before unfolding her own plans.

His eyes sparkled, and for the first time, she noticed they were brown. A very nice brown with flecks of amber to catch the light shining through the west window. "The guest rooms will of course be furnished with the finest oak and mahogany furniture from English carpenters and velvet drapes from France. Again, I have simply to wire the firms I've engaged, and they'll ship the items at once or build them to suit." He questioned her with one raised eyebrow, and she nodded for him to continue. "I've also engaged a French chef and a staff of English waiters. And of course a sommelier."

If he said "of course" one more time, she wouldn't be able to contain her annoyance. While he stood back, pride and satisfaction beaming across that well-formed face, she prayed for guidance as to how she might answer each of his ideas. As with her support of Beryl yesterday, maybe she should face this disagreement head-on.

"As generous as Westbourne is—" she refused to call any man *lord* "—his funds will go further if we make a few simple changes."

Garrick stiffened, and his chin hiked up considerably. "What changes?"

In light of all his work, she tried to put herself in his place but couldn't manage it. He had been reared in a culture that still believed in the Great Chain of Being, a view of mankind in which only people born into wealth and aristocracy mattered, only their plans and ideas were worthy of consideration. How could he comprehend American democracy, as imperfect as it was, where any person could rise above humble beginnings to accomplish whatever he or she dreamed of?

"A massive Palladian style hotel is all well and good in the proper setting, but not here. Never mind what your European aristocracy is used to. Americans visiting from the East can see such hotels in their own cities. Out here, they'll want to see something different, something out of the dime novels they love to read so much. So we don't need to import architects and workers from Europe. Not when any man in the San Luis Valley can build a two-story house. The hotel will simply be a bigger house. And, as my father said the other night, plenty of local men need work now that the railroad is completed. Our local carpenter can craft the woodwork, as he did in our ballroom. I saw you admiring it, so you know to what I refer."

The enthusiastic gleam in his eyes turned steely again, but she wouldn't stop until she'd said it all. "The rooms should be decorated in a Western theme, with furniture made by local craftsmen and drapes by our own very talented town seamstress. I envision antlers on the walls beside paintings of our mountain scenery. For the bed coverings, woolen blankets woven by Indian artisans."

What had she left out? Ah, yes. The restaurant. "As you may have noticed, we have excellent cooks in Esperanza. I'll take you to Miss Pam's café so you can taste her Western fare. She'd be the perfect manager for the hotel kitchen. As for waiters, we have many local young people who can learn quickly how to serve, and others who can clean the rooms. Mr. Chen's Chinese laundry should have our business."

She sat back and gave him the most sympathetic smile she could muster until she noticed the look of sheer resentment on his face. But his misbegotten ideas weren't her fault.

"I suppose," he said in a clipped tone, "that you simply forgot about the sommelier. Please don't tell me the bartender in your town saloon is the local wine expert."

"Not at all." She stood and walked toward the door feeling anything but a sense of victory. "We won't need a sommelier because Esperanza has no saloon. By agreement and vote of all of our citizens, we also have a no-alcohol ordinance. No wine will be served in our hotel."

A sommelier, indeed! Exiting Father's office, she felt the need to enlist an ally in this disagreement with Garrick. Mother would understand, but with her health still a concern, Rosamond couldn't burden her.

With each step she climbed up the stairs, her temper rose another degree, along with frustration and annoyance and several other unidentifiable emotions. She hoped Beryl was still settling in so she could get some support, some reassurance. Before she could enter her bedroom, Father emerged from his room dressed for travel.

"That was a mighty short meeting." He tugged at the sleeves of his frock coat. "How did it go?"

She reluctantly faced him. "I thought you left early." She really needed time to sort things out before telling him what had happened. "You shouldn't ride in the heat of the day, especially not while wearing that long jacket and high collar."

"I'll be fine. Don't change the subject." The scolding fondness in his eyes chastened her. "You may have been away for a while, but I can still read you like a book."

"Well." She sighed with resignation. "Your Englishman has some mighty highfalutin ideas for our humble little Valley. Palladian architecture, French chef. Really, Father, you didn't need to import a foreigner. I can supervise building the hotel by myself."

"And build your high school?" His thick, graying eyebrows arched in a challenge.

He'd hit a sore spot, but she wouldn't back down. "You won't be surprised to know I consider the school my highest priority."

He studied her briefly. "No reason the two projects can't be done at the same time, but one person can't do all of the planning and execution. I have a business arrangement with Westbourne. That's why Garrick's here. His involvement is essential." He moved toward the stairs again. "I must be on my way. The army's closing Fort Garland, and I want to keep my connections with the officers and soldiers so they'll recommend our beef for their next posts." He paused two steps down and stared back up at her with his no-nonsense Colonel face, the one she and her brothers knew better than to challenge. "I'm too busy to be pestered by every detail. That's why I assigned the hotel to you. You go work things out with the Englishman. Today."

"But—"

He waved his hand dismissively. "I don't want to hear about it." He continued down the stairs. "You two are adults. Find a way to work together."

She ground her teeth briefly, but concern for him overrode her problems with Garrick. She knew better than to stop Father now, but she'd discuss his health with Mother at the first opportunity. Both of her parents needed to slow down, so she'd also need to speak to her brothers about them.

In her room, she found Beryl primping before her

vanity table, her eyes bright with excitement. "Percy wants a tour of the ranch. Do you mind if I take him?"

"But—" Rosamond clamped down on her disappointment. She wouldn't spoil Beryl's happiness with her own troubles. "Not at all. You know Northam land as well as your own."

Beryl bit her lower lip. "Do you think I should ask Consuela to accompany us? For propriety's sake, I mean?"

"That's a good idea."

Once Beryl left, Rosamond sat in her favorite spot by the window. After Father's scolding, she needed to think, to pray about how to approach this difficult situation. In spite of his orders to work with Garrick, she simply couldn't dislodge her antagonism toward him.

Lord, how can I develop kinder feelings toward a stubborn man with whom I have nothing in common?

Garrick waited until Rosamond left the room and closed the door before he slumped down in the chair she'd just vacated. He rested his elbows on the desktop and put his head in his hands.

"Now what, Lord?" No answer came, as usual. The Lord had been silent from the moment Uncle announced his plans for this hotel. From the beginning, Garrick had doubted these Americans would appreciate finer living.

No, that wasn't fair. The Northams owned a charming house, quite pleasant in this setting. But Rosamond, for all of her talk of simpler ideas, was nothing short of a spoiled princess used to having her own way. Whereas an English lady would state her ideas and then politely acquiesce to his superior plans, Rosamond seemed to enjoy cutting down his every proposal in both her tone of voice and the determination on her pretty face. How could he give over control to her? Uncle would be horrified to learn the plans he'd approved had been rejected. But there was nothing to do for it.

Despite the roiling sea in his chest and belly, he retrieved stationery from the drawer and penned a letter to Uncle calmly stating why the project wouldn't work and requesting permission to return home. He'd post it this afternoon before his appointment with Reverend Thomas. Then perhaps he could seek the minister's counsel about how to recover from this disaster.

The possibility of speaking with a reasonable person served as an impetus to leave straightaway. Garrick went upstairs to change into something more suitable for riding, but Roberts was nowhere to be found, and this house had no bell pulls to summon servants. A search out the window revealed his valet working in the back garden alongside Mrs. Northam and, of course, Rita. Garrick put his hands on the window to raise it so he could call for Roberts but changed his mind after picturing how undignified that would be.

Instead, he searched through the wardrobe and found his riding breeches and boots and quickly made the change by himself. While the completed ensemble wouldn't be approved in London, these people wouldn't know that he should have changed his shirt and waistcoat. If he could have managed to tie on a different cravat, he would have. As it was, this one was only slightly askew. He fussed with it for a moment before going downstairs to inform his hostess of his plans. In the garden, he approached Mrs. Northam, who knelt beside a rosebush with pruning shears.

"Sir?" Roberts hurried over from the next flowerbed and eyed him up and down, his mouth briefly agape. "May I help you?" He held up hands covered with sandy gray soil. "It'll just take me a moment to wash…"

Garrick waved away the idea. "Don't bother." To Mrs. Northam, he said, "With your permission, I'm riding into town. May I bring you anything?"

Her plump cheeks rosy from exertion, Mrs. Northam stood. "My, you look so handsome, Garrick." She brushed the back of her hand over her forehead and looked beyond him. "Isn't Rosamond going with you?"

His throat suddenly closed, and he cleared it with a cough. "No, madam. She, um—" How should he finish the sentence when he didn't know where Rosamond had gone after she left the office?

"Hmm." Mrs. Northam tilted her head and gazed at him thoughtfully. "Well, I don't need anything, but thank you for asking. You go on now and enjoy your ride. Pete's out in the stables, and he'll saddle a horse for you."

"Thank you, madam." Garrick strode across the barn-yard. By the time he reached the barn, his shiny black Hessians sported a coat of fine gray dust. Inside the building, the smells of fresh hay and discarded muck collided, making him dizzy for a moment.

Pete, the groom, provided Garrick with Gypsy, the excellent bay mare he'd ridden the day before, and he was soon on his way. The road into town was as straight as London's Pall Mall, just the sort of stretch that invited a full-out, mind-clearing gallop. But Pete had warned him that these cow-ponies weren't bred for long distance runs, so he settled for alternating between an easy canter and a brisk trot. Gypsy seemed to enjoy being out, and Garrick tried to do the same. After all, he'd made a firm decision about the hotel, so he should be pleased to have that door shut, even if he'd always count it as a failure.

He sent up a prayer for wisdom about his next move, ever mindful that Helena's future came before his own ambitions. He must find an occupation in which he could make enough money to provide a respectable dowry, even if said occupation gave him no personal satisfaction. Nothing came to mind. Who in London would hire him after he'd botched this endeavor?

As his emotions dipped lower, a large blue-gray crane burst into flight from the swampy area that ran beside of the road. Gypsy started briefly, then resumed her pace. Garrick wished he could sprout wings and fly away from all of the mess he'd made of the hotel project. Not really. Better to be like Gypsy and quickly overcome this bit of adversity. The idea cheered him. With one door shut, surely God would open another one. Garrick simply must look for it.

Rosamond's beautiful but resolute face came to mind, accompanied by a strange grief-like longing that sent his heart plummeting again. What could they have accomplished if she weren't so intractable? If she hadn't dashed all of his dreams? He doubted he'd ever answer those questions.

With her friend out at least until dinnertime, Rosamond unpacked some of her textbooks and carried them to Father's office to work on lesson plans for the fall. She always worked ahead on her responsibilities, and she'd need all summer to prepare a year's worth of lessons for three subjects: history, literature and composition.

She opened Goodrich's *A History of the United States of America* and took a sheet of paper from Father's desk to make notes. Indentations marred the stationery. Maybe someone, probably Tolley, had used it for padding rather than write directly on the desktop. Father really needed a new blotter to write on.

Curious, and perhaps a bit nosey, to see what her younger brother had written, she held the page up to the light. She made out the words *Dear Uncle, failure, rejection, disappointment* and *return home as soon as possible.*

Tolley hadn't written this. Garrick had.

A dull ache formed in Rosamond's chest. Garrick Wakefield felt like a failure, and it was all her doing. She could have, should have, been kinder to him from the outset. Could have tried to compromise. If he hadn't been so arrogant and dismissive of all that she loved, maybe she would have felt more inclined to do so. No, that wasn't right. No matter how he behaved, no matter what silly ideas he proposed for the hotel, she should do the right thing. She should at least try to understand him.

She heard the front door open and shut, and then the sound of Beryl's and Percy's laughter wafted into the office. If Garrick left, Percy would leave with him. That might break Beryl's heart. Somehow Rosamond must find a way to work with Garrick so he'd stay.

But that didn't mean she must agree to pretentious Palladian architecture sticking out like a sore thumb smack in the middle of Esperanza. Did it?

Chapter Five

Once he reached Esperanza, Garrick located the livery stable and left Gypsy with Ben, the man in charge. "Just put her in there." He nodded to an empty stall.

"You're a busy man." Chafing at the man's curt order, Garrick led Gypsy into the space and closed the gate.

"Yep." Ben exited the other stall. "Sure could use a regular helper, but this time of year most local boys work in the fields or with the herds up in the mountains." He eyed Garrick. "Any of the hands out at Four Stones free?"

Why would the man think he knew such a thing? "I've no idea."

"Well, send 'em to me if you hear of one."

Garrick strode out of the stable. It was enough that he'd put his own horse in the stall, beyond enough to be expected to find an employee for the man. At home, even after he'd lost his expectations, Uncle's servants always showed him proper respect.

He marched up the street toward the mercantile, where a sign on the door read Post Office. His energetic walk cooled his temper. He must remember these Americans had different customs regarding, well, just about everything. Exhibit A: Miss Rosamond Northam and her quickly concocted plans for a Western-style hotel. But he was through with all of that and wouldn't think about her.

Inside the mercantile, several people he'd seen at church gave Garrick pleasant greetings. Two young girls eyed him with obvious admiration, giggling until the matron with them shushed their silliness. If Rosamond were of a different temperament, he wouldn't mind such admiring looks from her, but he doubted she would ever view him favorably.

The proprietress greeted him warmly and assured him his letter would go out on the morning train. He paid the pricey postage and walked back out into the sunshine, his mood anything but bright. Uncle wouldn't receive the bad news for weeks. Several more would pass before he responded. How could Garrick endure the endless days before he received permission to return home? How could he go back to Four Stones and face Rosamond for a good part of the summer? If only he could contact Uncle more quickly.

The telegraph. He should have thought of that first. Though the expense would cut into his funds, he'd send the wire: *Hotel project failed. Request permission to return to England straightaway*, thus reducing a two-page letter to ten words.

Buoyed by the thought, he strode down the dusty streets. Ahead he saw Adam Starling speaking to a man, who waved him away. The boy approached another person, who also spurned him. Was he begging? Had no one met the family after they arrived? Garrick lifted a hand to hail the lad.

"Adam."

He turned lethargically, and Garrick reached him just as he fell forward. Garrick caught him in his arms.

"Easy now, lad." Garrick looked around indignantly. Why hadn't anyone helped this needy boy?

Adam swiped a grimy hand over his eyes. "Oh, it's you, sir. From the train." His voice weak, he struggled to stand on his own.

"Yes." With considerable difficulty, Garrick subdued his emotions. "I'm Wakefield. Where's your mother? Where's Jack?"

"Over yonder." Adam pointed to the rear of the train station.

Garrick saw only a makeshift canvas tent.

"She's pretty wrung out," Adam said. "Probably sleeping."

In the distance, the whistle of the morning train pierced the air. Bile rose in Garrick's throat. If Adam's mother was sleeping, would Jack wander off again?

"Come along." To help the boy walk, Garrick put an arm around his waist, feeling gaunt ribs through the tattered cotton shirt. He urged him over the tracks to the tent. "Mrs. Starling, are you there?"

Adam lifted the canvas side to reveal a heartbreaking sight. Garrick needn't have feared Jack would get away from her again, for the child lay limp in his mother's arms. Beside them sat the little sister, her round blue eyes staring at nothing.

"Right." Garrick ground his teeth. Where was the man of this family? Where was the compassion in this town? He doubted Rosamond would stand for this, considering the charitable way she cared for her friend. "Come with me."

Mrs. Starling blinked and shaded her eyes. "Will you help us?"

The plaintive tone in her voice deeply moved Garrick. With her children's lives at stake, she couldn't afford to be proud. "Yes. Come along now." He knew he sounded cross, but he could barely speak over the emotions clogging his throat.

Not caring what the provincials on the street thought, Garrick half carried, half herded the little family to Williams's Café next to the mercantile. Once he explained the family's dilemma to the proprietress, Miss Pam expressed great dismay.

"Why, I had no idea. My Charlie's the telegraph operator, and he's usually right there at the train station. But he's been checking the wires between here and Del Norte for the past several days. Otherwise, he'd have brought them here to me." She instructed her waitress to bring four bowls of chicken and dumplings. "Are you hungry, too?" she asked Garrick.

Until that moment, he hadn't been, but the aroma of the food generated an embarrassing growl in his stomach. "Yes, I suppose I am."

"Make that five bowls, Leah," she called to the waitress.

He gave her a wry grin, and she chuckled on her way to the kitchen. The woman's goodness stirred more unruly emotions in Garrick. He forced his attention to Mrs. Starling, who sat across from him with Jack in her lap. Beside her, Adam held the little girl, Molly. Just the promise of food seemed to give them strength to sit up and await their dinner.

Garrick marveled at God's hand in the day. The Almighty was using him, perhaps not to build a hotel, but to save a family. While it didn't redeem his own future, or Helena's, it was good. It was right.

As she ate, Mrs. Starling told her story. Her husband had worked on this leg of the railroad and wanted to settle in Esperanza. He sent money for their fare from

St. Louis, but when they arrived, no one knew anything about Bob Starling, and her money ran out.

"I need a job." Tears reddened her eyes. "Any decent job."

"Me, too." Adam's pallor lessened with each bite of food.

Garrick felt better himself. This might not be French cuisine, but at least he now understood Rosamond's preference for Miss Pam becoming the hotel chef. Perhaps the idea had merit. Or perhaps they could offer both European and American cuisine. On the wall, next to a lovely painting of a snow-capped mountain, a menu listed venison, beef, pork, duck, turkey and chicken dishes, along with a variety of desserts. While limited and somewhat plain, the bill of fare would satisfy hungry travelers. Perhaps—

"You know of any jobs, sir?" Adam recaptured Garrick's attention.

He'd been offended by the livery stable owner's request, yet now God's plan became clear. "Have you worked with horses?"

Adam's brown eyes lit up. "Yessir. I've got a way with 'em, don't I, Ma?"

She spooned a fluffy bite of dumpling into Jack's mouth. "You sure do."

"Brilliant. The livery stable owner requires an assistant. I shall take you there after we finish eating." Even if Ben had already found someone, Garrick would find a way to employ the boy. Anything to keep Garrick busy and away from Four Stones, away from the lovely, maddening Rosamond Northam.

Other customers now filled the restaurant, giving Garrick a moment of unease. What would his friends back in London think if they saw him eating with this ragtag family? The look of gratitude in Mrs. Starling's eyes and the sweet grins from Molly, Adam and Jack dispelled all such thoughts. When God was at work, what difference did other people's thoughts make? Now, what should he do next to help the Starling family?

Miss Pam brought several slices of apple pie and a small pitcher of thick cream. "You gonna take these folks out to Four Stones?"

"Hmm." Garrick mulled the question over briefly. He mustn't assume the Northams would welcome unexpected guests, especially now that he and Rosamond were at odds. And, of course, Adam should live closer to the livery stable. "I believe lodgings in town would serve better. Do you know of any for rent?"

Her warm brown eyes twinkled, and the smile permanently etched in her kind face beamed brighter. "I do."

When Garrick didn't return for the noon meal, Rosamond fretted until she remembered his appointment with Reverend Thomas. Maybe he and the minister had eaten dinner at Williams's Café. She chuckled to herself. After tasting Miss Pam's cooking, maybe he'd change his mind about bringing a chef all the way from France.

After the meal, she sent Beryl, Percy and Mother away and stayed to help Rita clean up the kitchen. She enjoyed being back in the routine of the ranch. Of course before she went to Boston, no valet tried to shoo her from the kitchen and take over her duties.

"Please, Miss Rosamond, do let me help Rita." Roberts took a freshly washed dish from her and dried it with a tea towel. "You must have more important things to do."

The hopeful look in Rita's eyes was all the reason Rosamond needed to make her exit. Two romances were blossoming right under her nose, and she'd do all she could to encourage them both. And she did have something important to do: figure out how to manage Garrick and his impossible plans. Maybe if he understood how short summers in the Valley were and how winters sometimes made building impossible, he'd realize they couldn't wait until workmen arrived from England. And since Father had already provided much of the building materials, they could get to work right away.

With much more to ponder, she took a writing tablet from Father's desk and made her way to the front porch. Beryl and Percy sat on the swing, deep in conversation, so Rosamond turned to go back inside.

"Rosamond, wait." Beryl beckoned her to a nearby chair. "I want you to hear something." While Rosamond obeyed, Beryl nudged Percy. "Tell her."

"Oh, well…" He tugged at his collar. "Don't really want to tell tales out of school."

"It's not gossip," Beryl said. "I think she needs to know."

Rosamond's curiosity was piqued. "Is this about Garrick?" *And why he's so arrogant?*

"Yes, actually." Percy shifted in his seat, setting the swing in motion. "I was just explaining to Beryl—" he cast an admiring look her way "—why this hotel business is so important to him."

Rosamond did her best not to gape. Hadn't she prayed just this morning for a way to understand Garrick? "How interesting. I'd like to know, too."

At Miss Pam's recommendation, as soon as their meal was finished—with leftovers packed up in a tin pail for later—Garrick took the family to the Chinese laundry, where he paid the proprietor a week's rent for two upstairs rooms and meals. Mr. Chen even offered Mrs.

Starling part-time work ironing shirts. Garrick surveyed the establishment. It was clean and efficient in every respect. Perhaps Rosamond was right about using their services for the hotel.

At the livery stable, Ben was more than pleased to put Adam to work straightaway. Before Garrick left, the boy pumped his hand in gratitude. "You saved our lives, sir."

"Oh, I may have helped a little." While his praise was encouraging, Garrick reminded himself that he'd merely done his duty before God. Of course that always lifted his spirits. "Now, you must take care of your mother."

With all things managed by early afternoon, he rode to the parsonage beside the church. A note on the door bearing his name informed him that Reverend Thomas had had an emergency call. He apologized for missing their meeting and requested another, if convenient, on Thursday. Garrick scrawled an affirmative answer on the page and left it in the door.

This was no doubt best. After all, helping the Starlings had cheered him so much that he might blurt the story to the minister. Once his emotions settled, he'd consider telling the cleric about the Starlings, but only to ask his help in watching over the little family. On the other hand, he wouldn't tell Rosamond or any of the Northams about what had happened today. The Lord commanded that alms should be done in secret, so such boasting was unseemly.

Still, as he rode south toward the ranch, his heart overflowed with peace and joy. Even his resentment against Rosamond dissipated. He couldn't comprehend why God brought him over five thousand miles from home just to help Adam's family, but a sense of satisfaction and trust filled his soul nonetheless.

"Very well, Lord, what's next?"

Gypsy perked up her ears at his words, and he laughed clear down to his still-full stomach. How very good the laughter felt. So good that a new energy and motivation to complete the hotel project swept through him. Was this the Lord's answer? If not, then why did he have a sudden desire to find a way to please Rosamond? If her ideas about the cook and laundry weren't unreasonable, which of her other ideas had merit? That exquisite mountain painting in the café might be a sample of some local painter's work, so perhaps her thoughts about the decor of the rooms might also have worth. Even the carpentry work in the Northams' ballroom compared well with the furniture in Uncle's manor house.

But how could he compromise with her without giving way in every decision they must make? Somehow he must try. If young Adam could forge ahead despite difficulties, Garrick could do no less. The moment he returned to the ranch, he'd find Rosamond and attempt to negotiate with her.

The letter! Why had he so hastily sent it? Why had he given up so easily? Now when Uncle received it, he'd lose all confidence in Garrick, all respect for him.

Reining Gypsy around, he urged her to a gallop, his heart dropping lower with every beat of her hooves on the roadway. At Mrs. Winsted's shop, he leapt from the saddle, lashed the reins around the hitching post and hurried inside.

"Madam—" he gasped for air, for calm, lest he appear like the numbskull he was "—my letter?"

She gave him a maternal smile. "Don't worry, my boy. I took special care to see that it went out on the noon train."

* * *

"So you're telling me Westbourne can't bequeath even one of his properties to Garrick?" Rosamond was tempted to chew her thumbnail, a habit she'd overcome with some difficulty only last year. Percy's revelations about his cousin being replaced as his uncle's heir stunned her. No wonder Garrick seemed surprised that she and her brothers shared ownership of Four Stones with their parents. Yet in spite of his loss, Garrick was still arrogant. Anyone who grew up expecting to inherit an earldom would surely be devastated, even humbled once he was replaced by his uncle's direct heir. Perhaps being an aristocrat gave him that attitude of superiority. How very medieval. Still, she felt some sympathy for Garrick, especially after seeing what he had written to his uncle.

"Not even a rental house." Percy nudged the porch swing into motion, and Beryl smiled as if he'd handed her the moon. "According to English law, everything Lord Westbourne owns was entailed generations ago and must go to his eldest son, little Viscount Lord Eddington. Even his second and third sons won't inherit, although Westbourne will no doubt make some financial arrangements to provide them with a means to earn their living."

"Well, I should hope." Rosamond considered how diligently Father endeavored to help her and her older brothers achieve their dreams, providing money and any other resources they needed. What parent wouldn't do that? And even though Westbourne was Garrick's uncle, he still should be allowed to bequeath him something if he wanted to. "Where does that leave you, Percy?"

He laughed and traded a look with Beryl as if they'd known each other for years. "I'm not related to Lord

Westbourne. Garrick and I are cousins through our mothers, who were sisters."

"Are your properties entailed?" Rosamond knew the question was terribly rude, but if Percy couldn't provide for Beryl, she wasn't sure the romance should go forward. Not if some relative could be born or come out of the woodwork and claim Percy's fortune.

He laughed again, as he often did. "No. My late father earned his fortune from the sweat of his own brow in trade, and I'm his only heir."

"What a blessing for you." The anxiety she'd felt for her friend's future ebbed away. Marrying Percy was just the thing for Beryl. In addition to being kind and romantic, he'd grown up knowing how to take care of himself. He'd probably observed his father's hard work, maybe even worked beside him, as Rosamond and Beryl worked alongside their parents.

"Oh, look." Beryl pointed west toward the road from town. "Looks like the object of our discussion is coming back."

"I say." Percy glanced at each of them. "Let's not tell the old boy we were talking about him." A guilty frown wrinkled his fair brow.

"I can't promise that, Percy," Rosamond said. "It doesn't seem honest. Besides, I don't keep secrets well. Why not just tell him you explained the English system of inheritance to us."

"Brilliant. I'll do that." He didn't seem in the least dismayed by her refusal. "He's truly trying to make something of himself with this hotel business. I'm not certain, but I believe Lord Westbourne contrived the project just for him, and I'll do anything to help him succeed."

In that moment, with these new insights, Rosamond knew she also wanted Garrick to succeed, knew she'd go far to help him. But not at the cost of building an impractical eyesore in the middle of Esperanza. If he agreed to compromise on some of his plans, she'd change some of hers.

As he rode closer, she could see his shoulders slumped as though he was depressed. He looked toward the house and straightened, lifting his riding crop in salute. Once again, her heart stung for him. She might not think much of arrogant English aristocrats, but in his short time in Colorado, Garrick hadn't displayed the least bit of bitterness toward being replaced as his uncle's heir. She could certainly admire him for that.

Riding down the lane toward the house, Garrick was dismayed to see he was being watched. If they noticed his dejected mood and asked him about it, he'd blame the altitude. No one needed to know about the letter, any more than they needed to know about the Starlings. He'd go on as if he hadn't written to Uncle. Tomorrow he'd post a letter of apology and pray for understanding.

After Father and Mother died when Garrick was five years old and Helena newly born, Uncle had been a kind, if distant, parent to them. He'd excused and forgiven many childhood mistakes. Surely he'd regard Garrick's letter as a mistake if he sent a speedy retraction.

He pasted on a grin and rode up to the front of the house before remembering that no groom would dash out of the barn to take charge of his horse. *Bother!* He really must get used to these American customs, even if that meant learning how to curry a horse.

"Good afternoon." He raised his bowler hat in greeting to Percy and the young ladies. "What mischief did you three plan while I was away?"

Percy laughed, and Beryl echoed him—not a good

sign. They were already too fond of each other. When
Rosamond gave him a faint smile, however, his spirits
lifted considerably. Perhaps their association would improve. With her long dark hair curling around her face
and shoulders, she looked particularly fetching. Even
agreeable. He could only hope.

"Come join us in our mischief," she called. "I'll have
Rita bring out some lemonade and cookies." From her
friendly tone, she could be inviting him to afternoon tea.
One would never know they'd parted at odds this morning. Another good sign.

"Must see to the horse first." He smiled and tilted
his head in the direction of the barn. He'd need to tell
the groom about riding Gypsy so hard and offer to pay
for any harm done. Actually, he could tell the mare had
enjoyed the gallop and seemed no worse for it, but one
could never be too careful with horses.

"Just leave her with Pete," Rosamond said. "He likes
to feel needed."

Garrick pondered her remark as he rode Gypsy across
the barnyard. Obviously the bow-legged, gray-haired
groom was too old for such strenuous cowboy duties
as branding, perhaps even herding cattle. Yet, like an
old pensioner on one of Uncle's estates, Pete remained
employed on the ranch. Garrick could only admire Colonel Northam's sense of *noblesse oblige* toward those
who served him. Such generosity must cost him a pretty
penny, possibly a sign of sufficient wealth to match Uncle's investment in the hotel.

Pete assured him that Gypsy had suffered no harm
and refused the coin Garrick tried to give him. "Just
doing my job," the old fellow protested. Garrick had
never encountered an English servant who rejected a
gratuity.

As he left the stable, several black-and-white puppies—sheepdogs, by the look of them—scampered out of a stall and followed, tripping over each other in their eagerness to catch him.

"Hello, you little rascals." He made the mistake of bending down to scratch the ear of the most aggressive pup, only to have the others—five more, he now realized—jump and whimper for the same favor. When Garrick tried to step away, they were just large enough to knock him off balance. He landed on his backside with an *umph*. Barnyard dust flew up to cover his black boots and coat and tan riding breeches. His bowler hat tipped dangerously and dropped to the ground. One of the pups grabbed it by the brim and raced away.

"Come back here, you little beast."

Garrick scrambled to his feet and gave chase. The pup ducked under the bottom slat of the barn corral, denting and then ripping the black crown on a nail. The little scamp's brothers and sisters were right behind him in hot pursuit, barking and yipping as they ran. Garrick started to climb over the fence but stopped with one foot on the lowest rail. Three of the dogs grabbed the hat and growled and tugged as if it were a rabbit they'd caught for their dinner. In seconds, the brim separated from the crown.

Garrick stepped down, rested his forehead on the rough wood and heaved out a long sigh. What else could go wrong this day?

Chapter Six

Anticipating Garrick's return, Rosamond left Beryl and Percy long enough to go to the kitchen and ask Rita to prepare the refreshments. When Garrick had offered a smile before going to the barn, she sensed it had been forced, yet she still hoped his time away from her had improved his thoughts as it had hers. Maybe his talk with Reverend Thomas helped him sort things out in some way.

Shortly after she returned to the front porch, the sound of high-pitched barking reached them.

"The puppies!" Rosamond hadn't paid attention to them since returning home. "Let's go find out what they're up to."

"Capital." Percy stood and took Beryl's hand. "I'm quite fond of dogs."

They rounded the corner of the house and saw Garrick resting his head against the top rail of the corral, his clothes dusty and rumpled, his hair blowing loosely in the breeze.

"What on earth?" Rosamond and the others hurried across the barnyard.

"I say, old man." Percy reached his cousin first. "What happened?"

Garrick turned a frustrated look in his direction and waved a hand toward the puppies. "Those little scamps decided to eat my hat for dinner."

"Oh, no." Rosamond's heart sank. "They've ruined it. Oh, Garrick, I'm so sorry."

Percy burst out laughing and slapped Garrick on the shoulder. "I say, now you'll have to purchase one of those cowboy hats."

"Yes," Rosamond said. "And I'll pay for it."

Garrick shook his head. "That won't be necessary." Before she could insist, he eyed the puppies and gave a snort of exasperation. "Are they always so aggressive?"

Rosamond shrugged. "I've been away for two and a half years and haven't met this litter. Tolley's supposed to be in charge of their training." For a moment, she watched them roll in the dust, growling in their puppy ways and chasing each other around in the otherwise empty corral. Before she could stop herself, she began to giggle at their silly antics.

Beryl and Percy joined in, and soon Garrick chuckled.

"Ah, well. It's only a hat." He heaved out a resigned sigh. "Now, what's this I hear about biscuits and lemonade?"

"I believe they're called cookies, old boy." Percy looked to Beryl for approval. When she gave him a smile and a nod, he beamed like a boy just commended by his teacher.

"Ah, yes. Cookies."

As Garrick viewed the two, worry skittered across his brow. Rosamond bit her lip to keep from asking why. She truly wanted to feel kindly toward him, but if he hurt Beryl, she must protect her friend.

They traipsed back to the front of the house just as Rita and Roberts brought out lemonade, cookies and small sandwiches. At the sight of his employer, Roberts almost dropped his tray full of pitcher and glasses.

"Oh, sir!" He set his load down on the small wicker table and whipped a small brush from his pocket as fast as Rosamond's brother Rand could draw his Colt .45. "You must permit me to assist you."

"Never mind." Garrick waved him away, giving Rosamond a sheepish glance. "I should like to sit for a moment before I change."

"As you wish, sir." Roberts eyed his employer doubtfully, but nevertheless, he and Rita quietly withdrew.

"Did you enjoy your visit with Reverend Thomas?" Determined to be a gracious hostess, Rosamond poured glasses of lemonade and passed them around. At her nod, Beryl offered the sandwiches and cookies.

Garrick took a long draft and released a quiet, satisfied sigh. Then color crept up his neck. Instead of a well-bred Englishman, he sounded more like one of the cowboys as he drank. "Forgive me. I didn't realize how thirsty I was." He shrugged sheepishly. "Unfortunately, the good Reverend was away on an emergency. I plan to go back on Thursday." He took a sandwich from the platter.

Rosamond tried to guess why he'd stayed in town for several hours, but wouldn't ask. She'd needed the time away from him. Now she felt as if she were meeting him for the first time, only this time she was prepared. Now that she knew more about his past and knew what Father's expectations were, she could move forward with more confidence. Garrick seemed to be relaxing, too. Maybe they could talk about the hotel after supper. She'd come up with several ideas and would make this consultation go better than their first.

Rather reluctantly, Garrick carried his portfolio back to Colonel Northam's office. With an hour or so of pleasant chitchat on the porch, a change of clothes, a delicious supper of beef stew and the American version of biscuits, he hadn't yet written down his ideas for compromise. One thing remained firm in his mind: the Palladian facade. A grand building like that would enhance the appearance of the little town and raise its status as a tourist destination for European aristocracy eager for an experience in the Wild West and willing to pay a pretty penny for it. Rosamond might well be right about wealthy eastern Americans wishing to visit the West as well, but he wouldn't have Uncle shamed in front of his friends by offering inferior accommodations.

She entered the room on an airy cloud of rose perfume and wearing a frilly white shirtwaist and a green skirt that reflected in her eyes, intensifying their emerald color. To his shock and horror, Garrick's heart jumped to his throat and then plunged to his stomach. *Lord, I must not develop feelings for Rosamond.* He couldn't marry, couldn't even fall in love, at least not until Helena's future was secure. Not until his own future was settled.

"Shall we begin?" Her agreeable smile suggested this meeting would go well. "If you'll permit me?" She sat at the desk and glanced up at him, those bright green eyes twinkling in the light of the kerosene lamp. Once again Garrick's heart leapt into his throat.

"One thing you may not have realized as you made your plans," she continued, "is that our winters are long and harsh here in the San Luis Valley. Sometimes it's impossible to do any building. If we're going to please my father and your uncle in a timely fashion, we need to get this hotel built this summer. Agreed?"

Still lost in the fragrance of her perfume and gem-like color of her eyes, he took a moment to grasp what she'd asked. He coughed into his fist and swallowed. He'd spent very little time with young ladies other than his sister. Was Rosamond flirting with him?

"Well?" She blinked, but not in a way to suggest she was batting her eyelashes at him. Still, it was a becoming gesture, and his pulse increased.

"Yes. Yes, of course." He tugged at his collar. This cool, pleasant evening suddenly felt warm. "I'll wire my building contractors first thing tomorrow morning."

She shook her head and frowned. "It'll take too long for them to arrive. We need to start building right away."

So she wouldn't compromise. All of his pleasant thoughts fled. "But—"

She held up a hand to silence him. "Please let me explain."

He gave her a curt nod. Not the most gentlemanly thing to do. He instantly regretted it.

In response, she wrinkled her nose in a rather attractive way, which nonetheless signified her displeasure with him. "Father already ordered the stones to be cut from our local stone quarry. The quarry's over near Del Norte, and they have beautiful pink rock of the finest quality just perfect for our hotel."

Now Garrick blinked. "Pink stone available from local quarries? And you say the Colonel has already ordered them to be cut to our specifications?" Right away he could envision the carved pediments above the portico, just as Messrs. Henman and Harrison designed it. Like the Parthenon in its heyday, it would gleam in the sunlight. Too bad the local landscape was so flat. Such a stately building should stand on a hilltop like the Acropolis. Still, her information recharged him and made him certain this project would work after all.

"Tell me more."

Rosamond couldn't ignore the way her heart tripped when Garrick's handsome face lit up with interest and excitement. She'd been around strong, attractive men all her life yet never reacted this way to a single one of them. To her chagrin, she was behaving like a giddy schoolgirl. In fact, she had to force her thoughts back to the purpose for this meeting.

"The stonemasons who built our town bank used that pink stone," she said. "Father likes the look of it, so that's why he chose it. When he and Mother first returned from Italy, he ordered enough stones to be cut to supply the outer walls for the hotel. The master mason who supervised the bank project still lives in Del Norte. We'll hire him to adjust your exterior design and a master carpenter to complete the interior. I think we'll both be pleased with the results."

The amber flecks in his brown eyes caught the lamplight and twinkled like gold. Then he frowned, and the light went out. "What did you mean about adjusting my exterior design? It's flawless. What's more, with the drafts supplied by Messrs. Henman and Harrison, the plans are ready to execute."

She sat back, resisting that perpetual urge to chew her thumbnail. Instead, she gave him a conciliatory smile. "Do you like the idea of using the stone?"

His guarded look shouted his distrust. "Well, yes. Of course. Who wouldn't agree a stone building is superior to a wooden one?"

She bristled at the haughty tone permeating his words

but quickly calmed herself. Father had said to work things out, so she would ignore Garrick's aristocratic attitude. Maybe he couldn't help how arrogant he sounded. His English accent seemed to resonate with an air of superiority.

"Well, then." She gave him a businesslike smile. "Shall we agree to have the stones sent over right away?"

Puzzlement crossed his face. Had he expected her to argue? "Yes, of course. Right away." He frowned again. "Although I should like to inspect them first, of course."

"Of course." She gritted her teeth for a moment. Another thing she must ignore was his favorite phrase, *of course*. "We can go tomorrow. Rita can pack a picnic, and Beryl and Percy can go with us."

He frowned again. "Well, perhaps Percy—"

Would he disapprove of every idea she offered? She stood abruptly, not willing to listen any further. "Chaperones." She brushed past him.

"Ah, yes. Of course."

Of course. Again! She whipped around, one scolding finger raised and cross words on the tip of her tongue. At his look of innocent puzzlement, she shook her head, turned and sailed out of the room. She'd get along with him. She *would*.

What on earth had he said to annoy her? This woman was entirely too temperamental. But then, Garrick hadn't been a model of pleasantness himself, so he must accept some of the blame for their lack of compatibility. Of course, if she simply wouldn't disagree with almost every one of his concepts, if she'd simply acquiesce to his master plans, they could get along famously. But no. She had her own ideas. He huffed out a sigh, a snort, actually. This was what came from trying to accomplish something in partnership with an American, and a female, at that.

He lowered the wick on the kerosene lamp to douse the flame, then followed Rosamond out of the office into the hallways lit by candles in wall sconces. In England, most upper-class houses and businesses used gaslight for illumination. Would gaslight work in the hotel? Or would Rosamond find fault with that idea, too?

Upstairs, as Garrick started to enter his room, Percy offered him a cheerful goodnight, lifting his mood a little. Maybe his jolly cousin could serve as a sort of buffer between Garrick and Rosamond—if he wasn't too busy dancing in attendance on Beryl. But that was a problem for another day. Garrick fell asleep trying to sort out which items on his planning list could be modified and on which ones he must stand firm.

The next day's weather was agreeable, if a little warm. Shortly after breakfast, Garrick made his way to the barn. With no footman to inform the stable boy of their need for a carriage, Garrick volunteered to carry the message, mainly to avoid another conflict with Rosamond. She'd barely spoken to him at breakfast. Nor had Tolley been the most pleasant meal companion. He'd glared at Garrick across the table, his dislike obvious. Of course, he laughed when he learned how his pups had destroyed Garrick's hat, as though he'd instructed the beasts to do it. When Mrs. Northam suggested that her youngest son lend Garrick one of his hats, Tolley had pretended not to hear her, instead asking Rosamond to pass the bacon and eggs.

As Garrick strode across the barnyard, an odd little thought—revolutionary almost—took root in his mind. He'd sensed from the beginning that Rosamond didn't care much for him. While she didn't completely ignore him, as the young ladies in London had, she also didn't seem to respect him. What sort of man did she respect?

She clearly adored her three brothers. Unlike wealthy, indolent English sons, all of the Northam offspring worked alongside their cowhands. Yet, as Garrick had noticed at church on Sunday, they received the community's highest regard. In England, such esteem was reserved for the wellborn, their birthright, so to speak. Perhaps to earn similar regard from these Americans, Garrick should follow the customs of the land and lend a hand around the ranch. He hadn't found the branding enjoyable in the least. Thankfully that job was completed for the year, so he needn't attempt to master the skill. But he might prove useful at other tasks. He sent a silent request upward asking the Lord for wisdom in how to proceed.

Encouraged by the promise of *James* 1:5—"If any of you lack wisdom, let him ask of God, who giveth to all men liberally and upbraideth not, and it shall be given to him"—Garrick strode into the barn. On guard against an attack by the rascal puppies, he was relieved to see them curled up in a furry black-and-white mass in the first stall. Only one lifted a sleepy head to eye him before dropping back to sleep.

Garrick found Pete cleaning an already spotless harness with saddle soap on a cotton rag. The wiry old cowboy set aside his work, stood from his seat on a hay bale and tipped his wide-brimmed hat.

"Mornin', Mr. Wakefield. What can I do for you?" His wide grin, which revealed a few teeth missing and many years of wear on those that remained, bespoke the very kind of regard Garrick sought. His piercing blue eyes also exuded warmth that went a long way to soothing Garrick's sense of rejection.

"Pete, I want your job."

The old man blinked. Then he burst into a loud guffaw. "Awright, boy. You're hired." He fisted calloused hands at his waist. "What do you want to learn first?"

Pleased to be so quickly understood, Garrick waved a hand toward a back stall. "We're going into town, so I'd like to learn how to prepare that surrey for the trip."

"Didn't I hear tell that you and Mr. Morrow learnt about hitchin' up wagons on Sunday from Miss Rosamond and Miss Beryl?"

"I'm afraid I didn't do much to help." And could kick himself for having missed the opportunity. His foolish pride had kept him from accepting Rosamond's tutelage.

"I'll be happy to oblige." Pete walked toward the stall. "Let me get it."

"Permit me." Garrick strode after him. "I want to know how to manage by myself."

That comment earned him another one of those piercing looks, along with a nod of approval. With some difficulty, Garrick managed to pull the conveyance out into the barnyard. Thankfully, he'd not lost all his strength despite not exercising these past weeks as he traveled.

Pete told Garrick how to make certain the carriage was clean and sound and then sent Garrick into the back corral to fetch Old Sam, a large brown gelding, out to the barnyard. At Pete's instruction, he gave him a good brushing, attached the freshly cleaned harness, guided the beast backward between the shafts and secured the trappings.

Garrick worked up quite a sweat, but completing the job alone brought him an unfamiliar sense of satisfaction. When Pete patted him on the shoulder and commended his work, satisfaction threatened to turn to pride. Should he tell Rosamond he'd prepared the surrey? No.

That would be boasting. She might even laugh at him for thinking the deed remarkable.

He climbed onto the front bench and lifted the reins, only to discover his hands stung from his labors. If he drove to town, as he intended to do, he ought to wear gloves. The gelding had a soft mouth and required little direction as he guided him to the front of the house. Garrick left the animal to nibble on the front lawn while he went inside to fetch the others.

Rosamond wore a pretty blue gingham frock that turned her green eyes a lovely shade of turquoise. Her thick, dark brown hair was swept up into a charming coiffure beneath a pretty straw bonnet, and tiny gold-and-pearl earrings dangled from her ears. As Garrick helped her into the front seat of the surrey, he caught the scent of her rose perfume. Her elegance and grace stirred his heart dangerously...until she assumed the driver's seat on the right and took up the reins.

"Do permit me to drive, Rosamond." Garrick hoped she wouldn't argue.

To his relief, she merely turned a quizzical look his way. "Do you know how?"

He chuckled softly. If only he could tell her how many curricle races he'd won. But again, that would be boasting. "I did manage to bring the surrey around from the barn."

"Oh, pish-tosh." Percy thumped him on the shoulder before climbing into the back beside Beryl. "My cousin is far too modest. He was a champion driver at Oxford. You can trust him entirely."

Garrick couldn't stop the flush of pleasure creeping up his neck. Good old Percy, bragging about him that way.

With a shrug, Rosamond scooted over to the left side. "Very well. Let's see how you manage."

Had she decided not to approve of anything about him? Disappointment dispelled his momentary elation. In its place, wounded pride reared its ugly head, and Garrick did nothing to stifle it. He must remember his purpose for being here, not only for his sister's benefit, but for his own sense of self-worth. Miss Rosamond Northam might not think much of him, but he'd prove himself worthy of Uncle's trust by building the grandest hotel possible in this inhospitable wilderness.

Rosamond watched Garrick from the corner of her eye, silently approving the way he drove up the lane and onto the main road into town as though driving were second nature to him. As Percy had indicated, Garrick did know how to handle the reins. Yet she couldn't bring herself to compliment him for his skill, even when he carefully guided the mare around a hole in the road. Any cowboy could do the same. She and her brothers didn't expect praise for knowing how to do such a simple task. Besides, if she told him he was doing a good job, he'd probably say, "Of course."

Lord, forgive me. This morning while reading her Bible and praying, she'd promised the Lord she'd try to get along with Garrick, even be hospitable. But the dark looks he'd given Tolley over the breakfast table made the promise hard to keep. Yesterday when the puppies destroyed his hat, he'd been rightfully displeased, yet eventually laughed it off. When Tolley laughed at the story, however, Garrick reacted poorly. No wonder Tolley ignored Mother's request to lend the Englishman a hat.

How she wished she could enjoy this lovely day like her friends in the backseat. Beryl and Percy talked softly, with Percy remarking about this or that bit of scenery and Beryl explaining some historical note about the site.

Rosamond released a quiet sigh, wishing she could think of a pleasant topic of conversation. She noticed Garrick's bare head and his dark, curly hair being tossed across his forehead by the breeze in an attractive way. She squelched the giddy jump of her heart over his manly presence. They had nothing in common, and she refused to become fond of him. On the other hand, she owed him a hat and would purchase one for him.

"Let's stop at Winsted's General Store before we go out to the quarry."

He gave her a sober nod, while a slight flicker in his eyes suggested he was pleased with the idea. "As you wish."

At the store, Mrs. Winsted greeted the party in her usual welcoming fashion, even speaking to Garrick like an old friend. "I guess that letter you sent yesterday is halfway across Kansas by now." She chuckled. "Don't think I'll ever get over how fast letters can get from one place to another since the railroad came."

While Beryl and Percy traipsed off to shop, Garrick pulled an envelope from his inside jacket pocket and held it out to Mrs. Winsted. "Would you be so kind as to post this one on today's train?"

Curiosity seized Rosamond, but she couldn't ask to whom he'd written. Nor could she read the address before Mrs. Winsted took it in hand.

"Another one to that Lord Westbourne, eh?" Mrs. Winsted eyed him with obvious admiration as she accepted his coin, stamped the missive and placed it in her outgoing mail pouch. "You'll end up broke writing to him every day."

Garrick glanced at Rosamond, puzzlement in his eyes. Did he wonder how to answer Mrs. Winsted's harmless comment? Was he actually looking to Rosamond to help him out? The urge to rescue him swept away all curiosity about why he'd written to his uncle twice in two days.

"Mrs. Winsted, our English guest lost his lovely black bowler hat yesterday in an unfortunate incident." Rosamond grasped Garrick's upper arm, surprised at the bulging muscle beneath the black linen frock coat. She tugged him toward the display of men's hats. "Oh, look, Garrick, she has several bowlers. But I'd suggest a Stetson, since you'll be out of doors a great deal. Their wider brims protect you from the sun. Here, this white one's perfect for you."

Before he could object, she placed the headpiece on him and gently shoved him toward the mirror on the counter. "See how handsome you look?" Had she actually said that? Heat rose up her neck and into her cheeks. "Just like a cowboy."

"A cowboy?" He snorted out a mirthless laugh. "Ah, yes, the epitome of manliness."

Was that sarcasm or resignation in his voice?

"I say." Percy approached with Beryl at his side. "What a ripping good hat, old boy. Don't you think?"

Garrick grimaced. "Maybe in another color. Perhaps a black one?" He handed the hat to Mrs. Winsted. At her negative response, he said, "Tan? Brown?"

She offered a brown one, but it was too small. "I'm afraid white is all I have in your size, Mr. Wakefield. We'll have a new shipment from Philadelphia next week."

"White it is, then." Percy triumphantly placed it back on Garrick's head.

A few minutes of animated debate between the cousins gave Rosamond a chance to whisper to Mrs. Winsted that she must put the cost of the hat on the Northam account. The storekeeper nodded and then put an end to the discussion with "Wear it for a few days, Mr. Wakefield. If you decide it's not for you, bring it back."

"Please do that, Garrick," Rosamond added. "If we're going to get out to the quarry and do everything else we need to do today, we can't spend any more time here."

Before Garrick could object, they bustled him out to the buggy, and soon they were on their way west to the quarry.

Rosamond watched Garrick from the corner of her eye. He really did look handsome in that white hat. Maybe she'd made a mistake to insist that he take it. The last thing she needed was something else to make him more attractive to her. Even his befuddlement over their insisting that he take the hat caused her heart to hiccup. Like Father when Mother took charge of some clothing issue, Garrick exuded a charming vulnerability in the face of his quandary. No wonder he needed a valet to see to his attire.

Garrick felt as if everyone on the street were staring at him. In fact, several people he recognized from church did take a second look after waving at the surrey's occupants. He felt ridiculous in the hat, almost like a fraud. While he had no doubt he could master any skill a cowboy performed, he hadn't the slightest desire to make it his life's work. He certainly didn't want anyone to mistake him for a rancher.

Once they arrived at the quarry some seven or so miles west of Esperanza, however, he gave over his objections to the hat. The sun beat down relentlessly as they toured the vast stone works, and the wide brim did indeed protect him from its burning rays. By the time they'd settled their business with the master mason and headed back toward town, Percy, being of a fairer complexion and wearing his black bowler, had turned quite red around the edges.

"We'll get you a Stetson, too," Beryl said. "And as soon as we get back to Four Stones, we'll apply some aloe to keep those spots from blistering." Her maternal tone set Garrick's nerves on edge. How could the two of them become so familiar with each other in less than five days? And how could he keep them from growing any closer?

Halfway back to town, at Rosamond's direction, Garrick drove the mare to a shady spot beside the river that ran some hundred yards north of the road.

"I love to picnic here," she said as he helped her down from the surrey.

"Me, too," Beryl added. "I chaperoned Marybeth and Rand on a picnic a few miles up the road when they were courting." She giggled like a schoolgirl. "Right then, they didn't know they were courting. Everybody else did, though."

Percy found her observation particularly humorous, if his jolly laughter was any indication. "I've observed that sort of thing from time to time in my few years of life." As he helped Beryl lay out the picnic blanket, he cast a look at Garrick. "Some people just don't realize the value of what's right in front of them."

Garrick glared at his cousin. He most certainly was not courting Rosamond, nor did she seem the slightest bit interested in his doing so.

They settled down on blankets and began to dine on the fine picnic packed by the Northams' cook. Garrick made up his mind to enjoy this grassy scene of pine and cottonwood trees, with wildflowers blooming in little patches here and there. The air was fresh but thin, which tired him and made him long for a nap. But the exquisite pink stone in the quarry fired his imagination, making sleep impossible.

One thing was now settled in his mind. When Garrick had taken the master stonemason aside to ask about payment, the man told him Colonel Northam had paid in full for the entire shipment. That settled at last his concerns about the Colonel having sufficient wealth for his share of the project.

Mr. Frisk, the master stonemason, added that his workmen would begin transporting the prepared stones to Esperanza straightaway. The foundation would have to be laid first, and then the masonry frame walls would go up. They hoped to finish the exterior before the end of June, leaving the interior to carpenters, who would frame in the interior walls with wooden studs, cover them over with lath and plaster and finally apply wallpaper. Artesian wells would supply water throughout the building. The main section of the hotel should be completed and ready for guests by early September before the weather turned cold. After that, the workmen would continue to build a second wing of the hotel as long as the weather remained agreeable.

Garrick could now report to Colonel Northam that the hotel would soon become a reality.

Rosamond appeared as excited as he. She'd made notes in a small journal along the way and now retrieved it from her reticule and focused on him.

"I noticed in your plans that you've already ordered the furniture and velvet drapes, but only for the first wing guest rooms. Our local carpenter can make the furniture for the second wing." She paused to take a bite of her roast beef sandwich. "What about cotton curtains for the less expensive accommodations?" She gave him a glorious smile that gave no hint of their previous disagreements.

That annoying little hitch in his chest happened again, not unlike when Uncle had given him his first pony. Percy nudged him and smirked, and he realized he was sitting frozen with a sandwich halfway to his lips.

"Yes, of course. Cotton curtains. Brilliant idea."

Rosamond seemed to hide a laugh as she stared down at her journal. "Mrs. Winsted can order the fabric. Mrs. Beal, our town seamstress, will appreciate the work." She cast a frown in his direction as though she expected disagreement. "She owns a Singer, and her work is of professional quality."

"Very good." Garrick's first thought was Mrs. Starling, but he wouldn't contradict Rosamond now that they seemed to be getting along and the subject was as simple as curtains. In any event, he hadn't seen a sewing machine among her few belongings. "Perhaps she could use an assistant."

Rosamond regarded him, curiosity beaming from those bright green eyes. "Probably. Do you know of anyone?"

He'd spoken without thinking. How could he explain that he knew someone in Esperanza, especially a woman, to whom he'd not been properly introduced? There was nothing for it. His pride mustn't keep Mrs. Starling from additional employment. "I do. I met a lad in town whose mother might be interested in the position."

The girls didn't seem to find it strange, but Percy questioned him with a look and then shrugged when Garrick didn't answer. Instead, Garrick accepted a biscuit—*cookie*—from Rosamond and ate it to avoid further comment. The less anyone knew about his helping the Starling family, the better.

* * *

Rosamond couldn't have been more pleased with the day. After they had finished their picnic, they'd traveled to the carpenter's establishment in Esperanza. They'd finally arrived home to find Father back from his travels. As they sat around the supper table, she and Garrick had much to report to him on their activities.

"Mr. Schmidt welcomed the opportunity to work on the hotel," she said. "He's happy to make time in his busy schedule to construct the interior walls and build furniture for the hotel." Rosamond couldn't keep the excitement from her voice. "He's going to write to his sons in Denver to come down and help. He'll also hire other qualified local workers."

"From what I've seen of his work," Garrick added, "I'm quite pleased. And he has no difficulty reading my drafts."

Father gave an approving nod to Garrick, who was seated on his right and across the table from Rosamond. "I knew I could count on you two to get this project underway. Now, how about that high school of yours?" His eyes twinkled with interest and a bit of teasing.

A warm feeling swept through Rosamond. So he did care about her school. "I haven't had time to plan anything, but I'll get busy right away." She might as well give voice to her main concern. "With workers needed for the hotel, I'm wondering who'll be left to build it."

"I can help." Tolley, seated adjacent to Mother at the other end of the table, wore that familiar puppy-dog look that begged for Father's approval. "Seems like—"

"What do you think, Garrick?" Father didn't even look at Tolley, whose face fell.

Rosamond's heart ached for her younger brother. Father never listened to him, only gave him orders. If he were a troublemaker, she'd understand, at least somewhat. But Tolley only ever tried to do what was right, just like their older brothers.

Garrick gave no indication he'd noticed the way Father interrupted Tolley. "I'm certain Rosamond will devise the perfect plan." He smiled at her across the table. "Please let me know if I can be of any assistance."

"Thank you. I will." Any other time, that charming smile and agreeable attitude would stir her feminine appreciation. Yet she couldn't let go of her concerns about Tolley, who now glared at Garrick as if he were the reason Father ignored him. Intervening never worked, so after dinner she'd ask her brother for his ideas.

As for Garrick, she decided they'd worked through their differences almost effortlessly, although she wasn't quite sure how. Nor was she certain she could trust him for further details in completing the hotel. Only time would tell. In the meantime, she'd try to figure out why Tolley didn't seem to like Garrick. Maybe he saw something in the Englishman the rest of them had missed.

Chapter Seven

Rosamond fidgeted in her chair in the parlor as she and Beryl watched Garrick and Percy battle over a chess game. Beryl watched with interest, but Rosamond found the game too slow and quiet. Besides, her mind was on Tolley, who still hadn't returned to the house from evening chores.

"Checkmate," Percy cried. "I've beat you at last."

"Good match." Garrick laughed, clearly not bothered by his loss. "Ladies, would one of you like to try?" He stood and waved a hand toward the chair he'd vacated.

"I would." Beryl moved quickly to take his place. "At home, I'm the only one who plays, other than Pa." She set about putting her chessmen in order with graceful hands that belied her cowgirl upbringing, hands that used to lasso calves and harvest hay fields. Percy watched her, his blue eyes bright with admiration.

Delighted at her friend's blossoming romance, Rosamond smiled to herself...until she caught Garrick's frown. If he disapproved of Beryl, he never should have let her take his place at the chessboard. Annoyed, she stood and moved toward the door. "I'll be on the front porch."

She hoped Tolley hadn't decided to sleep in the bunk-house but would soon return to the house. She wanted to know about his ideas for the high school. More important, she wanted him to know she thought he was a smart, capable man. After all, with Nate and Rand living in their own houses some distance away from the big house, Tolley was responsible for many of the duties close to home. Nobody had to tell him to go out and milk the cows or organize branding time. He also commanded the respect of the cowhands. Even the older ones didn't seem to mind taking orders from him, though he was only twenty years old.

Outside, she sat in the porch swing and gazed toward the western range, barely outlined in the fading twilight. Lantern beams from the house cast shadows on the front lawn, and a mild breeze kept insects at bay. How she loved to sit here alone in the evenings and watch the stars sprinkle themselves across the inky sky.

"Would I be imposing if I joined you?" Garrick didn't make a sound as he came out the door.

"Not at all." His presence didn't bother Rosamond as much as it should have, considering her annoyance with him only a few moments ago.

In truth, he did bother her, but the disturbance was of another sort. They'd all washed up after their trip, and now his bergamot cologne wafted through the air in a most pleasant way. He'd given Mother the Earl Grey tea, and the aroma of bergamot was becoming one of Rosamond's new favorites, a dangerous situation. In his presence, every bit of good sense seemed to fly out of her head.

"Are you pleased with the events of the day?" Garrick settled in the nearby rocking chair and regarded her with an uncertain look. He wasn't at all like the young men in Boston who'd sought her out, usually trying to court her. Instead of a confident, aggressive approach, he seemed a bit awkward, even bashful. Not that he was courting her. Certainly not. On the other hand, he was never shy when they discussed plans for the hotel. And he'd been quite authoritative at the quarry, impressing even the master mason with his knowledge of stonework.

"I'd say the day turned out very well." Rosamond gave him a guarded smile. She mustn't forget Tolley's obvious reservations about Garrick. "Not only did we find our builders, but I believe we settled most of our concerns." She wouldn't mention the hotel facade. She had a suspicion Garrick had spoken privately to Mr. Frisk about the Palladian design. But at this late hour she was too tired to start an argument.

"Hey, sis." Tolley emerged from the house, a sweet grin on his still-boyish face. Until he saw Garrick. "Wakefield." He gave him a curt nod as he sat beside Rosamond and flung an arm over the back of the swing. The protective gesture wasn't necessary, but if she playfully shrugged him off, he'd be embarrassed in front of Garrick. Besides, for some reason, he seemed to want to protect her from the Englishman, and she'd never discourage any of her brothers from such inclinations.

"Tolley." Garrick returned Tolley's nod, but the sigh that followed suggested he wasn't pleased with the interruption.

Now she wouldn't have a chance to ask why he came out to join her. As far as Tolley was concerned, however, she knew exactly what to ask, even if Garrick heard it.

"Hey." She gently elbowed him in the ribs. "I'm dying to know your ideas for my school. Any help you can give…"

Even in the shadows, she saw his face light up. He

glanced at Garrick and then turned a shoulder to him, as though to exclude him. "Seems to me the ones to build the school ought to be the ones who'll attend it."

Weary as she was from a long day, Rosamond felt a rush of energy. "Yes! What a grand idea. Thank you." She gripped his free hand, even as a problem occurred to her. "But won't the school-age boys be too busy with ranching and farming to help? Summer's not the best time to take them away from their families, but we need the building before fall."

"True. But most of the fellas want to attend high school bad enough to use their free time to help out." He lifted his chin and gave her a triumphant smile. "I've been talking it up since last fall when Mom told me about your plans."

Grateful tears stung her eyes. "Oh, Tolley, how can I ever thank you?" She nestled under his arm and gave him a tight hug, ignoring the scent of a day's hard work emanating from his shirt. Why couldn't Father see what a wonderful, hard-working man his third son had become?

"And if you need a foreman to manage the project," he said, "my time off is yours to command. Just tell me what you want."

She pulled back and regarded him with a playfully skeptical look. "And exactly what have you built, Mr. Foreman, that gives you sufficient experience for the position?" She injected a teasing tone into her words so as not to reveal the pinch of doubt in her mind.

"You been over to Rand and Marybeth's house? It's two full stories, and I did as much as Rand and more than Nate in building it."

"I'm sure it's beautiful. That reminds me. I've neglected my sisters-in-law since coming home and should visit both of them. I'll inspect Marybeth's home closely."

Even though she still teased him, she felt certain Nate had taught him everything about building a solid house. As they were growing up, Nate was always more father than brother to Tolley. Which helped, considering the way Father ignored him.

"All right, then. Once you tell me what you want, I'll start rounding up those volunteers." Tolley stood, pulled her up beside him and started to tug her toward the door. "Time to go in."

"Oh." She hung back. "I think Garrick wants to discuss the hotel." He might want to discuss something else, but she couldn't just abandon him here on the porch.

"If he does—" Tolley shot a warning look at Garrick "—he can come inside where the rest of us are."

Rosamond barely managed to swallow a laugh. She mustn't make him feel bad for wanting to protect her reputation. She reached up on tiptoes and kissed his cheek. My, how tall he'd become. If she wasn't mistaken, he had at least an inch on Nate, maybe two on Rand. Her baby brother had become quite a man over the past two and a half years, and somehow she must make their father see it.

Garrick followed Rosamond and Tolley inside. He'd hoped for a private chat with her, perhaps to inquire about her interests beyond ranching. From the first, he'd been fascinated by her plans to establish an upper school for the local youths. Even more remarkable, she not only planned to teach at the school but also to take on the duties of headmistress. Although some young ladies back home involved themselves in charitable works, most were too busy with their social lives to think of those less fortunate.

Tolley's suggestion of using local boys to build the

school was quite brilliant, if they were all as capable of building as he'd boasted. Before Garrick could compliment the younger man, however, Tolley had insisted that they go inside. While his concern for his sister's reputation was commendable, something Garrick himself would do for Helena, his persistent hostility was mystifying since the two of them had barely spoken a few dozen words to each other since Garrick had arrived in Esperanza. How could Garrick make peace with him? He had noticed the way Colonel Northam ignored his youngest son, another mystifying situation. Should Garrick mimic the Colonel's behavior or go out of his way to show respect for Tolley? Rosamond obviously loved all of her brothers, but her eyes held a hint of compassion for Tolley. Perhaps Garrick should follow her example.

Later that evening, as Roberts helped him prepare for bed, Garrick experienced an odd moment of impatience. How ridiculous that he couldn't manage a simple task such as shedding his clothes and putting on a nightshirt. Even the Colonel didn't employ a valet, yet he was always well groomed and impeccably dressed. Did Garrick's need for such assistance diminish him in the eyes of these self-sufficient cowboys? While he wasn't at all prepared to dismiss Roberts, perhaps Tolley's disdain could be overcome if Garrick continued his plan to learn cowboy ways.

Tomorrow he'd rise before the sun, dress himself and make his way out to the barn. Pete had offered to teach him ranch duties, so he'd make good use of his time until the work crew and materials arrived for the hotel. Maybe he'd even learn how to milk a cow. Well, no. That was a bit too much.

Before falling asleep, he once again considered the differences between English and American customs, even their diverse ideals. At home, he'd been respected and honored simply because of his family's wealth and position and, of course, his own expectations within the hierarchy of British Society. How quickly that had changed when Uncle sired a direct heir and Garrick learned he must earn his own living, not to mention Helena's dowry.

Here in America, any footloose wanderer could buy a piece of property, settle down and build a respectable life within a community of good people. Considering his own loss of expectations, Garrick suddenly found that idea appealing. Where in England could he change the course of his life rather than suffer the whims of heredity?

With a weary yawn reminding him of how much energy he'd expended that day, he sent up a sleepy prayer that the Lord would waken him before dawn so he could find Pete and start on his new project. Perhaps he should spare his Hessians any damage and purchase a pair of those boots everyone wore out here. After all, he already possessed a very fine cowboy hat. Might as well complete the ensemble. Perhaps even one of those garish plaid shirts...

"Come with me," Rosamond said to Beryl and Percy, who sat very close to each other on the other side of the round breakfast table. Fortunately, Garrick wasn't there to frown at them. "Marybeth will enjoy the company. Ranch wives get pretty lonely, especially during the summer when their husbands are so busy." She wouldn't tell them she'd be inspecting the house Tolley built or that he'd volunteered to round up workers and build the high school. If his work wasn't satisfactory, she'd tell him she'd made other arrangements. That would break her heart—and his—so she prayed he'd done a good job.

"Would you enjoy visiting Marybeth?" Percy gazed at Beryl like a lovesick puppy.

"If you would, I would." Beryl returned his fond look.

"It's settled, then." Rosamond didn't give them a chance to change their minds. "We'll leave in ten minutes." Taking a last sip of coffee, she rose from the table.

Courtesy demanded that she must also invite Garrick to go with them. Except that he wasn't in his room, and even Roberts didn't know where his employer was. Rosamond wouldn't waste time searching for him. If they arrived at Marybeth's early enough, they could help her with morning chores and give the new mother a rest. Tomorrow they'd do the same for Susanna.

Sure enough, they found Rosamond's newest sister-in-law sitting in the parlor rocker, trying to comfort seven-month-old Randy, who was teething.

"We brought you some fresh milk, Marybeth." Rosamond put two full mason jars into the ice box. "I see Rand's been to the ice house recently."

"Thanks. Yes, he's good about keeping a supply in the house." Marybeth held Randy against her shoulder and patted his back as he whimpered. "There's coffee on the stove, so help yourselves. No cinnamon rolls this morning. I haven't even fed the chickens or gathered eggs."

"What can we do to help?" Rosamond brushed a hand over Randy's damp, down-like brown hair.

"Well…" Despite Marybeth's weary gaze, her face shone with a sweet, maternal peace.

"Permit Beryl and me to help you." Percy bent down to peer closely at Randy. The baby's crying became a whimper. Percy made a ridiculous face at him, and Randy hiccoughed out a giggle. "I say, what a delightful little lad."

Marybeth laughed. "You're good with him. Why don't you hold him and I'll gather the eggs." Her eyes sparkled with teasing, and she lifted up her son toward Percy.

"May I?" Percy took the baby in hand as if he'd done so before.

"I didn't really mean to trouble you." Marybeth stood and placed a clean diaper over Percy's shoulder.

"Nonsense. No trouble at all." Percy clearly enjoyed what he was doing, even when Randy grasped the end of his nose with damp fingers.

Rosamond, Marybeth and Beryl stared at him, mouths agape.

"Whyever are you looking at me that way? Can you not see that Randall Jr. and I have formed a bond?" He bounced as he spoke, further delighting Randy. "You ladies run along and tend those chickens. We gentlemen will do just fine."

Beryl gazed at him as if he'd parted the Rio Grande during flood season. "Where did you learn to manage babies?"

He gave her a modest smile. "When Lord Westbourne and his new bride began filling their nursery, I visited with each new addition. Jolly little lads, they are." He slid a glance toward Rosamond. "I must say, for a man who's been displaced as his uncle's heir, Garrick certainly does dote on his little cousins."

How generous of Percy to turn the attention to Garrick. Obviously, he wanted to stir up a romance between his cousin and her. While that would never happen, Rosamond was still moved by his comments, which she fully believed. When they'd all arrived in Esperanza last Friday, Garrick had made friends right away with Nate and Susanna's two children. And he spoke of meeting some boy in town whose mother needed work. The arrogant Englishman she'd overheard in the Denver train station hadn't sounded at all like a man who cared for children or needy mothers.

Tolley might still have his problems with Garrick's English ways, but Rosamond must consider this other side of his character. His privileged upbringing wasn't a fault any more than hers was—simply a fact of life. In spite of it, he appeared to have a generous spirit. Maybe she should try to dig a bit deeper and find out just what motivated him.

Beryl stayed inside to help Percy while Rosamond and Marybeth tended the chickens and gathered eggs. They came back inside to find Beryl in the rocking chair, holding a very happy baby sucking on a white cotton cloth.

"See how clever Percy is." Beryl beamed up at him. "He put a piece of ice in this napkin, and it's soothing Randy's teething pain."

"I'd never have thought of that." Marybeth sighed. "Mother Northam and Angela, Susanna's stepmother, come over when they can to teach me about mothering, but I've lots to learn." She smiled at Percy. "Thank you." She reached out for her son, but Beryl held tight and rose from the chair.

"Now, how about a tour of this pretty little home?"

The house turned out to be everything Tolley had said. With four rooms on each floor, the growing family had plenty of space. The bedrooms and parlor walls boasted flawlessly applied wallpaper. Further, Marybeth felt secure during winter storms and fierce spring winds.

"The windows barely rattle, even upstairs, and only a little sand blows in around the edges from time to time." She laughed. "No house in the Valley can escape that."

Delighted with Tolley's excellent work, Rosamond turned her attention to helping Marybeth in the kitchen. She and Beryl made bread, killed and dressed a chicken, peeled potatoes and carrots and set a pot of stew to boiling. Plenty of wood already sat stacked in a bin near the cast-iron stove, so Percy brought in water from the outside pump and refilled the stove's water tank.

With another trip to town on their agenda, they declined Marybeth's invitation to stay for dinner and rode back to the big house in time to freshen up and eat with Mother and Father. And Garrick.

"I say, old man." Percy clapped his cousin on the shoulder. "Where've you been? What did you do all morning?"

Garrick shrugged. "I managed to keep busy." He stared down at his plate and began to eat.

Rosamond thought she saw him grin before he took his first bite. What was he hiding?

Garrick hid his smile by taking a bite of a gravy-covered muffin—or biscuit? He still had much to learn about translating Americans' misusage of the language into proper English. The cooking, on the other hand, was varied and delicious—at least everything Rita prepared. And devouring this delightful concoction before him kept him from having to answer Percy about his activities.

Until today, he hadn't been terribly concerned about keeping his lessons with Pete a secret. Yet as the morning progressed, he realized learning a cowboy's work would require considerable effort. If it took too much time away from the hotel project, he might reconsider his hopes of impressing Tolley and Rosamond on their own ground. Then, if he failed at the attempt, only he and Pete would know.

He had, however, ordered a pair of boots from Joe, who operated a tannery at Four Stones Ranch. Joe promised to deliver them within a week. Further, Garrick successfully saddled Gypsy, the bay mare the Northams had assigned to him. Before putting the blanket or saddle on her, he brushed her carefully to remove any possible burrs or other debris from her sleek, reddish-brown coat. She leaned into the brush, clearly enjoying the attention. Then, as he shook out the blanket, she turned her finely shaped head and acknowledged him with a friendly nudge. Grooms had always taken care of his ponies and horses on Uncle's estate, so until today he'd had no idea that grooming a horse helped one make friends with the creature. Gypsy had minded him from the start, but now she actually seemed eager to please him.

Maybe if he did something nice for Rosamond, he could win her over, too. Not that he was comparing her to a horse, of course. In any event, pleasing her was a pointless goal. Uncle was the one whom he needed to satisfy. On the other hand, that didn't mean he couldn't enjoy himself away from the building project. Winning Rosamond's admiration somehow became his new objective. And Tolley's, of course, though he wasn't quite sure why. Perhaps because Rosamond cared so much for her younger brother.

"Shall we go into town and arrange for the hotel curtains?" Rosamond asked.

At her benign smile, his heart hopped like the little frog he'd seen by a stream this morning during his ride with Pete. He wanted to please Rosamond, wanted to return to England knowing he'd earned this strong, intelligent American woman's respect. Oddly, the thought of leaving her caused Rita's fluffy muffins to sit like a rock in his stomach.

"Well?" Rosamond asked across the table, her eyes filled with amusement.

"Yes." Garrick realized he'd been staring at her without responding to her question. "Yes, of course. Town. Curtains. And don't forget the bedding."

Beside him, Percy snickered. If Garrick weren't so set on limiting his cousin's contact with Beryl, he'd tell him to stay home. But he and Rosamond required a chaperone, so all four must go. At least that way, Garrick could keep an eye on the would-be lovebirds.

"Rosamond." Colonel Northam dabbed his lips with an elegance befitting an aristocrat. "Make sure you ask Mother whether she needs anything from town."

"Yes, sir." Rosamond turned to Mrs. Northam. "Mother?"

The older lady's pretty smile was identical to her daughter's. "I need to work in the kitchen garden this afternoon, so thank you for saving me a trip. I'll get my list."

At their first stop, Mrs. Beal welcomed them into her front parlor, which she'd turned into a showroom for her wares. While Rosamond explained the purpose of their visit, Garrick surreptitiously inspected the seams on a gown displayed on a dress form, pleased with what he saw. As Rosamond had said, the Singer machine stitches were even and secure, promising long wear for the garment. Curtains received less abuse than clothing, so they'd last for years. He fingered the cuffs of the dress. Perhaps he should engage the woman's services to make a plaid shirt for him.

"Oh, my. I'd be delighted to make the curtains and bedding." Mrs. Beal spoke with a genteel southern American accent. "Why, as soon as you provide the material, I'll set aside everything else to complete the work in time for the hotel opening."

So much for his new shirt. Garrick couldn't be too disappointed, however. With the start of each part of the hotel project, his enthusiasm for the work grew, something he hadn't anticipated when Uncle proposed it. "Perhaps you could use some help. I know of a woman who recently arrived in Esperanza who would welcome the work."

Rosamond gave him one of those pretty smiles, and that annoying frog hopped inside his chest again. "Would you like a helper, Mrs. Beal?"

The cheerful tone in her voice indicated her support of Garrick's idea, and the frog hopped higher and annoyed him even more. But then, he had a simple explanation for such odd excitement. After a rocky beginning to their collaboration, they were starting to see eye to eye on everything. Yes, of course. That was it. He wasn't forming an attachment to her. Not in the least.

"Why, yes, I would," Mrs. Beal said. "I'll speak to my daughter, Lucy, about working with me. With the twins and another one on the way, she and Seamus will welcome the extra income. But I'm sure with all those rooms to decorate, we'll need more than two seamstresses. Can you vouch for this other woman's sewing skills?"

Even though he'd inspected Mrs. Beal's work, Garrick hadn't considered whether Mrs. Starling could sew. Fortunately, when they found her hanging clothes behind the Chinese laundry and explained the purpose of their visit, she pointed to the dress she wore, one of her own creations. The well-worn garment was held together with small, tight stitching.

"In St. Louis, I sewed for some upper-class ladies, so I don't think you'll be ashamed of my work." Her eyes fell on Garrick. "Mr. Wakefield, you've surely been sent by the Lord to help us out. I've asked around town, but still haven't been able to find out what happened to my husband." Her voice broke, but she straightened her spine and lifted her chin. "Now, thanks to you, we'll manage until he shows up."

Rosamond eyed him, curiosity sparkling in her emerald eyes. He frowned and gave a quick shake of his head to forestall any questions, at least for now. Maybe she'd forget Mrs. Starling's grateful remarks and he wouldn't have to explain. He didn't want praise for doing what any decent man would do.

As Rosamond gave the woman directions to Mrs. Beal's house, an idea came to Garrick that would solve two problems. He'd challenge Percy to find this lost Mr. Starling. That would help the little family and keep Percy too busy to spend time with Beryl. Garrick had been quite uncomfortable watching the two of them traipse off to the mercantile while he and Rosamond went in search of their seamstress. This would put an end to the cozy pairing.

While he could see certain admirable qualities in the little ginger-haired girl, she simply wouldn't make an acceptable wife for Percy. His cousin was destined for great things at home in England. Marriage to an American, especially a cowgirl, would ruin his every chance to make his mark in Society. Garrick's duty was to see that didn't happen.

Chapter Eight

Rosamond thought the day went very well. Not only did they find their seamstress and an assistant for her, but Mrs. Winsted promised to order the fabric tomorrow. They also found everything on Mother's list in the mercantile. In former days, housewives had needed to order many items, but Mrs. Winsted now stocked a greater variety of goods to satisfy most household needs.

In celebration of the day's success, each of them found something personal to purchase: Percy a pocketknife, Beryl a pair of lace gloves, Rosamond ribbons for Lizzy and a top for Natty. Even Garrick, as particular as he was, found a ready-made plaid shirt he liked.

"What do you think?" He held it up for them to see. The golden strands woven through its brown pattern accented the amber highlights in his eyes and complemented his newly tanned complexion. The shirt more than suited him; it made him even more attractive.

Of course, Rosamond couldn't tell him that, so she simply said, "Looks good."

"I do wish Roberts were here to help me decide," he muttered to Percy.

Rosamond and Beryl giggled. Apparently, a well-bred

Englishman required his valet's approval for any clothing choices. Rosamond found his uncertainty both winsome and charming.

"Not at all, old boy." Percy smacked his cousin's shoulder. "As Rosamond says, it looks fine." He chuckled. "Just like a cowboy."

From the pleased look on Garrick's face, Percy's remark was the deciding factor. "I'll take it."

Interesting. So Garrick wanted to blend in with the locals. Rosamond could only wonder why, especially after he'd seemed so disdainful of cowboys. As he drove the surrey back toward Four Stones—quite handily, she admitted—she used the opportunity to keep her resolve to know him better.

"How did you say you met Mrs. Starling?" Her curiosity increased when he gave her a worried glance.

"Her son works at the livery stable." He refocused on the road ahead.

"I say, was that the lad—" Percy started.

"Stubble it, Percy." He shot a look over his shoulder that silenced his cousin.

How strange. Why didn't Garrick want Percy to ask about the boy? With his replies so cryptic, she might need to ask his cousin if she wanted to learn more about him. But that wasn't the easiest thing to do when they were usually all together. Maybe she should ride into town tomorrow and ask Mrs. Starling how she'd met the Englishman.

The following day, however, she remembered her plans to help Susanna. She, Beryl and Percy rode over to the one-story house Nate had built for his bride five years ago. Like Marybeth, this young mother also had her hands full with a home and two small children to care for. After they helped her catch up on chores, Susanna expressed heartfelt gratitude in her genteel Southern way. Lizzy and Natty loved their gifts. Playing with the children for a while was an added bonus of the visit.

They'd invited Garrick to go with them, but once again, he'd declined and, over dinner, brushed aside their questions about his morning's activities.

"Leave the man alone." Father waved his fork at Rosamond as if it were a royal scepter. "I'd imagine he's working on hotel plans. Isn't that right, son?"

In the corner of her eye, Rosamond saw Tolley wince and then glare at Garrick. She didn't recall ever hearing Father address her younger brother as "son" in that same paternal tone. She sent her brother a sympathetic smile, but he'd already turned his attention to his plate.

Oblivious to Tolley's wounded look, Garrick paused with his forkful of green beans halfway to his mouth. "Working. Yes, of course, sir." He ate the bite, and she suspected he'd done so to keep from giving Father a complete answer.

Now her curiosity grew like Jack's bean stalk. His complexion had tanned more than yesterday, a sure sign he'd been outside all morning. He even bore the telltale lighter color to his upper forehead to indicate he'd been wearing his new hat. Yet he probably wouldn't work on the hotel plans outdoors. Besides, he'd brought his completed plans with him from England and had already given copies to the master stonemason and the carpenter. Now all he had to do was wait for the materials to arrive and building crews to assemble.

"Sir," Garrick said, "what would you think of having a bit of a ceremony when we lay the hotel cornerstone?"

Father's eyebrows shot up, and he leaned back in his chair. "Fine idea. I like that. We can have Fred Brody photograph the event and print it in the *Esperanza Jour-*

nal. He mails his newspaper all over the country, so this will be excellent advance advertising. Maybe Boston and New York papers will reprint the story."

"I can speak to Brody this afternoon, sir. I'll be in town to meet with Reverend Thomas."

"Very good." Once again, Father sent him an approving smile.

Once again, Tolley glared at Garrick from the other end of the table.

Once again, Rosamond's heart split in two. She'd been taught never to contradict her parents, but with the passing of each day, each incident, she longed to tell Father he was making a terrible mistake giving such favor to a stranger while ignoring his own son.

Garrick settled into the chair in the parsonage kitchen. He still hadn't become accustomed to this Western practice of being entertained in a room the English considered "below stairs," the sacrosanct domain of servants, especially since most houses seemed to have perfectly charming little parlors. Ah, well. When in Rome…

He took a bite of the cinnamon roll Reverend Thomas offered him. "Quite tasty. My compliments, sir."

"I didn't make them," the minister said as he poured coffee into two cups. "Mrs. Foster, the church organist, sent these over. The local ladies keep me well supplied with hearty meals." He patted his flat abdomen as he sat down. "I'm always tempted to overeat."

Like most of the men Garrick had met in Esperanza, the young minister looked like a cowboy, even in his black linen frock coat and white shirt. A holstered gun hung on the hall tree by the front door, giving Garrick pause. Why would a minister need a gun?

"I can't thank you enough for this." Reverend Thomas

held up the book of Spurgeon's sermons Garrick had brought. "My own messages will be greatly improved by studying his insights into Scripture. I'll try to copy the most useful ones before you return to England."

"Do you envision yourself as one of the ancient Irish monks copying holy writings?" Garrick chuckled. He couldn't imagine such a task. "No, you mustn't bother. The book is yours to keep."

The minister eyed him for a moment and then nodded. "Thank you. That's very generous of you."

"Not at all." Garrick waved away his comment. That sort of praise always made him uncomfortable. "I appreciate your time today. Rand and Nate Northam asked me to address their Sunday school classes this Sunday, and I'm trying to think of an appropriate topic. Perhaps you can advise me."

The minister chuckled. "With that English accent, I think they'll just enjoy hearing you talk, whatever the topic." His eyes twinkled. "Don't think they intend to insult you. I'm one of the few Southerners in town, so I've received my share of mocking. No one means any harm by it." He poured more coffee into Garrick's cup and then picked up the book of sermons and thumbed through it. "I assume you've looked for inspiration here."

"I have, but preaching isn't my gift. I'd like to engage the lads in a bit of discussion, if they're responsive. Perhaps conduct the class as my professors at Oxford did, using Socrates' dialectical method."

"Ah. Very good."

They considered several ideas, finally deciding that Garrick should discuss England's church history with the boys.

"If you start with the Roman invasion, maybe talk

about some of the ruins, they'll hang on your every word," Reverend Thomas said.

With that settled, they spent an hour or so discussing Scripture. As he had last Sunday, Garrick found the minister far different from the ancient vicar who held the living at Uncle's manor. While he'd always enjoyed church liturgy, he'd never been close to the vicar, nor did the old man welcome such amity. Reverend Thomas's open demeanor invited friendship, and during their visit, Garrick gradually shed his natural reserve. If he ever required a confidant, this man would be his first choice, even before Percy, who so lightly dismissed every trouble.

As he stood to leave, the minister followed him to the door. "How are you and Rosamond progressing with your hotel plans? I've barely spoken with her since she came home. From what I observed on Sunday, she appears to have matured into a charming woman." He chuckled. "But then she always was a delightful girl. Her boarding-school experience seems to have enhanced her character."

An odd bit of jealousy pinched inside Garrick's chest, which was ridiculous. The unmarried minister might only be in his late twenties, but his regard for Rosamond was obviously pastoral rather than romantic. In any event, Garrick had no intention of letting his feelings for her go further than…what? Friendship? Admiration? Neither word seemed appropriate.

"She's a clever girl." He forced indifference into his tone. "And we are, indeed, progressing. If all goes well, we shall lay the cornerstone next week. Perhaps you can attend the ceremony and offer a blessing."

"I'd be honored."

With that matter nicely settled, Garrick made his way to the newspaper office, located on Main Street in a row with Mrs. Winsted's mercantile, the barber shop, Williams's Café, and several edifices in the process of being built. Across the dusty street, the newly built and freshly painted sheriff's office stood behind the pink stone bank. This town was expanding at an extraordinary rate. After his satisfying visit with the minister, the realization that he was doing his bit to help the growth of such a community bolstered Garrick's spirits even more.

When he entered the newspaper office, the heavy smell of ink washed over him and the clatter of the printer drowned out all thought. Fortunately, the newspaperman caught sight of him and stopped cranking out papers on the noisy machine. The tall, gangly young man strode across the length of the print shop, hand extended.

"Fred Brody." He swiped long strands of brown hair from his forehead with his free hand, leaving a streak of black across his freckled forehead. "And you are the Englishman who's building our new hotel." His voice held the same Southern inflections as Reverend Thomas's.

"Garrick Wakefield." Garrick shook the man's hand, choosing to ignore the ink that transferred to his own. As their hands clasped, convivial warmth shot up his arm. Once again, he felt that strange longing to be a part of this burgeoning community, to be welcomed by one and all instead of being shunted to the sidelines by former friends because he'd lost his expectations.

He apprised the newspaperman of the Colonel's interest in having the laying of the cornerstone photographed. Although the idea was his own, he decided to use the Colonel's name to give the request more impact, just as his using Uncle's name had influenced Messrs. Henman and Harrison to accept the commission to design the hotel.

"Of course. I'll write an article to go with the photograph." Brody again swiped at the strands of hair hanging over his brown eyes, further smearing the ink on his forehead. "That should give your hotel some good publicity." He leaned toward Garrick in a friendly way. "Say, if I may ask…" He bit his lip. "I mean, that is to say…I'd like to meet Miss Rosamond Northam. Would you present me to her after church this Sunday? That is, if you have no objections. I'd ask the Colonel, but, well, he can be a bit formidable." He laughed nervously. "The Northam men appeared a bit protective of her after church last Sunday."

In spite of the knot in his throat, which now sank into his chest, Garrick could think of no reason to deny his request. Yet the newsman's intent was clear. He was enamored of Rosamond, if only from a distance. But how could Garrick complain? He had no intention of courting her, so to refuse an introduction to an educated man of her class would be wrong. Assuming the fellow looked in the mirror before church and removed the ink from his face, of course.

As if the newsman's request weren't enough, Garrick repeated a similar conversation with Nolan Means when he went into the bank to confirm the financial arrangements Uncle had made. The young banker's appearance was pleasant enough. His refined manners and exquisitely tailored suit set him apart from the local cowboy culture. But for his somewhat cultured American accent, he'd be right at home in any London drawing room.

After they completed their business, Means said, "I have been out of town and regret missing church on Sunday as I have looked forward to meeting Miss Northam. We opened the bank shortly after she left for Boston. As you are residing at Four Stones Ranch, perhaps you could tell me of an appropriate time for my sister and me to pay her a call."

Garrick wanted to inform the banker that he wasn't Miss Northam's social secretary. Or that she wasn't receiving callers. Or that she was too busy to meet a stuffy banker. Or that she preferred the company of cowboys over gentleman in fine suits. Instead, he said, "The young lady does come and go quite a bit. Perhaps your best opportunity will be to approach the family this Sunday." Perhaps her *formidable* father would sort out her many suitors. If not, Tolley certainly would.

At least later, when he chatted with the new sheriff, he felt confident that married Abel Lawson wouldn't be interested in courting Rosamond.

"Good to see you, son." The lawman gripped his hand and slapped him on the back as one would an old friend. "I was mighty impressed by the way you and your friend handled those train robbers. When we boarded in Denver, I marked you both as tenderfoots, but you jumped right in and did your share to stop the robbery."

"Thank you, sir. Actually, Percy's my cousin, and we were glad to help." The man's compliment sounded a bit two-edged, but still positive. After all, Sheriff Lawson welcomed him with respect. Jumping into the fray earned that for him.

How he would welcome this same regard from others. When he went back to England, none of his acquaintances would admire him for his courage during the robbery, or even any success he might achieve either here or there. In London Society, wealth and position counted for everything, and he possessed neither.

Yet the longer he remained in America, the more he yearned for regard and respect, especially from a certain young lady whom every other unattached man in town seemed eager to court. Would his attempt to learn cowboy ways impress her? Or would he simply make a fool of himself?

Rosamond settled into the pew between Mother and Garrick, with Dad on Mother's other side and Percy and Beryl farther down the same row. Tolley sat in the back row with Nate, Rand and their families, and Rosamond could feel his glare aimed at Garrick.

Mother directed each of them to their places, just as she would at the family supper table, clearly with romance in mind. While that was all well and good for Beryl and Percy, Rosamond couldn't think of a worse idea for herself and Garrick. She didn't mind being friends with the handsome Englishman, but she couldn't both marry and fulfill her dreams of teaching.

Five years ago, she'd agreed with Mother about Nate and Susanna. After Susanna's father was severely beaten by outlaws up on La Veta Pass, Nate had come along, saved his life and brought the two of them to Four Stones Ranch while the old Southern gentleman recovered. Then Rosamond *and* her parents had encouraged Marybeth to travel from Boston to Esperanza to marry Rand. She could see her older brothers and their wives were happily married. Maybe she and Garrick… But she mustn't let her mind go in that direction. Not when she planned a teaching career. Not when Tolley kept sending those cross looks Garrick's way.

"How did your Sunday school talk go?" She whispered to Garrick even though the service hadn't yet begun and other people were talking in normal tones.

"Smashing." His whole face lit up, and her heart tripped. My, he was handsome. Every time he smiled like that, she had to lasso her heart and drag it back into place. "The boys were eager students, asking questions and giving opinions." He shook his head as if he couldn't quite believe it. "After this morning, I quite understand your desire to become a teacher."

A warm feeling radiated from Rosamond's heart, flowing throughout her whole being. "I'm so glad you enjoyed yourself." Later she must explore this common interest further.

She started to ask if he'd thought to invite Mrs. Starling's son to the class, but Reverend Thomas took his place at the front of the congregation, and the room grew silent.

"Good morning, everyone."

The minister opened the service with his usual warm welcome, and the joy in Rosamond's heart increased. How pleased she was to be here in her homey church to worship with dear friends who loved the Lord. How pleased she was that Garrick enjoyed teaching her brothers' Sunday school classes. While she hadn't discussed spiritual matters with him, she saw he was a man of faith, especially when his countenance beamed with holy joy as he sang the opening hymn, "What a Friend We Have in Jesus."

Maybe Mother was right—again—in her matchmaking ideas. If Garrick had an abiding faith in God and lived by godly principles motivated by that faith, if he believed in working hard to achieve his goals, if he liked children, even enjoyed teaching them, why shouldn't Rosamond permit herself to care for him?

She knew exactly why. Because once they finished the hotel, he'd return to England and his aristocratic friends, probably regaling them with stories about unsophisticated Americans and their unrefined ways.

Besides, she must stand firm in her plans not to marry.

While Garrick had enjoyed teaching the boys this morning, she did more than enjoy teaching on a rare occasion. She'd felt called to teach in this very sanctuary four years ago after Reverend Thomas gave one of his soul-inspiring sermons on spiritual gifts. The Lord had spoken in her heart and mind that day, and after graduating from the academy, she was all the more dedicated to the profession. She couldn't expect a husband to understand such ambitions, so she must forgo marriage. As never before, the thought wove a thread of sadness through her, diminishing her joy.

The following day, groups of workers assembled on both building sites, which were just over one block apart. Rosamond was torn between the two until Tolley reassured her that he and his "men" would manage without her supervision. After looking over Marybeth and Rand's house, she had full confidence in him. She'd inspect the school as work progressed, but surreptitiously when she brought the boys refreshments from Williams's Café.

The hotel building crew was another matter. Very few of the men appreciated having a woman at the site, especially one who gave orders. Being the Colonel's daughter, Rosamond had never encountered such cold-shoulder treatment on the ranch. Certainly none of the Four Stones cowhands ever refused her instructions. But then, she'd grown up among them, and most doted on her as a younger sister. After a quick prayer for guidance, she marched over to several men, who were digging the spot for the cornerstone.

"Excuse me, gentlemen." They were hardly gentlemen, but she knew good manners always accomplished more than shouted orders. "The cornerstone will go on the southeast corner." She smiled and pointed toward the correct spot.

None of the four men so much as lifted his head to acknowledge her. One spat to the side. Another murmured a word she wasn't familiar with, but which didn't sound in the least proper.

"I said the other corner." She raised her voice only slightly.

One by one, the men stopped, dug their shovels into the dirt and crossed their arms over the top of the handles, still not looking at her. Then one man slid an unpleasant glance her way. With a gasp, she took a step back.

"I beg your pardon, Miss Northam." Garrick appeared at her side, a rolled-up building draft under one arm. He gave her a slight bow and tipped his new hat to her. "When you've finished instructing these chaps, would you please inspect the water pipes with me? I want to be certain they're where you want them." His voice held no servility, merely respectful deference, something she guessed only an Englishman could accomplish. In fact, he sounded a bit like his valet. He looked at the men, one or two of whom shuffled their feet and sent worried looks his way. "When these men complete the task you gave them, perhaps they can assist in unloading the stones from the wagons. That is, if it's all right with you."

Rosamond's heart swelled with appreciation for his unexpected support. Where was the arrogant aristocrat who hadn't even wanted her to be a part of this project? She gave the men another pleasant smile. "The southeast corner."

"Yes, ma'am." They doffed hats and then scrambled diagonally across the building site, shovels in hand, two of them tripping on the way and almost falling headlong into the rectangular hole other workers were digging for the basement.

It was all Rosamond could do not to laugh out loud at their comical escape. Nor did she miss the looks of the other men who observed the incident. With just a few words—questions, actually—Garrick had established her authority before the entire hotel building crew.

She gazed up at Garrick from beneath the wide brim of her straw hat. "Thank you."

"Hmm?" He was busy scanning the draft, or seemed to be. Yet she didn't doubt he knew exactly what he'd just done. "Ready?" He offered an arm.

She placed a hand on it, feeling beneath the fabric even stronger muscles than a mere week ago. Whatever he was doing to improve, she couldn't help but admire him more and more with every passing day. This was no lazy aristocrat but a hard-working man, the only kind of man she could ever respect.

Garrick could barely restrain himself from planting a facer on the brute who'd looked at Rosamond as if she were a beefsteak he wished to devour. Never mind the other three who'd ignored her sweetly delivered order. Garrick knew many a titled lady who shouted orders like Lewis Carroll's Queen of Hearts, and would likely dismiss anyone who failed to promptly obey. That anyone could deny Rosamond her every wish was beyond him. Of course, in the matter of the Palladian facade, he must stand firm. But otherwise, he'd give her the moon if she asked.

Where had that come from? Perhaps the heat had affected his thinking. At Roberts's insistence, he'd worn his black suit, white linen shirt and a tie. His valet had insisted that a professional appearance would establish his authority. And it had. To a man, all the workers acknowledged him as if he were the lord of the manor. Such irony, since he'd never be that. But when Rosamond gazed up at him with gratitude beaming from those lovely emerald eyes, he did feel a bit like a knight in shining armor. Of course, he couldn't tell her that.

In any event, these men were being paid handsomely by Uncle and Colonel Northam, so they shouldn't mind which of their employers' agents gave them orders.

After he and Rosamond inspected the water lines, they moved out of the building area and under an open canvas-covered pavilion erected nearby.

"I'm utterly amazed at these artesian wells so prevalent in this area," he said, "not to mention the purity of the water." He filled glasses for each of them from a pitcher on the center table and handed one to Rosamond.

"Thank you." She took a sip, studying him over the rim of the crystal with those bright green eyes.

Somehow he sensed that she was thanking him for more than the water. But he wouldn't refer to the incident with the men. No need to boast of his support for her. He sipped from his glass, enjoying the cold water freshly pumped from beneath the earth and considering how he might change the subject.

"That lovely fountain in the center of town reminds me of the fountains in Rome. Did you know that during Rome's heyday, they used vast concrete aqueducts to pipe enough water into the city to supply the needs of two million people?"

"Do tell." She smirked playfully.

Oddly, his collar became tight, and he made up his mind to wear something looser tomorrow, no matter what Roberts said. "Indeed. Many of those aqueducts are still standing today."

"Hmm." She kept her gaze on him. Was that admiration in her eyes?

He coughed lightly. "Remarkable after all these centuries, wouldn't you say?"

"Quite remarkable." Her smirk softened into a sweet smile.

Again he tugged at his tie.

She laughed. "I suggest you wear your new plaid cotton shirt tomorrow."

"Right."

"I'm going over to watch the boys clear the plot for the high school." She set down her glass. "Want to go?"

"Yes." He glanced around the hotel site, pleased that work was progressing in all areas. "I'd enjoy that."

After informing Mr. Frisk, the master stonemason, of their plans, he held out his arm, wondering if she would squeeze it as she had a while ago. Odd how women did that. Was she taking the measure of his masculinity? If so, he hoped he came up to snuff.

She did squeeze, and he enjoyed the contact, even through his linen jacket and shirt. From her smile, he guessed his arm met with her approval. In fact, he was quite satisfied himself after only a week of lifting bales of hay every morning with Pete.

The short walk to the high school site took only a few minutes. Garrick looked for Adam among the boys chopping at weeds, raking away debris, moving supplies or taking directions from Tolley. He was pleased to see the lad focused on Tolley as he spoke. Garrick had invited Adam to Sunday school in hopes of introducing him to the others, and his plan had worked. They in turn must have invited Adam to help with this effort. Garrick must make certain Adam could still keep his position at the livery stable, but volunteering to help build the school would make him a part of the community.

No one understood the importance of such acceptance more than Garrick.

Tolley saw them approaching, and the friendly expression he'd directed toward the lads turned hostile. "I said I could handle this, sis."

Rosamond waved. "I know you can. We're on our way to Williams's Café. May we bring your men some refreshments?"

Garrick guessed she'd realized her mistake in inviting him to the site and quickly invented a plausible reason for the two of them coming this way.

The lads caught sight of Garrick and, to his chagrin, hurried over to him with greetings, questions, handshakes and all over jolly-good-fellow camaraderie. While he enjoyed their welcome, Tolley strode away and began to unload wooden beams from a wagon. Garrick's heart sank to his stomach. Once again he'd given Tolley cause to dislike him just by his presence.

"Would you boys like some lemonade?" Rosamond's gaze was on her brother as she asked.

"Yes, ma'am."

"Sounds good."

"Sure is hot today."

They all spoke at once.

"Perhaps I should go back to the hotel," Garrick said softly.

"Don't you dare," Rosamond returned in a whisper. "I need your help to carry the refreshments." To the lads, she said, "Now you get back to work. Our school won't be built before winter if you lollygag all day."

They laughed and made genial remarks as they returned to their work. Garrick guessed this worksite would be much more relaxed and enjoyable than the hotel's. Only Adam lingered.

Garrick gave him a brief nod, then took Rosamond's elbow and moved her toward Main Street. "Refreshments it is."

No sense in stirring up trouble. If Tolley learned that he was responsible for Adam being here, he might not let the lad work on the school, which could cause him to be left out of other activities. Garrick had forgiven Tolley for tripping him during the cattle branding, but he'd be foolish to trust him not to do some other bit of meanness. Adam shouldn't have to pay the price for Tolley's vindictiveness toward Garrick.

"We can set the trays there." Rosamond nodded toward the back of an empty wagon. Miss Pam had filled two pitchers with ice-cold lemonade and provided a platter filled with her delicious ginger cookies. "Why don't you go on back to the hotel site?" Rosamond asked Garrick. "I'd like to stay here for a while and watch the progress."

"Will Tolley permit you to stay?" Garrick glanced around. For some reason, he seemed reluctant to leave her.

"I can manage him. I know he's capable, but I also know he wants to prove himself without Big Sister watching over him. Still, this is my school." She gave Garrick her warmest smile and added in a teasing tone, "And while you're also capable, you can count on me to come check up on you in a little while."

"Hmm." He narrowed his eyes, but they still held a twinkle. "Don't hurry. We'll manage to keep busy."

As he strode away, she felt the loss. How easily she could fall in love with him. The beginning of their acquaintance had been rocky, yet in just over a week, they'd become friends. Even so, she still must consider Tolley's animosity toward him. She'd never seen her younger brother behave this way toward anyone, so why Garrick? Did he want to protect her? That hardly seemed necessary since Garrick was always a perfect gentleman, even protecting her just as her brothers would have from those rude workers. Did he resent Father's unreasonable favoritism toward Garrick? That didn't make sense, either. Father had never given Tolley much attention, as even Nate and Rand had observed. Maybe she'd never know because Tolley certainly wouldn't admit to such ill feelings.

She poured lemonade for the twelve boys, most of whom she'd known all their lives and whose ages ranged from thirteen to nineteen. The only boy she didn't know approached her, tattered hat in hand, and received his glass.

"Thank you, ma'am." He glanced beyond her. "Did Mr. Wakefield leave?"

"Yes. He's over at the other building site." She studied him briefly. Now she could get some answers about Garrick. "Are you Mrs. Starling's son?"

He grinned shyly. "Yes, ma'am. I'm Adam Starling. And you're Miss Northam. I want to thank you and Mr. Wakefield for getting that sewing job for my ma. She likes working with Mrs. Beal a whole lot, and sewing's a heap easier than washing clothes." His eyes reddened slightly. "I don't know what we'd have done without Mr. Wakefield's help. I suppose he told you about Jack and the train."

She managed to hide her surprise. "Why, no. Perhaps you could tell me."

Over the next ten or so minutes, she listened with rapt attention as Adam unfolded a startling, inspiring story about the man she was so reluctant to love. And gradually, as he spoke, that reluctance flowed away as dross from refined silver.

As they drove home that afternoon, they said very little. Perhaps Garrick was as tired as she was, but she also wanted to carefully assess what Adam had told her. He'd given her a whole new perspective on the man. Late into the night after she and Beryl went to bed, she could think of nothing else.

The arrogant Englishman who'd spoken so judgmentally of Americans in the Denver train station had nonetheless risked his life for a small American child. He'd saved a starving family and found them a home and honest work so they could survive on their own. And all without saying a word to anyone.

He'd even prevented Percy from asking about Adam in front of her and Beryl, probably to keep them from learning about and praising his kindness. And just today, when she'd tried to thank him for making sure the hotel builders respected her authority, he'd changed the subject and talked some nonsense about Roman fountains. All this from a man who'd grown up expecting to become an earl. She could hardly comprehend such humility and graciousness. Nor could she imagine him reporting to his friends back home in England that Americans were somehow lesser beings. Perhaps his haughty words in Denver were an attempt to cover some sort of uncertainty about being in a foreign country and working with people he didn't know. He truly was a fish out of water, and yet, in a short time he'd figured out how to cope.

Humble, handsome, charming, courageous, generous, hard-working. A man of faith and good humor. Unfailingly a gentleman.

Yes, she could love this man. But did she dare?

"Rosamond," Beryl whispered, rolling over to face her on the bed they shared. "Are you awake?"

"Yes." Rosamond wanted to giggle at the conspiratorial tone in her friend's voice. At the academy, they'd spent many a late night sharing secrets. "What's on your mind?"

"I'm so happy." Beryl sighed blissfully and then grasped Rosamond's hand in the dark. "Percy's done something wonderful, and I can't keep the secret from you any longer."

Rosamond's heart stalled. "He proposed." Garrick would be furious.

Beryl giggled. "No, but maybe one day soon." She lay back as if that were the end of it.

"Hey." Rosamond gently pinched her friend's arm. "What wonderful thing did he do?"

Another sigh. "He helped me get over my fear of guns."

Rosamond sat up with a gasp. "How? When?" Had the two of them been on their own long enough for such a remarkable change to happen?

"We've been working together since last week. When I told him what happened to me, he was horrified. And pleased to know the man who shot me is in prison for the rest of his life." She sat up and then leaned back against the mahogany headboard. "When I told him about my terror of every loud noise, he was so sweet and understanding. He said we'd overcome my fears together. First, he talked me into just holding my guns—the pearl handled Colt .45s I bought over in Del Norte—while we chatted about all sorts of things. His home in England, my folks' ranch. School. We did that for days."

She sat quiet for a moment. "I learned to shoot when I was five, just like you and my sisters. Then…well, you know. Getting shot scared me in ways I didn't understand. You've always been strong for me when some loud noise reminds me of that day at the bank, but I didn't think I'd ever get over it." A slight catch in her voice revealed the depth of her emotions.

Rosamond squeezed her hand in the dark.

"This afternoon," Beryl said, "we rode out a piece and set up cans on a log. Consuela went with us," she added quickly. Another brief silence. "He stood behind me with his hands on my shoulders. Not too heavy, of course, just enough so I'd feel his support. I was shaking real bad. But he kept saying how I could do it and not to be afraid. When I was ready, I took a shot." She giggled, and her gleeful tone brought tears of joy to Rosamond's eyes. "I flinched real bad. *Badly*, I mean. And missed, of course, being so out of practice. But I shot and shot until I didn't flinch anymore." She heaved out a great, satisfied sigh. "I'm over it, Rosamond, and all because of Percy."

"I'm happy for you, my dear, dear friend." Rosamond wiped away her happy tears on the corner of her sheet. But nipping at the heels of her joy was the memory of Garrick's disapproving frown whenever he saw Percy and Beryl together. Knowing how much influence Garrick held over his cousin, would he try to keep them apart?

If so, then the perfect man she was in danger of loving too much had a fault she couldn't overlook.

Chapter Nine

Even though he needed to rest for tomorrow, Garrick fought sleep. One moment, the successes of the day filled his thoughts and prompted fresh ideas for the hotel. The next moment, his stomach churned with anxiety on two fronts.

His growing fondness...attraction—he wished he could define these irresponsible feelings for Rosamond—filled his mind and heart and sent them in a direction he mustn't take. Friendship? That was insufficient to describe the depth of his emotions. Could he think of marriage? Impossible. Before he took such a sacred step, he must secure Helena's future.

Yet he couldn't help but think of his own future. If he wanted Rosamond to be a part of it, he must make his feelings known to her, especially since other potential suitors, such as Nolan Means and Fred Brody, seemed desperate to meet her.

For him, however, one thing was certain: responsibility must win out. Uncle had taught him that lesson well when they'd both thought Garrick would inherit the title and all that came with it. Even with the change in his expectations, the lesson held firm. Therefore, in spite of the other gentlemen attracted to her, he must put some distance between Rosamond and himself.

His other dilemma was no less distressing. He must separate Percy and Beryl. Something had happened today to intensify their attraction, if Beryl's moon-eyed gazes at Percy over supper and his secretive smiles at her were any indications. His cousin mustn't waste his life out in this wilderness when he could do so much good at home in England once he married well and entered Society.

There was nothing for it. Garrick must forget impressing Rosamond, surrender his cowboy lessons with Pete, take Percy away from Four Stones Ranch and seek lodgings in town. Reverend Thomas had mentioned that the widowed church organist had rooms to let. Perhaps she had enough beds for their valets, as well. Tomorrow he'd locate her house and make his inquiries. He'd introduce Percy to Mrs. Starling and ask him to search for her husband. He'd make his excuses to the Colonel by saying he must be closer to the hotel. And he would somehow keep his heart from shattering through it all.

The next morning over breakfast, he concluded that the Lord had paved his way. Beryl and Rosamond hadn't yet risen for the day, so he wouldn't be confronted by any questions they might ask. He also had plenty of time to explain his plans to Percy. Of course, he didn't tell his cousin all that was in his heart, only about the missing Starling family patriarch.

"You've always been clever at solving puzzles." He spoke softly so Rita couldn't hear him. "Finding the countess's stolen spaniel, and all that. If you take Richards along and perhaps hire a local man as a guide, you'll have everything you need for the task." He took a bite of Rita's delicious griddle cakes and then sipped his coffee.

"I've no doubt you can locate the chap or, at the least, find out what happened to him. Think of the adventure!"

"Well…" Percy's conflict was evident in his frown. "It's not that I mind helping the family, but perhaps the new sheriff would be the better man for the job."

Garrick hadn't thought of that. He scrambled to think of a truthful way to dismiss Percy's concern. "But he's just getting acquainted with the area himself, so he really wouldn't know much more than we do." He chewed his lip, feeling like a liar and a conniver. But he must go on for Percy's sake. "In any event, his duty is to protect the good people of Esperanza. I doubt he can take a week or even longer to search for a man no one's heard of."

Percy tapped his chin thoughtfully. "I wonder whether Beryl would like to accompany me on the hunt."

Garrick inhaled sharply. "That would hardly be proper." He needn't pretend his concern. At home, such a jaunt with a female could end up in a forced marriage. For all of their rustic ways, these ranchers did care about their daughters. He could well imagine George Eberly holding a shotgun on Percy as Reverend Thomas bound him in marriage to Beryl. "Think of the young lady's reputation."

Percy's eyes widened. "Yes, of course. How foolish of me." He stared down and shoved a bit of egg around on his plate. At last he gazed at Garrick, determination filling his eyes. "Very well. I'll do it. You and I both know the grief of losing our fathers, so we mustn't let this family do without theirs any longer."

Garrick sat back in his chair and nodded. He should feel satisfaction, victory, even. Instead, he felt a cold lump where his heart should be. But he must still accomplish more with his cousin. "I'm going to make arrangements for us to move into town. I need to be closer to the hotel site, and you should be closer to the telegraph office so you can send out inquiries."

"I suppose." Percy hadn't stopped frowning throughout this whole conversation. Now his shoulders slumped, and he breathed out a long sigh. Garrick's merry cousin was depressed, and Garrick was to blame.

Rosamond greeted Garrick just as he entered the worksite. "My, you were out early this morning." She had missed him at breakfast. After yesterday's flurry of emotions, she couldn't quite subdue a giddy hiccup in her chest. To her surprise and disappointment, he barely looked at her. "Where have you been?" Heat rushed to her cheeks. Why on earth had she asked such a nosey question?

"Personal errand." His tone was brusque, further deflating her spirits. "It came to mind last night that we should settle the matter of the chef. If we're going to hire your Mrs. Williams, perhaps we should let her know. Otherwise, I must send for the French chef I originally planned to import to manage our kitchen. Of course, it'll take him some time to sever his London connections and arrange his travels."

"Of course." Rosamond stiffened.

What had happened to destroy their blossoming friendship? Had he argued with Tolley? Whatever the problem, she wouldn't let him embarrass her in front of the builders, especially after the support he had given her yesterday. Two men were already staring at them with too much interest.

"Let's go speak to Miss Pam right away." She started to reach out and take his arm but thought better of it. Instead, she turned toward the street and walked away. To her relief, he fell into step beside her.

And held out his arm.

She gave him a sidelong glance before setting her hand on it. "Thank you." She injected a cool tone into the words. He must learn right away that she wouldn't accept rudeness from him any more than she would from the workers.

They walked in silence all the way to Williams's Café. Cross words and angry questions churned through Rosamond's mind, but she held her tongue. Mother never spoke in haste and rarely in anger. Rosamond always tried to follow her sweet example, but today it was harder than usual. She accepted responsibility for her part in this odd situation. Just because he had many admirable qualities, she'd let her feelings for him grow out of proportion. He was wise to take a step back from her. She'd step back from him, as well. After all, they'd only known each other for two weeks. Maybe he was frequently moody.

There! She'd found another fault and must remember it whenever her maverick heart tried to get away from her again.

He opened the café door and stepped aside so she could enter. The scent of freshly baked bread filled her senses, and her mouth watered. "Oh, my. That makes me hungry, and I ate plenty of breakfast just a short while ago." Silly how such an aroma could improve her disposition. Now who was being moody?

Garrick chuckled. "I know what you mean. I'm hungry all over again."

His laugh broke down the last of her crossness. Maybe she'd been mistaken about his mood. After all, she'd been terribly nosey to ask where he'd been.

"Morning, folks." Miss Pam emerged through the

swinging kitchen doors. "Have a seat." She waved to a table by the window. "What can I bring you?"

"Coffee for me," Rosamond said.

"And I'm guessing you want tea." Miss Pam gave Garrick a knowing look, as any good merchant gives a favored customer. "Right?"

"Right." He gave Miss Pam that glorious smile, and Rosamond's heart plunged into danger all over again.

Once again, Garrick felt at war with himself. He'd been pleased to find sufficient accommodations for himself, Percy and their valets at Mrs. Foster's house. Not quite so pleased that Rosamond awaited him at the building site and asked a perfectly innocent, entirely friendly question, to which he'd barked his reply. Hurt feelings flickered briefly in her lovely eyes before she'd lifted her chin and answered him in kind. Good for her for not cowering like a housemaid in fear of her master. In fact, he'd wanted to kick himself for inflicting even the slightest pain on this sweet, intelligent lady.

Why not answer her question? Why not tell her he was moving to town? Because he was a coward of the worst sort. Instead of straightaway confessing all, making amends and reaffirming her authority before the nearby workmen, he'd changed the subject.

Not that this business of the hotel restaurant could be delayed. What he'd said to Rosamond about time being of the essence in regard to importing the chef was certainly true. Then the instant they'd entered the café, the aromas of baked goods, roasting chicken and coffee had filled his nostrils and incited his appetite, and Chef Henri was forgotten. Garrick could easily imagine guests waking to such delightful smells and recommending the hotel based on the cuisine alone.

Miss Pam brought their beverages and set them on the table. "Would you like a cream puff fresh out of the oven?"

"Yes, indeed."

"Oh, yes."

Garrick and Rosamond answered in unison and then shared a smile. Perhaps their moment of discord truly was at an end. They watched as Miss Pam returned to the kitchen and came back with two small plates containing large fluffy yeast rolls with white icing drizzled across the top.

"Do you want to address the subject with the lady?" Garrick hoped that by deferring to Rosamond, he could regain more of her good opinion.

"What subject?" Miss Pam set the plates in front of them.

"Do you have a minute to chat?" Rosamond waved toward one of the empty chairs at the table.

Garrick quickly stood and held out the chair. "Please join us, won't you?"

"Well…" Miss Pam glanced toward the kitchen. "We need to get dinner ready for our customers."

Through the swinging doors, Garrick could see the waitress busy with some chore. "We won't take but a moment of your time."

The lady sat and looked from Rosamond to Garrick and back again. "How can I help you?"

"We'd like to offer you the position of head chef at our hotel." Rosamond's demeanor conveyed professionalism and authority, along with a generous measure of friendliness.

"Oh, my stars." Miss Pam sat back and again looked back and forth between Garrick and Rosamond. "Why, I never expected such a fine compliment. Naturally, I'm honored."

"Then you'll take the position?" Garrick sensed hesitation in the lady's voice.

For several moments, she gazed around her pretty little café like a proud mother, and he guessed what her answer would be.

"After owning my own place, being my own boss, I can't rightly say I'd enjoy working for someone else." She patted Rosamond's hand. "I hope you won't take offense."

"None taken. We understand," Rosamond said. "You established your café before we even named our town."

"Yes, I did." Miss Pam's warm smile held a hint of proper pride. "Tell you what. I'd be pleased to do some baking for you from time to time. Would that help out?"

Garrick's first thought labeled her offer as quaint. After all, the hotel would require a great deal of baked goods every day, not just the odd delivery. Then he bit into the fluffy pastry before him, and all such arrogance disappeared. "Keep us supplied with these, and you have a bargain." And if Henri didn't appreciate serving this lady's fine baking in his restaurant, he'd simply have to cope.

With one more issue out of the way, Garrick and Rosamond finished their refreshments and rose to leave. Rosamond ordered lemonade and cookies for the boys at the school site, and Garrick headed for the train depot to send wires to Uncle and Henri.

That evening over supper, Father announced that he'd been to town to talk to Mayor Jones and Reverend Thomas. They'd all agreed the hotel should share the cornerstone laying ceremony with the high school. "Both enterprises are important steps for our community, so we want everyone to take part. The town council will spread the word that we're having the big event on Sunday after church. Mayor Jones suggested that we start at the school and then move on to the hotel, then back to the church for dinner on the grounds."

Pleased beyond words, Rosamond glanced at Garrick as he nodded his approval. She also noticed Tolley sitting up straighter, so she flashed a grin at her brother. Right now, Father should commend Tolley for his fine leadership in clearing the school site, yet no such praise came. She started to say it, but Father spoke first.

"Garrick, I saw Mrs. Foster today. I understand you're moving into town. We'll miss you here, of course, but I understand your wanting to be closer to your work."

Rosamond could barely keep from choking on her bite of roast beef. She'd been with Garrick most of the day, and he hadn't mentioned a thing about this. So that was his "personal errand" this morning. She looked around the table. Seated beside Garrick, Percy gazed sadly at Beryl. Next to Rosamond, Beryl blinked back tears. Percy must be moving into town, too, and had probably already told Beryl. Why was Rosamond the last to know?

Anger welled up inside her, dousing all her former joy. This was Garrick's doing. While he might find this move necessary, perhaps to get away from her, she couldn't imagine why he'd deliberately hurt Beryl. Hadn't her friend suffered enough? Even though Percy had helped her overcome her fear of guns, she still needed his company, his growing affection, to overcome her feelings of rejection at the academy and misunderstanding by her family. Didn't Garrick realize Beryl had lost her place in the world? Percy was helping her find it again.

"Must you go?" Rosamond aimed her question at Percy, hearing the strain in her own voice. "You're welcome to stay here while your cousin tends to his duties in town."

Percy offered a weak smile. "Actually, he's putting me to work, as well." He looked at Garrick, as if for approval, setting Rosamond's teeth on edge. What actual authority did Garrick hold over his younger cousin? Was bossing Percy around another silly English custom?

"What work is that?" Mother asked Percy. Had she noticed Rosamond's anger and jumped in to stop a conflict? She always managed to smooth away any social unpleasantness.

"There's some chap missing, and Garrick thinks I'm the one to find him." He shrugged. "At home, I've done a bit of detective work—amateur, of course, because Scotland Yard says they aren't quite ready to hire me."

While the others chuckled at his humor, Mother hummed with interest, her mellow alto voice further soothing Rosamond's annoyance. "You must tell us all about this missing *chap*." She turned her attention to Garrick.

"Ah, well, a young lad in town, the new groom at the livery stable…"

He proceeded to give a very brief account of Adam Starling and his family, leaving out anything that might garner praise from his listeners. He made no mention of saving Adam's little brother in the Denver train station or of rescuing the family from starvation once they reached Esperanza. Rosamond's emotions churned, admiration mixing with a remnant of anger. How noble of him to send someone to search for Adam's father. But why Percy?

A quick glance at Tolley's cynical expression revived her own earlier thoughts. She had absolutely no doubt he'd chosen Percy for the job to get him away from Beryl.

Her opinion hadn't changed by Saturday, when the two Englishmen and their valets moved into town, leaving both Beryl and Rita depressed. Even Consuela sighed frequently as she went about her duties, suggesting she missed Richards. Rosamond learned from Rita that they'd also grown fond of each other. Garrick was ripping them all apart. But for what reason?

By Sunday morning, Rosamond needed to spend considerable time in prayer to prepare her mind for the worship service. She didn't want to see Garrick for fear she wouldn't be able to keep from scolding him. But she did want to see him, wanted to tell him she'd missed him yesterday, missed the parlor games and friendly chats they'd all enjoyed every night. If he'd just explain himself, maybe they could work everything out. But he was a closed book, so last evening both she and Beryl had languished about the house like sick puppies.

When they arrived at church, Mother directed everyone to their places, as usual. No one in the congregation claimed a pew as their own, so this morning she chose a row on the right side of the sanctuary, halfway between the front and back. Rosamond noticed she didn't save places for Garrick and Percy. To her amusement, however, when the two Englishmen entered, Beryl left her side and sat with Percy. Garrick nodded a greeting but offered no smile. Rosamond thought he looked sad, but if he was, it was his own fault.

As usual, Reverend Thomas's sermon suited the events of the day. "Reading from Psalm 127, verse one, 'Except the Lord build the house, they labour in vain that build it; except the Lord keep the city, the watchman waketh but in vain.'

"Since this small part of the San Luis Valley was first settled about fifteen years ago, the Lord's blessed every endeavor. But we've come a long way in that time, and we're growing bigger. The railroad came through, more folks came West hoping for a new life and willing to work for it. Businesses sprang up. This church was built so we can join together as a community to worship and experience spiritual growth. Homes were built, where we find love and comfort. Now we'll have a high school where young folks can learn about the world and their place in it. We'll have a hotel, a place of rest for the wayfarer."

His gaze moved slowly around the room. "In the six years since I became your pastor, I've watched families grow and offered this prayer from *Psalm* 144:12, 'That our sons may be as plants grown up in their youth; that our daughters may be as cornerstones, polished after the similitude of a palace.'

"But we have a more notable cornerstone to our faith. As the Lord says in *Isaiah* 28:16, 'Therefore thus saith the Lord God, Behold, I lay in Zion for a foundation a stone, a tried stone, a precious cornerstone, a sure foundation.' That cornerstone is none other than our Savior, Jesus Christ. If we do not make Him the cornerstone of all that we build, we labor in vain."

As was her custom when hearing a sermon, especially one delivered by Reverend Thomas, Rosamond listened for that still, small voice telling her, "This is my instruction for you." Today the Lord's meaning was clear, just as four years ago she'd felt the call to become a teacher. She must set aside personal concerns and dedicate all of her energies to helping build this community, especially her school.

In a way, her family was the cornerstone of Esperanza, but not one of them wished to rule over the town or become, in biblical terms, the "head of the corner." In fact, Father had begun to step back from leadership three years ago when Mother became ill. During their lengthy absence, first to Boston, then to Italy, the people of Esperanza had joined together to keep the town growing.

Last year, before Father and Mother returned from their travels, an election was held. Humble Edgar Jones, the barber, became Esperanza's first mayor, and several other men were chosen for the governing council. Everyone agreed to and signed the original town charter, which included stipulations that no saloon would be built within the city limits, no alcohol would be permitted and all businesses would be closed on Sundays. All this was done without Father's leadership, and upon his return, he'd been more than pleased to remain in the background.

Rosamond appreciated his wisdom and would try to emulate him. The school wouldn't be hers, but would belong to everyone. In organizing the curriculum, she would merely put into practice the tried-and-true methods of education she'd learned at Fairfield Young Ladies' Academy.

As for the hotel, with most of her disagreements with Garrick worked out, she could leave the rest of the project to him. Well, not the Palladian facade, of course. Yet, as she thought it, she felt another nudge from the Lord, and she knew she must surrender even that. *All right, Lord. If he insists upon such an out-of-place front for the hotel, I won't argue with him any further.* Right away, peace swept over her, and she knew she could deal with whatever came.

Garrick watched as Rosamond dug her shovel into the dirt alongside Beryl, Mayor Jones and several others. After Reverend Thomas prayed a blessing over the school and all the students who would learn there, a four-foot square pink stone was moved into place. Fred Brody captured the moment with his large black camera. Then the congregants moved on to the hotel site, and the ceremony was repeated, this time with Garrick joining Rosamond and Colonel Northam for the photograph. As the magnesium powder flashed for the second time, Garrick's emotions seemed to ignite, as well. With the cornerstone laid, this grand project would begin in earnest. When it was completed, he could return home to the life to which he was accustomed.

"Now let's eat," someone called from the crowd, and everyone laughed. Merriment ruled as they made the short trip back to the church, where the ladies promised to bring out baskets of food for the "dinner on the grounds."

Hungry though he was, Garrick lingered at the hotel site. Although only one day had passed since he'd left Four Stones Ranch, he no longer felt a sense of community with these people. He'd tried to dismiss his childish feelings by reminding himself of his first impression of these small-town American cowboys. They were rustics, one and all, even those with better education and manners. He was an English gentleman better suited to life at Uncle's country manor. That was what he'd known all his life. Even though he wouldn't inherit the title or estate, he'd find a way to serve his three little cousins, perhaps as their tutor. After all, he'd completed his studies at Oxford and possessed all the knowledge required for the post. That idea had come to him after he addressed the boys' Sunday school classes. Perhaps he had a gift for teaching. He'd certainly enjoyed it.

"You coming, Mr. Wakefield?" Adam Starling stood

nearby holding little Jack on his hip. "I'll walk over with you."

"You go ahead. Join the other lads." Garrick glanced beyond him. "Is your mother all right? And Molly?"

"Yessir." Adam brushed dust off Jack's short trousers— new ones, if Garrick wasn't mistaken. "They're over with the other ladies, fixin' dinner. You ought ta come. Lots of good food free for the taking."

The peaceful expression in Adam's eyes warmed Garrick's heart. He'd already been accepted by the other lads, as his mother was accepted by the ladies. Now they just needed their father to return, and all would be right with the world. For them.

As the lad walked away, Garrick sat on the newly placed cornerstone and surveyed the cleared site. The basement had been dug and concrete poured. Next week, a sump pump would be put in place to remove any water that might seep in from the region's high water table. From deep below the Valley's sandy surface, artesian water would be pumped to the hotel kitchen and guest bathrooms on the upper floors. This would be a luxurious, modern oasis in the middle of the wilderness.

"Father sent me to get you."

Garrick turned to see Rosamond standing some ten feet away, her hands fisted at her waist as though she didn't particularly relish the errand.

"How thoughtful." Garrick hoped he didn't sound sarcastic. After all, any animosity between them was his fault. "Please tell him I'll come straightaway." He waited to rise in case she didn't care to return to the church in his company.

Instead of leaving, however, she moved closer, looking around the site. "It's hard to imagine how it's all going to look when it's finished." The glint in her eyes bespoke some of the excitement he'd felt earlier.

"Indeed. Yes." He'd agree to almost anything to regain her good opinion. "The drawings on the drafts can never give one a sense of dimensions and ground space."

Nodding, she proceeded to the temporary wooden barrier around the basement and peered into the hole. "Too bad we can't install an elevator, but I suppose that would be silly for a hotel with only three stories and a basement."

"Not silly at all. Do you want to hire an engineer to take on the project?"

She smiled, triggering a mild disturbance in the vicinity of his heart. "Let's not cause a delay. The day may come when people are too lazy to climb stairs, but I think it's good exercise."

"I couldn't agree more." His stomach chose that moment to rumble, and she laughed.

"I'm hungry, too." She walked across the level ground toward the site's perimeter. "Let's hurry before all the cowboys eat everything in sight."

He stood and offered his arm. When she took it, his chest swelled with happiness and a hint of pride for having her at his side. Perhaps they'd progressed beyond the unpleasantness caused by his move to town. Perhaps now they could just be friends. Friends. Nothing more.

Now if he could only believe that lie, he might be able to sleep better at night.

Chapter Ten

Over the next days and weeks, the work progressed admirably at both sites. When Rosamond and Beryl weren't working on their lesson plans for the coming year, they rode into town to watch the high school take shape. With so much of their own work to do, they didn't have time for a close inspection of the hotel's progress, and only observed it from a distance. Or so Rosamond tried to tell herself. In truth, Garrick's withdrawal still hurt, and she didn't wish to risk further pain.

Although the Englishmen had come to dinner one Sunday in mid-June and appeared to enjoy themselves, they'd left early, giving no plausible reason for not spending a leisurely afternoon in the country, resting from their labors. Rosamond sensed that Garrick instigated the early departure to separate Beryl and Percy, but the two managed a short visit on the front porch while Garrick fetched the gentlemen's mounts. While Rosamond hoped to converse privately with him, she was impressed that he would take on such a menial chore instead of expecting a servant to tend to the matter. To his credit, the arrogant Englishman no longer rode his high horse.

Over time, the girls gathered supplies and equipment.

Beryl's father ordered charts and science equipment for her classroom, including an expensive microscope. Rosamond ordered textbooks, writing supplies and blackboards. Both girls experienced great excitement over having their dream come true, although Rosamond continued to see sadness in her friend's eyes. If she were honest, she'd own up to a bit of melancholy, too. She found herself unable to dismiss all thoughts of Garrick Wakefield.

In the last week of June, the girls inspected the interior of their school and commended Tolley on his work. Rosamond always made sure her brother knew how grateful she was and how much she admired and believed in him.

"Anything for you, sis. Gotta keep the princess happy." He always responded in a teasing, dismissive way, but she could tell from the twinkle in his eyes that he appreciated her praise. When the school was completed, she had every intention of requiring Father to voice his approval, as well.

After discussing the color of paint and placement of blackboards and desks for each room, they exited the school through the wide opening where the double front doors would soon be hung. Rosamond ran her gloved hand over the unpainted doorjamb without a single splinter catching the fabric. Tolley had done much of the woodwork himself.

"The hotel sure looks grand, don't you think?" Beryl shaded her eyes and stared down the street. "Let's go see how they're doing."

Her bold proposal surprised Rosamond. Hadn't they agreed to leave the Englishmen alone? She looked toward the beautiful three-story building with its pink stones gleaming in the sunlight. "Yes. Very grand."

When would they put up that horrid Palladian facade? She didn't mind admitting that Garrick did very well with everything else regarding the hotel. Let others inform him of his mistake about the entrance.

"Come on, then." Beryl grasped Rosamond's arm and tugged her away from the school.

As they walked, she couldn't keep her pulse from racing in her eagerness to see Garrick. Then she had a bold thought of her own, one that might help her friend. "Do you suppose Garrick and Percy will go to dinner with us at Williams's Café?" That was, if Percy remained in town. He might be away searching for the elusive Mr. Starling.

"We can only hope." Beryl's pace picked up, and Rosamond hurried to catch her.

Her heart skipped when she caught sight of Garrick. Dressed, as always, in his black linen suit, he stood with Mr. Frisk beside the south wall, which was set back some ten feet from Main Street. Garrick raised his hand in a salute, and his smile promised a warm welcome. Had he watched them approach? Did he admire her as she admired him? Oh, my, these silly thoughts would never do. If his eyes spoke the truth, Garrick clearly did admire her appearance, but he just as clearly didn't want their friendship to grow into something more. Nor did she wish to give her heart to a man who would keep Beryl and Percy apart for no good reason, or a man whom Tolley so strongly disliked.

Once again, she lassoed her maverick heart and tied it firmly in place. Even there, however, the closer she came to Garrick, the more she felt it struggle to get free.

Garrick's heart tripped all over itself as he watched Rosamond approach. She was, without doubt, the most exquisite young lady he'd ever met, carrying herself with the grace and dignity befitting a duchess even when walking along this dusty roadway. If not for his obligation to secure Helena's future, he could permit himself to imagine strolling beside Rosamond along the Serpentine River in London's Hyde Park. Every gentleman would envy him. Every lady would seek to emulate her style.

Beside Rosamond, Beryl walked with the more boyish gait he'd noticed in all of her sisters, although she'd been far more graceful a mere six weeks ago. How easily she'd fallen back into her Western ways—all the more reason for Percy not to pursue and marry her. After love's first bloom faded, how would his cousin bear to watch his wife swagger across an elegant London drawing room? She'd hold back his every chance at social advancement. Garrick had the unpleasant duty of preventing that, but he felt assured that once they returned home, Percy would recover from his ill-advised attachment to the girl.

As they drew near, Garrick and the master stonemason tipped their hats and bowed.

"Good morning, ladies," Garrick said. "To what do we owe the pleasure of this call?"

"Would you give us a tour of the hotel?" Rosamond's lovely smile redirected his thoughts. He could easily love her entirely. If he surrendered his heart to her, would she wait for him to take care of family responsibilities? Or would that stuffy banker or enterprising newspaperman win her hand while he was away?

"Is Percy here?" Beryl approached the side of the hotel and peered beneath the balcony through a large opening soon to hold a glass display window for a shop, one of six set in the hotel's west side along Main Street.

"Ah. Well. No." Garrick felt an odd pang of regret when the girl's pretty smile disappeared. She truly was a gentle creature, far less boisterous than her sisters. He had no wish to cause her pain. "He's found a man who worked on the crew laying railroad track from here to Del Norte and who recalled our Bob Starling. The fellow said Starling later joined the crew on the southern arm of the Denver and Rio Grande line. Percy, Richards and the Northams' man, Pete, left yesterday morning to 'hunt 'im down,' as Pete said." Garrick added a humorous tone to his words in hopes of cheering the dear girl.

She rewarded him with a sweet, sad smile. "Well, if he's there to be found, I'm sure they'll find him." She turned away and appeared to be studying the unfinished storefronts along the side of the building, but he could hear her soft sigh.

"Shall we have that tour of the inside?" Rosamond stepped closer and eyed Garrick's arm as if expecting him to comply.

This was a bad idea, but he couldn't deny her request. Coward that he was, he turned to Mr. Frisk. "Sir, what do you advise?"

"Ma'am, I can't rightly say it's a good idea. Won't be safe for anybody but workmen to go inside for another six or seven weeks." The stocky, middle-aged man shook his head for emphasis. "The men are busy putting up the wood framing for the staircases and inside walls. There's building supplies all over the place."

"I'm terribly sorry." Garrick gave Rosamond an apologetic shrug, grateful to Frisk for voicing his own concerns.

"May we peek in the front door?" Her question was amiably delivered, one any passing stranger might ask.

"Of course." At least he could grant her this request. Mr. Frisk excused himself to see to other matters, and

Garrick held out an arm to each lady. They trod through the dust around the corner to the front of the building.

"The boardwalk will extend along these two sides of the hotel. Those partitioned spaces you saw will house businesses, of course." Did he sound proprietary, as if this were his project, not a shared effort? That wouldn't do at all. "Rosamond, have you heard from the milliner in Saint Louis?"

"Yes. Mrs. Ryan will arrive in September to open her millinery shop." She granted him one of her lovely smiles, perhaps a reward for his including her. "What other businesses have applied for space?"

"A Swiss watchmaker. A hatmaker. A tailor." He ticked the list off on his fingers. "Many of the necessary services a hotel should make available for its guests."

"Very good." Rosamond was all business now, staring into the cavernous insides of the work in progress. She and Beryl pointed at various things and shared a few whispered remarks. "I see the braces for the lobby chandelier, but can you move it to the center?"

"Yes. Yes, of course." He knew he must grant her some authority in these matters, even though she appeared to have abdicated her position. Had she completely given up? That didn't please him. He missed the spirited lady who'd fought him on the hotel's every detail.

Was this the moment to tell her that the Palladian facade wouldn't be possible? Frisk had explained to Garrick that when the builders had laid the borders of the foundation, they'd set it too close to the street to accommodate a portico. Once laid, the foundation couldn't be changed, nor the street narrowed. Frisk had noticed the misplacement only two days ago and had informed Garrick. Now only the boardwalk would separate the hotel from the street. Would that please her?

No, he wouldn't tell her but instead let her see the actuality. Her idea had prevailed without even the slightest ado. Of course, he wasn't at all pleased, but he was no stranger to such disappointments. Life rarely gave him what he expected, what he hoped for. Why should the front of the hotel, one he could be proud of, be any different? He wouldn't even bother to write to Uncle to explain how the approved designs hadn't been followed. Photographs of the completed hotel would tell the tale.

"Garrick, come to dinner with us," Rosamond said.

It was a command sweetly delivered, and although he knew of the danger of spending too much time in her company, he could only obey. Soon the three of them were seated around a table in Williams's Café.

After they'd ordered their meals, Rosamond removed her white lace gloves, laid them in her lap and sipped the coffee the waitress brought. "Did you receive a response from Chef Henri?"

"I did. He'll be most pleased to come to America. One of his ancestors fought under Lafayette's command in your rebellion against the Crown, and the family's been keen to immigrate since then." He chuckled, expecting his remark to bring a laugh. Everyone at home laughed at the French, despite preferring their cuisine. But Rosamond and Beryl nodded solemnly.

"Considering all the conflicts France has endured since our Revolution, with an outcome so different from ours," Rosamond said, "I believe he's made a wise decision."

"Oh, yes," Beryl echoed. "Too bad he won't be here in time for next Wednesday's celebration."

Garrick blinked. What had he missed? "Celebration? For what?"

The ladies traded a look and giggled.

"Why, the Fourth of July, of course." Rosamond's green eyes sparkled with amusement. "To celebrate the signing of our Declaration of Independence and our first victory over the British."

"*First* victory?" Garrick's defensive pride in his home country welled up in his chest. "Whatever are you talking about? I'll grant that you won your independence, but what other victory are you claiming?"

"Oh, please." Rosamond stiffened her spine and gave him that look his governess had always used to set him straight. "Beginning in 1812, while your Wellington was busy fighting Napoleon, we successfully resisted the attempts of other British military to reclaim their former colonies."

"Reclaim—"

"What else would you call your navy's impressment of American seamen, completely ignoring their citizenship papers? Your disregard for our borders? Your blocking of our trade with other countries?" To her credit, Rosamond's voice didn't increase in volume, although her eyes held a fiery pride. "But by 1815, once again, ordinary Americans banded together to drive the mighty British army and navy back to the other side of the Atlantic, where they belonged." She lifted her chin proudly as though she'd won the war herself.

The waitress chose that moment to bring their meals, a welcome distraction. After a prayer of thanks, he considered how to return to the subject about which Rosamond felt so passionate. This was the young lady he so much admired.

He buttered a muffin and took a bite before speaking. "I must make a study of that war. It sounds…fascinating." He was certain she spoke the truth. Odd that his own studies of British history at Oxford hadn't informed him of that particular conflict. Did Rosamond somehow consider him one of those invading Englishmen? Perhaps the only way to overcome her obvious distaste for all things British was to acknowledge the ills of the past. After all, despite his own earlier disdain for Americans, he'd quickly learned to respect their ingenuity and courage in bringing a form of civilization to this vast wilderness.

"You said your celebration next Wednesday has to do with your first victory over my wretched ancestors." He grinned playfully, hoping to show his kind intentions with a bit of self-deprecating humor. "Would I be correct in assuming your activities will be something similar to our Guy Fawkes Day?"

Rosamond laughed. He'd struck the right chord. "If you mean will we be burning King George in effigy, as you do Guy Fawkes, the answer is no. But we may have a bonfire along with our fireworks. The town council may have one planned. We always celebrate in fine style."

"Everyone here takes the day off," Beryl said. "Even the ranchers and farmers. We all come to town for the Independence Day Fair. We have baking contests, shooting contests, horse races."

"And more food than you could eat in a year." Rosamond took a bite of her chicken sandwich and then dabbed her lips with her linen napkin.

As always, her graceful manners held Garrick's attention…until he realized what Beryl had said. "Take the day off? Everyone?" The men already refused to work on Saturdays so they might see to their own properties. How could the hotel be completed on time if the workers constantly took holidays?

* * *

Rosamond set Rita's pies on the long plank dessert table outside the church and then returned to the surrey to bring her own gingerbread cookies and a cake for the cakewalk. She never entered the cooking contests because so many other ladies prepared excellent dishes. With cooks such as Mrs. Foster, Pam Williams and Rita's mother, Angela, vying for the prizes, Rosamond knew better than to waste her efforts in the competition.

When she was younger, however, she'd won a blue ribbon for reciting Longfellow's poem "Paul Revere's Ride." She could still remember every thrilling word and planned to recite it to her students. The poem wasn't entirely accurate, so she'd give her students a truer account of the events of April 18, 1775, when the British began their assault on their American colonies. But her former anger toward England, generated by a passionate history teacher at the academy, seemed silly now, as did her initial animosity toward Garrick simply because he was English.

Did he find it difficult being so far from home? She could almost forgive him for separating Beryl and Percy, considering that he'd sent Percy on a truly noble mission. She lifted a silent prayer that the search for Mr. Starling would be successful. And be completed very soon.

She scanned the busy churchyard to see if Garrick had come. Would he stay in his room at Mrs. Foster's, finding this holiday offensive? Or had his humorous remarks last week meant he'd dismissed their countries' former animosities, as she had? She couldn't find him right away among the milling crowd, but she did locate her friends.

Beryl was talking with her oldest sister, Maisie, who was married to Doc Henshaw. Maisie seemed to have put on weight since just six weeks ago, especially around the middle. Maybe after five years of marriage, she finally expected a blessed event. But Rosamond's joy for her friend mingled with sorrow that no such event would ever happen to her.

"Please permit us to carry those, Mrs. Foster." Garrick nudged Roberts toward one of the large hampers on their landlady's kitchen table, and he picked up the other one. In two short months, he'd grown quite familiar with kitchens, something he'd never be able to confess to friends at home or he'd become a laughingstock.

"Oh, thank you, dear boys." Mrs. Foster reminded Garrick of Uncle's housekeeper, a spritely, maternal sort who could nonetheless keep Uncle's household running smoothly. "I knew I could count on you."

"What delicious dishes have you prepared for today's party?" Garrick caught the scent of apples and cinnamon, but the apples on the tree in the yard hadn't yet ripened.

"Dried apple pie, lemon cookies, biscuits, chicken and dumplings, sweet potatoes." Mrs. Foster looked around the room. "That's everything. Shall we go?"

They exited the house, walked through the front gate and began the two-block trek to the church. Mrs. Foster reached for Garrick's free arm with one hand and Roberts's free arm with the other. Over the little lady's head, Roberts gave Garrick a worried, wide-eyed look and started to protest, but Garrick shook his head. The dear woman had no idea her friendly gesture placed master and valet on equal footing, something that would never be tolerated at home. But then, in this case the valet wore a suit and the master wore cowboy garb. Maybe Garrick should have worn something more suited to his station. Too late to change now.

They drew near the crowded park by the church, and the aroma of roasted beef wafted through the air, further inciting Garrick's appetite. In the center of the park stood a bandstand where a group of surprisingly talented musicians practiced their songs. The bandstand was festooned with red, white and blue bunting, as were most of the buildings in town. Across Main Street in front of the bank, a colorful banner proclaimed, Esperanza, July 4, 1883. The hubbub of music and cheerful voices stirred Garrick's emotions unexpectedly, and he decided to surrender himself to the enjoyments of the day.

After they deposited the hampers on the proper tables, Garrick took his leave of Mrs. Foster and dismissed Roberts to enjoy the day as he wished. Straightaway, Roberts fairly bounded over to another table where the Northams' cook, Rita, was arranging desserts. The girl's happy countenance upon seeing Roberts caused Garrick no small alarm. What would he do if his valet wanted to marry the girl and take her home to England? That would never do for more reasons than Garrick cared to list—not the least of which was that he couldn't afford another servant.

"Wakefield!" Colonel Northam hailed him from across the churchyard. Beside him, Mrs. Northam offered a smile and wave. The Colonel wore a striking brown tweed suit, with a black string tie held in place with a large silver and turquoise tie pin. His brown boots boasted a pair of ornate silver and turquoise spurs. Mrs. Northam was resplendent in a dark green cotton gown and matching sunbonnet. With such handsome parents, no wonder Rosamond was such a beauty.

Garrick returned their waves and strode across the

space to greet them. After proper greetings, he asked, "Did Rosamond come, too?" The words were out before he could stop them. Of course she'd be here, and Mrs. Northam's knowing smile proclaimed that she knew exactly why he'd asked. *Bother.* Couldn't a chap keep his feelings hidden any better than that?

"Yes, she's here," Mrs. Northam said. "She's probably helping to organize the children's games." She indicated a small field beyond the church. Sure enough, the lady who too often invaded his dreams was directing a group of boys and girls in some sort of activity.

"I see you've taken to wearing Western clothes." Colonel Northam placed a hand on Garrick's shoulder as he eyed his hat, plaid shirt and new boots. "Makes you fit right in."

"Thank you, sir." A warm feeling settled in Garrick's chest. The gentleman was the founder of this community and was respected by everyone who lived here. His public welcome to this event meant a great deal to Garrick.

Tolley stood not ten feet away wearing his usual scowl. "Say, tenderfoot, you gonna ride in the race this morning?"

Garrick glanced at the Colonel before answering. "Is that an invitation?" He injected as much friendliness into his tone as he could, to no avail.

"No. It's a challenge." Tolley continued to scowl.

"Bartholomew!" The Colonel growled as he sent an identical angry look in his son's direction.

Tolley winced and took a step back.

Bartholomew? Garrick had wondered about Tolley's unusual name.

"Then I accept your challenge." He just short of chirped his answer to try to smooth over the moment of rancor. He'd probably never understand the younger man's resentment, but he certainly wouldn't stand between father and son.

"Sir, I'll fetch your horse when it's time." Adam Starling appeared at Garrick's side, as he often did at the building site, no doubt eager to learn any possible news about his father. "I've been exercising her every day, just like you asked."

"Thank you, Adam." Garrick turned to the Colonel. "I appreciate your making Gypsy available for my use. May I have your permission to ride her in the race?"

"Indeed you may. She's one of our best and will give the other horses some serious competition." The older man squeezed Garrick's shoulder in a paternal way. "Now, if you'll excuse us, Mrs. Northam and I need to greet some other folks." He offered his arm to his wife. "Shall we go, my dear?"

Garrick tipped his hat and gave a little bow as the Northams walked away to join a group of other dignitaries dressed in their finest. He then took a step toward Rosamond and her little charges. Before he could take a second step, Tolley grabbed his upper arm and spun him around.

"Gypsy may be fast, but don't get your hopes up, tenderfoot. You'll be eating my dust in the race." He spat to the side. "Boots and hats don't make you a cowboy. Or a man." Before Garrick could react, Tolley gave him a shove and strode away.

Sick to his stomach with confusion and rage, Garrick knew he must collect himself before approaching Rosamond. What had he done to warrant such abuse? He hadn't felt this way since a fellow student at Oxford had taunted him about losing his place as Uncle's heir presumptive and tried to goad him into a fight.

"Mr. Wakefield, you gonna let him treat you that

way?" Wide-eyed Adam watched the whole thing, further creating conflict for Garrick. He mustn't set a bad example for the lad.

He cleared his throat. "The Lord tells us to forgive our—" He couldn't honestly call Tolley his "enemy." The animosity was entirely one-sided. "Forgive those who dislike us."

"Yessir. And I know all about turnin' the other cheek." Adam stared at the ground and shuffled his feet. "But my pa says there ain't no sin in a man defending himself when he's attacked, 'specially in front of everybody, the way Mr. Tolley done just now."

"Ain't?" Garrick wouldn't argue with the absent Mr. Starling. He thought about ruffling Adam's hair, but decided the lad was too old for such a playful gesture. "Don't let Miss Rosamond hear you say that or she'll have you sitting in the corner wearing a dunce's cap before classes even begin."

"Yessir," Adam repeated with a grin. "I think she's about to put you in the corner." He jutted his chin toward the field. There stood Rosamond staring in his direction, hands fisted at her waist. "You gonna run? If a girl looked at me like that, I'd run."

Garrick laughed, and his ill feelings dissolved. "Your perspective will change when you're my age." He gave Adam's shoulder a squeeze, as the Colonel had done to him. Surprising what encouragement such a gesture could give a man. If the Colonel thought well of Garrick, Tolley's dislike could be overlooked. Rosamond's apparent anger was another matter altogether.

Rosamond didn't know what to think. When she'd tried to ask Tolley why he disliked Garrick, he'd brushed aside her questions and told her it was between the two of them. Now, seeing their brief confrontation—in front of her parents, no less—she was determined to uncover the cause. Father had taken Garrick's side against her brother. Why?

But as Garrick walked toward her, that perfect smile on his handsome face, she couldn't be stern with him. Not with her heart fluttering like a baby bird trying to fly for the first time. On the other hand, how could he appear so calm while Tolley was storming the other way across the churchyard, clearly still angry?

Garrick reached her in seconds, and thoughts of her brother fled. If she didn't know better, she'd think he was one fine-looking cowboy. Fine-looking, yes. Cowboy, definitely no. During his short stay at Four Stones, he'd shown very little interest in ranch life.

"Good morning, Rosamond. You're the picture of beauty, as always." Was that a hint of humor in his eyes? How quickly he'd forgotten his confrontation with Tolley. Was that good or bad?

Unclenching her fists, she smiled. "You're not so bad yourself, cowboy."

He doffed that silly white Stetson she'd forced him to accept and gave her a sweeping bow. "My lady, at your service. Do you have steers to rope? Calves to brand? Cows to milk? I am yours to command."

His offer, delivered in the English accent she was beginning to love, brought laughter from the children nearby. At a glance, she could see they were entirely too interested in her conversation with Garrick.

"No branding today, but you can help me round up these mavericks so we can get their three-legged race started."

"I can do that." He studied the children almost like a schoolmaster, giving her heart another lurch. Where had that thought come from? "Now you young'uns line up right here." As he pointed to the chalk line in the grass, his perfect imitation of Pete's Western drawl brought more giggles.

For the next few minutes, they instructed the children in the rules for the race. Once they'd lined up, Rosamond nodded to Beryl, who rang a bronze handbell.

"Three-legged race," she called out as parents and other spectators gathered.

The event, which took place even before the mayor officially opened the Independence Day celebration, was designed to focus on the children and expend some of their energy so they'd settle down for that austere ceremony. Beginning with the five-year-olds on a twenty-foot course, ending with the youngsters in their teens tripping down the fifty-foot path, the races were a favorite and always started the celebration off with laughter and good spirits.

Winners were announced, ribbons distributed and then everyone surrounded the bandstand where the mayor would make his opening speech.

"May I accompany you?" Garrick offered his arm to Rosamond.

"Indeed, you may." Rather than placing her hand on his arm, she looped her own arm around it. Maybe she was being too familiar with him, but after they'd shared the fun and hoopla of the children's races, it seemed the perfect way to accept his offer. If his pleased smile was any indication, she'd made the right choice.

"Ladies and gentlemen." Standing behind a wooden lectern, Mayor Jones shouted to be heard above the chatter. "Reverend Thomas will lead us in the invocation." The crowd immediately grew quiet.

After the minister's prayer for God's blessings on the

events of the day, the mayor resumed his place before the crowd. "Today we gather to celebrate the founding of our nation. While our festivities are filled with gaiety and laughter, we must never forget the solemn events of July 4, 1776. One hundred and seven years ago today, courageous representatives of thirteen colonies signed a document that would change the world. Now people of many nations come to our shores to find freedom to worship, freedom to govern themselves, freedom to build whatever enterprise their ingenuity and determination leads them to create."

He paused and surveyed the crowd. "We aren't a perfect nation. We aren't a perfect community. But let us strive to continue the work of our Founding Fathers that we may work toward a better life for all." He beckoned to Mrs. Winsted, who stood among the people behind him on the bandstand. "And let us never forget the words of our Declaration of Independence."

With that, he took his seat. Mrs. Winsted moved into his place and unrolled a large scroll.

"CONGRESS, July 4, 1776. The unanimous Declaration of the thirteen united States of America. When in the course of human events, it becomes necessary for one people to dissolve the political bands which have connected them with another..."

Rosamond looked up at Garrick, whose rapt gaze was focused on Mrs. Winsted. Had he ever heard these words? Did he know how countless men and women had suffered and died to turn the thirteen colonies into the United States of America? Rosamond knew at once that she must pray for him to grasp that understanding in a way that would change his life...and maybe hers.

From the moment Mrs. Winsted began to speak, everything and everyone in the churchyard seemed to disappear, and Garrick could hear only the words that had separated forever this country from his own. The lady didn't read for long, soon giving place to Bert, the former slave who worked as a blacksmith and farrier at Four Stones Ranch.

"We hold these truths to be self-evident, that all men are created equal, that they are endowed by their Creator with certain unalienable Rights, that among these are Life, Liberty and the pursuit of Happiness."

A chill shot down Garrick's spine. What a remarkable thing, having this man, this former slave, recite this particular part of the document. Even more remarkable was the reverent silence in the churchyard. Not even a baby cried.

Mr. Chen took the next turn, reading about governments among men. Like Bert, he wasn't the typical settler here in Esperanza. Had he fled from some sort of oppression in China's vast empire? At Oxford, Garrick had only briefly read about the Asian continent.

Rafael Trujillo, owner of a large ranch north of town, spoke next, listing many complaints against the Crown. Did this man harbor complaints against those who had driven most of the Mexicans out of this area due to the Treaty of Guadalupe Hidalgo? One evening before he moved into town, Garrick had read that bit of history in Colonel Northam's library.

Others whom Garrick hadn't met read a paragraph or two of the document. Finally, Nate Northam summed up the well-reasoned argument against the "tyranny" of King George III, citing the authority of the men who now dissolved all former ties with England to declare their colonies to be free and independent *states*.

"And for the support of this Declaration, with a firm reliance on the protection of divine Providence, we mutually pledge to each other our Lives, our Fortunes and our sacred Honor."

Another chill raced down Garrick's spine. The American colonists had risked everything for their freedom. He could only aspire to that sort of courage.

Mayor Jones made a few more remarks about never forgetting and other thoughts about how the community could honor their past. Garrick tried to gather his thoughts before speaking to Rosamond. From the changing pressure of her arm around his, he knew the document was important to her, but he'd been too engrossed in the reading to look her way.

Across the yard, Garrick noticed Roberts standing beside the little cook, Rita. To his dismay, Roberts's face bore a bright glow about it, as though he'd just discovered some life-altering truth. Would he make this Declaration his own? For a moment, Garrick felt a bit like King George, angry that someone who served at his convenience now might want the freedom to do as he chose.

But then, why would this loss be any different from the many others in Garrick's life? Of course, he couldn't force his valet to remain in his employ. Only he, Garrick, was a slave to his duty, to his lack of fortune, and he wouldn't easily be able to break his chains, metaphorical though they might be.

Chapter Eleven

"Shall we visit the booths?" Rosamond sensed Garrick had much to think about, if his pensive expression was any indication, so she wouldn't press him. He seemed content to be with her, however. A relaxing stroll among the shaded stalls where local craftsmen sold their wares might be just the thing to help him.

"If that would please you." He smiled, and her heart skipped, as usual.

Father always tried to please Mother, and Rosamond had always hoped for a husband who'd consider her preferences. That was before her call to become a teacher had made marriage an impossibility. Or, at the least, too impractical.

"There's Bert." She led Garrick to the table under a canvas awning. "Bert, have you met Mr. Wakefield?"

"Yes, ma'am." The burly man gave Garrick a friendly nod. "We miss you at Four Stones, Mr. Wakefield. But with Pete gone—"

"Hello, Bert," Garrick interrupted him and stuck out his hand. "No, we haven't heard from Pete and Mr. Morrow. I'm hoping to any day."

Bert blinked and paused before reaching out to shake

Garrick's hand. "Ah. Yes. Sure. It'll take some time to find that man. I've added my prayers to the effort."

Rosamond couldn't guess what had just passed between the two men. Maybe Garrick had spent some time in the blacksmith shop. But when?

"Very good." Garrick looked down at the table, which was covered with spurs, knives, belt buckles, silver-and-turquoise items, all etched with varied designs. "Did you make all of these?"

"Yessir." Bert grinned proudly. "Keeping the horses shod don't take all my time, so I get to do some fancy work."

"Bert made Father's spurs," Rosamond said. "Did you notice them?"

"I did. They are exquisite." Garrick picked up a small oval silver tray etched with floral designs. "As is this. What's its purpose?"

Bert's eyes lit up. "Well, sir, the ladies like 'em for their vanities to put rings and ribbons and other gewgaws in."

"Ah, very good." Garrick took a brown wallet from inside his coat. "I must purchase it for my sister."

Rosamond's heart warmed. She knew very little about his sister, but such devotion could only be admired.

"How pretty." Garrick held up a silver-and-turquoise comb with long teeth for holding an upswept hairdo in place. "Would it be improper for me to give you such a gift?"

At Bert's hopeful look, Rosamond shook her head. "Not improper at all. After all, we're colleagues. It's merely a friendship gift." Wasn't it? "And of course you must let me buy something for you." She studied Bert's display and decided on a braided black leather bolo tie with silver tips, not as ornate as Father's, but still quite fine. With great ceremony, she buttoned his open shirt, strung the tie around his neck and secured the silver and turquoise slide in place. "What do you think?"

"I like it." He fingered the silver tips and chuckled. "You needn't give me anything." Then his lips quirked into a cute little grin. "But you may."

They completed their purchases, and Rosamond directed Garrick to another table where Mrs. Starling displayed newly sewn shirts, aprons, kerchiefs and other items. "Can I help you folks?" Dark circles under her eyes gave evidence of late-night work. Rearing three children alone must be difficult, all the time worrying about what had happened to her husband. The two younger children played with blocks on the grass behind their mother.

"Yes, indeed." Garrick looked to Rosamond. "You must help me select a new shirt. I've become quite fond of these American styles."

"Very well." She looked over the dozen or so shirts. "Mrs. Starling, I can't imagine how you had time to make these with all the sewing for the hotel."

The woman gave her a weary smile. "Mrs. Beal's been very kind to let me use her Singer in the evenings. It's a grand invention and makes sewing a pleasure."

"And such nice even stitches, too." Rosamond selected a solid burgundy shirt. "Let's see if this fits." She instructed Garrick to turn around so she could hold up the garment to check for a good fit. "Perfect through the back. Mrs. Starling, can you let down the sleeves an inch?"

"Yes, ma'am." The woman's eyes were bright. "I'll have that for you by dinnertime." Other people now gathered around to admire her work.

Although Rosamond never liked to use the Northam name for selfish purposes, perhaps this was an appropriate way to influence other people. She made a show of holding the shirt up to Garrick's chest. "Do you like it?"

"Very much," he said. "And I'd like two of those neckerchiefs as well." He selected a green and a red.

"Um, no." Rosamond took them from him and set them back on the table. Several people nearby laughed. "Now I know why you need a valet." She matched the burgundy shirt to a paisley kerchief woven with similar colors and then selected another to match the shirt he was wearing. "There. Looks good. Don't ever select your own clothes without help, understand?"

The crowd clearly enjoyed this interchange, for several added their own humorous comments about men choosing their own clothes.

"Yes, ma'am." Garrick laughed, and Rosamond enjoyed the pleasing sound—a sound she could get used to hearing.

He paid Mrs. Starling three dollars, although the woman protested it was too much. "Never mind. I'm sure I don't pay Adam enough for taking care of Gypsy."

They left their purchases with Mrs. Starling to pick up at dinnertime and continued their stroll just as the handbell rang again.

Mrs. Winsted called out, "Egg race!"

"Egg race?" Garrick laughed again. "And that is—?"

Rosamond sighed. She'd forgotten about this event, one she'd taken part in only one time before going to Boston. If they didn't go to the race course, maybe she could avoid being trapped into running. "All of the unmarried girls carry an egg on a wooden spoon and race to the finish line."

"Cooked eggs?" The amused look in his eyes showed he knew the answer.

"Where would the sport be in that?"

"Well, come along, then." He nudged her toward the field. "We mustn't let someone else win the ribbon."

"Oh, no. Don't make me do this." She'd brought a change of clothes but hoped her pink dress would last longer than this. The last time, her egg had broken all over her skirt before she'd run halfway down the raceway. "My students mustn't see their teacher behaving in such an undignified manner."

She turned in the opposite direction, but his firm grip on her elbow told her he had no intention of letting her escape.

"Nonsense, Rosamond. Your students will be delighted to see you're a good sport." Garrick had no idea why this whole idea amused him. Perhaps it was the gaiety surrounding them. Perhaps the merry mood in his own heart after choosing a shirt with this delightful lady's assistance. "After all, as a Northam, you must set the example of sportsmanship."

How often had his governess told him that very thing? *You will one day be Lord Westbourne, therefore you must set the example.* Even after losing his expectations, he still believed in doing the right thing in all matters big and small. One never knew who was watching and who might emulate his actions. "If I must ride in the horse race, you surely can make a go of this little contest."

"You're riding? Oh, Garrick, I'm so proud of you. Let's go see to Gypsy right now. I think the horse race is the next event."

"Don't change the subject." Garrick held her as gently as possible without letting her escape, and they continued toward the field. "What prize does the winner of this race receive?"

"A blue ribbon and china bowl for her hope chest."

She ceased her struggles and walked calmly beside him. "And the right to kiss the man of her choice. On the cheek, of course."

"A kiss!" Garrick stopped, still holding her arm. "Well, perhaps—" If she won, whom would she choose? He wasn't sure he wanted to know the answer to that question.

She gave him a saucy smile. "All right, then. You've convinced me. I'm sure Nolan Means—he's the banker, you know—would like for me to win. Shall we proceed?"

She broke away and marched in the most ladylike way toward the starting line, where some twelve or so girls lined up, including the two younger Eberly daughters. Beryl was passing out spoons, and her sister Grace was placing a large brown egg on each one. No doubt Beryl didn't enter because Percy wasn't there to kiss—a fortuitous situation to Garrick's way of thinking. Perhaps Grace considered the race too undignified for a deputy sheriff.

As with the children's events, Grace fired her Colt .45 to start the race. Cheers erupted from the crowd, along with cries of encouragement. From his place on the sidelines, Garrick had a good view of the proceedings, and he cheered Rosamond on. Several girls started too quickly and lost their eggs straightaway or tripped and fell. Yolks and whites splattered down blouses, aprons or skirts. He'd feel quite the cad if Rosamond ruined her lovely pink dress. Too late to purchase one of Mrs. Starling's aprons. Too late to tell her she needn't race to please him. But her determined expression as she glided down the course gave evidence that she was thoroughly enjoying the competition.

To his surprise and delight, she won, stepping across the chalked finish line a half step in front of Laurie Eberly. The crowd cheered even louder while the rest of the girls completed the course.

Rosamond carefully lifted her egg from the spoon and carried it back to the starting line, where one of the judges cracked it into a bowl to prove her an honest winner. Garrick made his way over to congratulate her but couldn't reach her for the cheering crowd. The ribbons were distributed, and the third place winner planted an enthusiastic kiss on her beau's lips. Laurie accepted the second place award and then looked around as if searching for someone. She shrugged and gave her father a kiss on the cheek.

Rosamond looked around the crowd. Garrick's heart stuttered. If only he'd planned this better and not insisted she enter the race. Nolan Means stood close by her, his young sister having participated in the event. For all of his banker's dignity, he looked at Rosamond rather longingly. Or perhaps Garrick was merely seeing his own longing in the other man's eyes. Still, if she kissed Nolan, Garrick would have all the more reason for stifling his attraction to her. Which, of course, would continue to be quite impossible.

"Hurry up and kiss somebody, Rosamond," Grace Eberly called out. "We got a horse race to run."

Her emerald eyes bright, her ivory cheeks flaming, Rosamond stared across the crowd, straight at Garrick. His pulse pounded in his ears. Would she kiss him? Was it even proper for him to let her? Certainly not in England, but these Americans held a different and interesting view of such things.

Rosamond essentially shoved her way through the mob, placed her hands on his cheeks, stood on tiptoes and—to his shock—planted a warm kiss on his lips. She stood back briefly and then kissed him again. Before he realized what he was doing, his arms went around her waist, and he answered in kind, kissing her in a way he'd never dared to dream of. Somewhere in the distance, he heard laughter and cheers and many foolish remarks. But all he could truly know was that this was right, this was good and he loved Rosamond Northam with all of his heart.

She broke from him gently and whispered, "The first kiss was for my race. The second was my best wishes for yours."

"Thank you." For the kiss. For the good wishes. For simply being her wonderful self.

He raised his head and looked beyond her. There stood Tolley, hatred burning in his eyes, a shocking yet predictable reminder of one of the reasons why Garrick could never pursue a further relationship with the beautiful lady in his arms.

Rosamond felt Garrick's embrace tighten and then suddenly go slack. Hadn't he enjoyed being kissed? She certainly had. Yes, she could tell he'd liked it from the surprise and delight on his face between the two kisses *and* his enthusiastic response to the second one. What had changed? She released him and glanced over her shoulder but saw nothing to explain why his mood had shifted. Tolley was making his way through the crowd toward the horses, so he couldn't be the cause of Garrick's change.

"I'm sorry." She stepped back from him. "So much for the teacher and her dignity."

He gave her a rueful smile. "Don't be sorry. Please." A frown darted across his forehead. "I'm quite pleased that you chose me, though I think your banker friend is a bit disappointed." He added a laugh that seemed forced, not at all like his carefree laughter before her race. "Well, I suppose I should see to Gypsy. Your father tells me she'll give the other horses some healthy competition. Now let's hope I can be the jockey she deserves."

Always the gentleman, he offered his arm. When Rosamond looped hers around it, a pleasing warmth spread through her that was becoming all too familiar—the warmth of belonging, caring, perhaps even loving. Oh, that maverick heart of hers. How would she manage to tame it?

She could feel Garrick's tension in the corded muscles of his arm as they walked toward the starting line under the Independence Day banner strung across Main Street. Was he merely eager to compete, as many of the men were? Or was something else bothering him?

"Here we are." Garrick met Adam at the starting line and took Gypsy's reins in hand. "Hello, my girl." He ran a hand over the mare's head and received a nudge in return. "Rosamond, you've already given me a token of your best wishes, but I'd welcome your prayers as well."

She tilted her head and gave him a teasing grin. "Now, now, Mr. Wakefield, you're an excellent rider. Have no fear."

He returned a gentle smile that didn't reflect in his eyes. "You're kind to say so." He gave her a quick kiss on the cheek and then swung into the saddle. "By the by, would you kindly keep my hat?" He handed it down to her. "Roberts won't be at all pleased if it's ruined."

"Yes, of course."

Sheriff Lawson strode into the street in front of the excited horses and riders milling about. "Hold your horses, folks. Brody wants to get a photograph of everybody under the sign." He beckoned to the newspaperman, who lumbered into the center of the street carrying his large camera and made quick work of photographing the participants. When he finished, the sheriff addressed the competitors again.

"Now you all know the rules. No interfering with the other riders. Just run your own race. There's watchers along the way in case anybody decides to cause trouble. The course is laid out with red flags so you can find your way if the dust gets too thick. You head west on Main." He pointed toward the San Juan Mountains. "Turn south on Foster, east on Patterson, north on Kirkland." He swung his arm over his head to accompany his words. "Last, turn west again on Main. Homer Bean and I are your judges, and a few other folks will watch as you cross the finish line. The winner will receive a ten-dollar prize and a blue ribbon."

After repeating her good wishes and her promise to pray for Garrick, Rosamond stepped up on the boardwalk to join the crowd in front of Mrs. Winsted's mercantile.

Laurie Eberly gave her hand a welcoming squeeze. "Congratulations on winning first place in the egg race. Who're you rooting for in this one?"

"I can't decide between Garrick and Tolley." Not true, but she wouldn't admit to anyone that she hoped Garrick would win.

Laurie laughed. "From the way you kissed Garrick, I think I can guess which one's your favorite."

"Nonsense." Rosamond sniffed artificially. "I was just overly excited about winning." She must turn this conversation around. "What about you? Any special rider you'll be cheering for?"

"I can't decide between Grace and—" Her cheeks reddened. "All the rest of 'em."

Rosamond studied the girl. At sixteen, she was becoming every bit as pretty and grown up as her three

older sisters. Did she have feelings for one of the cowboys? Surely not Tolley. The Eberly girls thought of Nate,
Rand and Tolley as brothers. Maybe one of their cowhands had caught her eye.

"Are you ready, men?" Sheriff Lawson bellowed.
"And lady?" He tipped his hat to Grace, and everyone
laughed. He moved out of the street, took his gun from
his holster and fired into the air.

Riders whooped, horses took off and the crowd roared.
Gypsy bucked briefly before springing into action. She
soon caught up with the pack. Within less than a minute, most of the horses turned the corner and disappeared down Foster Street, although the pounding of
their hooves could still be heard.

Almost too late, Rosamond remembered her promise to pray for Garrick. *Lord, please take care of Garrick and all of the riders. Keep them safe. Let Garrick
win. No, that's not fair. I don't mean that.* But as she
whispered "amen," she knew that was exactly what she
did mean.

The moment the sheriff fired the starting shot, Garrick knew he should drop out of the race. Gypsy was running her brave little heart out, but something was wrong
with her stride. He'd checked her legs before mounting
and knew her to be sound. Adam had agreed. And she
clearly wanted to run.

Hugging close to her neck, he glanced ahead, surprised not to see Tolley on his black stallion, Thor. In
fact, Gypsy was pulling into the lead ahead of two other
horses just as they made their second turn. She swung
wide, and Tolley came into view on Garrick's left. Even
with his hat low on his face, his sneering grin was visible. He whipped his mount with a crop, something

Garrick never cared to do. If the horse didn't want to compete, why force him? Garrick turned his eyes forward, urging Gypsy on, just as he felt something sting his left arm. No time to check it.

Gypsy and Thor ran neck and neck the entire length of Patterson Street, but as they turned onto Kirkland, Thor's longer legs and inside position put him ahead. Garrick let the stallion pass before moving closer to the red flags at the edge of the course. If he could just maneuver past Thor on the next turn, he could still win. A sudden craving to win exploded inside him. He hadn't entered any sort of race since his Oxford days and had forgotten the wild thrill of it all.

They swept around the corner onto Main Street to the roar of the crowd. Garrick gave Gypsy her head, and she galloped hard. They swept under the banner only inches behind Thor. Had she been only a little larger, they could have won. He kept the reins slack and let her slow down on her own before turning her back to the celebration at the finish line. Rosamond and Adam met him as he dismounted.

"Great race!" Rosamond plopped his hat on his head and then threw her arms around his neck and kissed his cheek. "You were wonderful."

"Thank you." Garrick huffed out a breath. Surprising how winded a chap got in a race when he was merely the rider. He started to tease Rosamond about the dangers of all these kisses, but Adam waved at him to catch his attention.

"Hey, Mr. Wakefield." The lad stood beside Gypsy, inspecting her rump. "She's bleeding."

"What?" Garrick checked the slight stream of blood oozing from beneath the saddle. "Let's get this off." He lifted the left stirrup and loosened the girth so Adam could lift off the saddle and blanket. Underneath they found a prickly bur. "What's this?" Picking the offending pod out of the wound, Garrick gritted his teeth to keep from yelling at Adam. "Didn't you brush her before you saddled her?"

Adam blanched. "Yessir. I always brush 'em clean before I put a saddle on any horse." He glanced at Rosamond and then stared at the ground.

"What are you not telling me?" Garrick softened his tone.

Adam bit his lip. "While I was saddling her at the livery stable, Mr. Tolley said he wanted to check her, her being a Northam horse and all."

"Surely you don't think my brother would harm one of our best horses just to win a race." Rosamond crossed her arms, and her eyes blazed. "Or any horse, for that matter."

Indeed, I do. "No, of course not. The bur must have caught in the blanket and Adam simply didn't notice it." Garrick turned toward Adam and warned him with a look. They would discuss this later. "Take her to the livery stable, tell Ben to check her wound and make sure to put salve on it."

"Yessir." His head hanging, Adam led Gypsy away.

Garrick's heart went out to him. Later he must assure the lad of his full confidence.

"Garrick, you're bleeding, too." Rosamond grasped Garrick's left arm. His shirtsleeve was ripped open, and blood caked on a stinging wound. "What happened?"

"I haven't the faintest idea." But he did have an idea. Tolley had struck him with his crop, and he would call him into account for these injuries. Not for himself but for brave Gypsy, who'd run a magnificent race despite the nasty bur that must have been driven farther into her hide with every stride she took.

To Rosamond's disappointment, Garrick refused her offer to tend his scratch. He located Roberts, claimed his new shirt from Mrs. Starling and went to Mrs. Foster's house to change. In his absence, Nolan Means and Fred Brody each invited her to eat dinner with them, but she declined. She'd wait for Garrick. Not that she assumed he wanted to spend the entire day with her, but he certainly hadn't shown interest in anyone else. Besides, she suspected he blamed Tolley for both his injury and Gypsy's, and she wanted to set him straight. Tolley simply wouldn't do anything so downright mean.

When Garrick and his valet didn't return in time for Reverend Thomas's blessing for the meal, Rosamond found Rita and suggested that they save some fried chicken and all the trimmings for the two men. "If we don't, they won't get any."

"*Sí*, Senorita Rosamond." Rita's sweet face lit up in a smile as they walked toward the food lines. "We must take care of our men, no?"

Rosamond stopped. "Well, I, um…" She mustn't foster the idea that Garrick was *hers*. "I'd just say we're being thoughtful of our guests."

"Oh, *sí*. Our *guests*." Rita's merry laugh showed she didn't believe Rosamond for a single moment. But then, she was free to fall in love and marry, if she wished. Rosamond didn't enjoy that same self-determination. Maybe those kisses had been a bad idea. What on earth had made her so bold?

They'd endured some teasing from friends for piling four plates high with food but were rewarded when

Garrick and Roberts found them seated on a blanket on the church lawn.

"How very thoughtful." Roberts sank down beside Rita and took the plate she offered. "We passed the serving tables, and they looked as if a swarm of locusts had eaten every bite. I assumed we'd lost out."

Holding a sheathed rifle, Garrick remained on his feet several yards away. From the way he kept glancing between Rosamond and Roberts, he appeared uncertain about whether to sit. Did he feel above eating with servants? She'd fix that.

"Oh, do sit down." She didn't bother to keep the annoyance from her voice.

He blinked in his charming way, still uncertain, but he laid his rifle on the blanket and did as he was told. "Thank you." He accepted the plate she handed him and began to eat.

Rosamond nibbled the last morsel of meat off of a drumstick, savoring Miss Pam's perfect fried chicken. Chef Henri would never be able to improve on this, no matter what delicious French dishes he brought to Esperanza's hotel. She waved a hand toward Garrick's rifle. "Are you entering the shooting match?" She'd never noticed him carrying a weapon.

"I am." He offered nothing further, and his mood hadn't improved since the horse race.

Rosamond's own mood plummeted, and she no longer felt the inclination to set him straight about Tolley. She finished her dinner and dug into Mother's lemon cake with buttercream frosting. That would probably be the only sweet thing happening at this meal. Even Rita and Roberts barely spoke, probably because of Garrick's grumpiness.

None too soon, the bell rang for the shooting compe-

tition. Excusing himself, Garrick picked up his rifle and
strode away, leaving Roberts to see to his plate. Or Rita.
Or Rosamond. She couldn't guess whom he expected
to clean up after him, nor could she decide whether she
was hurt or irritated. Maybe spilling a drop or two of his
aristocratic blood had offended him more than she realized. If so, maybe he was a sissy, just as Tolley claimed.
Cowboys got scratches and broken bones all the time but
never took offense. In fact, many took pride in enumer-
ating their many injuries in comical narratives. Clearly,
Garrick's pride allowed for no such good humor.

In spite of herself, she couldn't squelch the urge to
watch him shoot, even though many of the ladies were
busy cleaning up after dinner. She approached the long
tables where pans of soapy water held dishes ready to be
washed and the ladies' sleeves were rolled up.

"Mother, if I promise to wash supper dishes, may I
be excused this time?"

Mother gave her that familiar knowing, matchmaking look. "Why, Rosamond, what on earth could be more
important than washing dishes?"

"My, my, Rosamond. You young girls today." Mabel
Eberly laughed. "I saw you kiss that Englishman. That
story will be repeated for some time." She waved a soapy
dishrag toward the field behind the church. "Go on, join
my girls. They're over at the shooting range getting ready
to compete."

More ladies joined in the teasing, although one or two
others sent cross looks Rosamond's way. Did they disapprove of her for not washing dishes or for kissing Garrick? Her cheeks burning, she made her escape.

She'd always enjoyed watching the shooting matches.
Rand used to win all the time, but years ago, after he
killed an outlaw, he'd lost interest. She hadn't seen Tol-

ley shoot since she came home from Boston and didn't know anything about his marksmanship. Would he beat Garrick in this contest, too? Feeling more than a little disloyal to her brother and entirely contradictory to her own earlier thoughts, she said a little prayer for Garrick to win the blue ribbon and ten-dollar gold piece.

"Hey, Rosamond." Beryl joined her among the spectators for the event. "Has Garrick heard from Percy?"

Rosamond shrugged, her heart aching for her friend. "If he did, he didn't mention it."

Beryl sighed. "Oh, well." She waved toward the shooters. "Looks like some healthy competition."

"Yes, it does." Rosamond linked arms with Beryl out of habit. How often she'd steadied her friend before Percy came along. Yet here she stood, unafraid to watch and listen to the shooting match. What possible reason could Garrick have for not wanting his cousin to court Beryl? Once again, she suspected his aristocratic snobbery. Maybe her original opinion of him in the Denver train station had been right, after all. Maybe all of his friendliness since that time had simply been his way of coping in a society so different from his own.

Garrick watched as the youngsters took their turns on the shooting range, getting help when necessary from parents or older brothers. Most missed their targets entirely, but several hit the plate fragments propped on bales of hay. After winners were declared, the contest opened up to anyone thirteen years or older.

The hay bales were moved back, pottery shards set up and numbers drawn by the marksmen to decide the order in which each would shoot. Garrick drew a seven of perhaps thirty.

He hadn't practiced in recent weeks, but he'd thoroughly cleaned his rifle after shooting with Pete in a field several miles from Four Stones Ranch. His weapon was ready. He was ready. He'd always done well at grouse shooting on Uncle's estate, so stationary targets should offer very little challenge. If nothing else, he'd enjoy testing himself in the contest.

In the first round, most participants hit their marks and moved on. By the third round, however, only six competitors remained: Garrick, Tolley, Laurie and Grace Eberly, and two cowboys Garrick didn't know. The bales were set at about one hundred fifty yards, and the judges set out three smaller pottery shards for each contestant. They must hit all three to continue. Laurie and the cowboys each missed one, so only three shooters remained.

Each time Garrick advanced to the next round, he hoped he might gain Tolley's respect, however grudging, even though he still intended to settle the matter of Gypsy's injury. Yet, after each round, the younger man muttered insults to him when no one else was close enough to hear them. Now, with only three of them competing, Garrick steeled himself to the possibility that Tolley might try to distract him. Anyone who would injure a horse or strike a man during a race, simply for the sake of winning, couldn't be counted on to display good sportsmanship.

Suddenly, winning this event became even more important to Garrick than the horse race. Someone must show this young ruffian his behavior wouldn't be tolerated. Garrick would gladly volunteer for the task.

Once again the targets were moved farther away. Grace, taller than many men and as boisterous as all of her sisters, took the first turn. Using a Winchester '76, she fired the repeating rifle, quickly blasting away two of the shards but missing the third. Garrick had brought his single shot .577 Snider-Enfield to America almost as an afterthought, yet its accuracy never failed him. Neither did it fail this time. Three shots, two quick cartridge reloads at the breech, three hits.

He didn't intend to look at Tolley, didn't intend to speak to him, but his eyes seemed to turn of their own volition while his mouth blurted out, "Your turn, *Bartholomew.*"

A mistake. A terrible mistake. Tolley's temper exploded in an oath. He took his place on the firing line and raised his Winchester. Shaking the way he was, he'd never hit his targets. And he didn't.

Garrick's heart sank like a stone. He'd expected poor sportsmanship from Tolley, but he'd been the one to distract his opponent. *Lord, forgive me.* Now he'd never be able to befriend the disagreeable, hot-headed younger man. An apology must be offered straightaway.

He saw Tolley stalk away from the match and started to follow him, but others crowded around to congratulate him, and he was unable to move. Several yards beyond the mob, he saw Rosamond and Beryl strolling from the field arm-in-arm. He'd won this event, including the blue ribbon and a ten-dollar gold piece, but apparently a kiss wasn't part of the prize. And perhaps in winning the shooting match, he'd forever lost something far more valuable: Rosamond's good opinion.

The mouth-watering aromas of a side of beef and a whole hog sizzling over open pits had tantalized everyone since morning. Rosamond was no more resistant to the temptation than anyone else. After a fine day of competitions and fun, and with memories of dinner long forgotten, supper commenced. Lines once again formed at the food tables, plates were piled high and everyone hoped for a piece of one of the prize-winning pies or cakes to finish off the feast.

Rosamond hadn't bothered to look for Garrick that afternoon, partly because she'd been teased all day about kissing him and partly because she'd heard him goad Tolley at the shooting match. No wonder her brother disliked the Englishman. What else did Garrick say to him when she wasn't around?

Even if he'd never before insulted her brother, calling him by his given name was sufficient to incite her brother's rage. Tolley always hated being called Bartholomew. Never mind that he'd been named for their paternal grandfather, an honor because the old gentleman had served as a judge and later spent two terms in congress. When Tolley was born, she'd just begun to talk and couldn't pronounce the long, complicated biblical name, so she'd called him Tolley, a nickname that had stuck. Only Father called him Bartholomew, and only when her brother displeased him. Garrick's words, delivered in that arrogant, aristocratic English accent, were clearly meant to goad Tolley, and the ploy had worked. After such meanness, how could she respect or even like Garrick?

Then again, growing up with three brothers and knowing countless hard-riding cowboys, Rosamond had learned that most men had a strong sense of competition and usually goaded each other with a fierce exchange of words. Maybe in the heat of the shooting match, Garrick's true nature had finally emerged. Maybe he wasn't such a perfect gentleman, after all. That was hardly her concern. No matter how much she'd been attracted to him, no matter how polite she must be to him socially, she had three important reasons for dismissing any romantic notions toward him: Tolley, Beryl and her own call to teaching.

Even as she made up her mind about the matter, Rosamond saw Garrick striding toward her across the park. How handsome he looked in his new burgundy shirt and the bolo tie she'd impulsively bought for him. Her traitorous heart jumped. With no little struggle, she turned in the opposite direction and joined the other women for washing dishes. As she took her place between two of the ladies who'd disapproved of her actions earlier, she noticed that Garrick was now headed in the opposite direction. Nosey Mrs. Casper harrumphed, and busybody Mrs. Norton muttered, "Now, that's more like it, missy." Obviously, they'd been watching her. Everyone watched the Northams. Like Caesar's wife, each member of the family must be above reproach, must set an example of proper behavior. All the more reason for Rosamond not to give in to her foolish sentiments toward Garrick. At the thought, her heart ached with disappointment.

Garrick had no intention of following Rosamond to the dish-washing tables. The two women standing on either side of her looked like harpies ready to fly in and devour her. Sweet girl that she was, she smiled at the women as she set to work. Such grace was hard to find, especially when Rosamond's younger brother was more inclined to answer sharply. Genteel Mrs. Northam had taught her daughter well.

After considering the situation all afternoon, he'd decided he must discover the true nature of his feelings for Rosamond. When she'd kissed him and he'd returned the kiss with a decidedly unfamiliar depth of feeling, he'd been ready to call it love. Perhaps it was, but how could he be certain? From the moment he'd seen her in the Denver train station, he'd admired her. Even their disagreements over the hotel had soon dissipated and even generated his respect for her intelligence. Before returning to England, he must discover whether he loved her and whether she felt anything for him. As in the children's fairy tales his governess had read to him, the knight must go on a quest, then return to claim the hand of his lady love. Could Garrick do that?

He needed a plan, just as he'd planned how to build the hotel. Only this time he'd be building the rest of his life. If Rosamond cared for him, perhaps she'd be willing to wait until he earned Helena's dowry. Then he'd take a job, any job, to support her. He'd even consider asking Percy to hire him as his man-of-all-business. He simply *must* make a way for his dreams of a life with Rosamond to come true. He couldn't speak to her now, so he'd wait until the dance and try to claim every set with her. That would be his first step. If all went well, he'd plan the rest of his strategy for courting her.

At sundown, Mr. Chen and his family lit the brightly colored paper lanterns they'd strung around the park and on Main Street. The musicians took their places in the bandstand and began to play their lively tunes. As everyone gathered in the park, Garrick felt as nervous as a schoolboy. The bandmaster summoned everyone to assemble for the opening dance, the Virginia reel. Perhaps it was similar to an old English country dance. Or perhaps a Scottish reel. Garrick could manage either of those.

He spied Rosamond approaching the grassy area cropped short for the dancing. She'd changed into a green silk dress appropriate for evening wear, and even at a distance, he could see how the dress brightened her green eyes. If he were a wealthy man, he'd buy an emerald necklace and earrings to complement those enchanting eyes.

Nolan Means also strode toward Rosamond, his intent clear in his focused gaze. Garrick reached her first.

"Rosamond, you are a vision of loveliness." Garrick sketched a bow that would have made all of his titled ancestors proud. "May I have the first dance?"

"Miss Northam, may I have this dance?" Nolan moved into her line of vision and gave a similar bow.

Rosamond looked from Nolan to Garrick and back again. "Mr. Means, I believe Garrick spoke first. I'll save the next dance for you."

Her acceptance filled Garrick with relief, and he resisted the urge to gloat. Instead, he gave Means a polite nod. "Rosamond." He held out his arm, she set a hand on it and he led her to the dance area. Her rosewater perfume wafted gently into his awareness, teasing him with a pleasant, heady sensation. "I must confess I'm not familiar with the Virginia reel. Do forgive me if I misstep." He gave her an impish grin.

Her returning smile seemed forced, and his heart dropped. Was she angry with him about his regrettable words to Tolley? If so, why had she accepted his request to dance? As soon as possible, he must tell her how wrong he'd been to blurt out those thoughtless, provoking words.

"The caller will tell you what the steps are." She waved a hand toward the bandmaster. "Just listen, do as he says and watch me."

"Ah. Very good."

As she took her place in the line of ladies and he took his with the other men, her stiff smile faded. The music began, the caller instructed the head couple to move forward and bow, followed by several variations of turns, ending with the two weaving in and out of the opposite lines. By the time Garrick and Rosamond moved up to become the head couple, he felt fairly confident he was making a good showing.

They reached the end of their progression down the line of dancers, and, as they swung around and started back up, something caught his foot and held it fast. He found himself spinning and falling, flailing his arms in a desperate attempt to regain his balance. Instead, he landed on his back with a *whomp!* The air went out of his lungs, the world spun and everything went black.

He awoke to find himself seated on the grass, a crowd around him, and Doctor Henshaw examining the back of his head. Where was Rosamond? Was she all right? Had she fallen, too?

"Blacked out for a minute, didn't you?" The doctor moved his index finger back and forth in front of Garrick. His eyes instinctively followed the movement. "You'll be all right. Why not sit out this next dance."

"Yes. Yes, of course." Garrick permitted the doctor to help him to his feet and over to the wooden steps to the bandstand.

Across the way, he saw Tolley, a smug expression of satisfaction on his face, a lariat in his hands. The blighter had somehow tripped him with that rope! Just as he'd done at the branding. Before he knew what he was doing, Garrick charged across the space and grabbed Tolley by the front of his shirt.

"Having fun today, are we?" Garrick's right hand fisted, his arm ached for action, but he sent up a desperate prayer for restraint.

Tolley struggled to twist free, and his eyes widened when he couldn't. He obviously hadn't expected Garrick to possess the strength to hold him. "Let go of me," he growled.

Despite cries from the gathering crowd urging him to give Tolley the thrashing he deserved, Garrick released his adversary. With Tolley's own community wishing him ill, Garrick couldn't bring himself to add to his shame. Further, Garrick saw some of the boys from Sunday school nearby, the same boys who were building Rosamond's school. He mustn't do anything to diminish their regard for Tolley.

"This is for kissing my sister." Tolley swung at him, knocking him to the ground for a second time.

His jaw stung, but with help from others, Garrick leapt back to his feet and planted a facer on the younger man. "That was for Gypsy."

Tolley stumbled back as though shocked, his Stetson flying off.

"What's going on here?" Colonel Northam's unmistakable voice boomed over the clamor of the mob. "Bartholomew, what have you done?"

"What have *I* done?" Tolley shook with a rage far worse than at the shooting match. "Why don't you ask your Englishman what he's done?"

The Colonel didn't even glance at Garrick. "Boy, go home. Now." His commanding voice brooked no response. Eyes blazing, Tolley grabbed up his hat and slapped it against his leg before striding away toward the improvised corral beyond the church. The tormented look on his face cut into Garrick far worse than his stinging jaw. Couldn't he do anything right in regard to Rosamond's younger brother?

A stunned silence fell over the park for a few moments. The fiddle player timidly began to play, and soon the other musicians joined in. People milled about as though trying to remember what they'd been doing before the unpleasantness began. Someone remarked that the fireworks had started early. Someone else laughed. Garrick's jaw ached.

"Fire!" Dub Staley, one of the younger hotel workers, raced into the park, terror in his eyes. "Fire at the hotel!"

Chapter Twelve

Holding a tight rein on her emotions, Rosamond helped Mrs. Winsted pass out new tin pails from the general store. With the last of them distributed, they joined the two lines passing buckets of water one block from the city's fountain. Rosamond pushed into a spot between Nate and Rand near the hotel's double front doors.

To her dismay, Father stationed himself just inside, next to Garrick. Father was too old for such exertion. Yet as each filled bucket reached him, he flung the contents onto the blaze with as much vigor as Garrick. Still the flames climbed up the studs and licked at the ceiling beams. If they couldn't contain the fire on the first floor, the entire inside of the structure might collapse. How had it started? Was it deliberately set?

"Father," she shouted over the clamor of the crowd, "can't we open the pipes to the artesian well?"

He didn't seem to hear her, but Garrick responded. "The flames are blocking the way to the valves."

His soot-streaked face wore a stricken expression that reflected her own feelings. This was *their* hotel, *their* project. Neither one of them could bear to see it destroyed.

"Garrick, no!" Father shouted.

In spite of his command, the Englishman poured the next bucketful of water over his own head and clothing and then ran toward a smoldering pile of rubble. He leaped over it and disappeared behind a wall.

Horror gripped Rosamond. Had her words incited this foolish bravery? She'd never forgive herself if something happened to him.

Moments later, water gushed down from above, spraying over the blaze and making quick work of dousing it. Nate, Rand and several other younger men used wet burlap bags to beat down the last of the flames.

To Rosamond's relief, Father at last surrendered his place and stepped out into the open air. He bent over and coughed hoarsely but didn't appear to be in distress. She looked beyond him but couldn't see Garrick. She grabbed her nearest brother's arm.

"Nate, Garrick's back there." She waved a weary hand toward the black interior of the building.

Nate gave her a brief nod. "I'll find him."

Before he could take three steps, Garrick emerged from the darkness, coughing into a soot-stained white handkerchief.

Without a thought, her heart bursting with joy, Rosamond flung herself at him with a sob. "Garrick, you're all right."

His arms around her, he gave her a crooked smile. "I am. Yes. Thank you." His smile disappeared. "Where's Tolley?"

The implication of his question felt like a slap in the face, the feel of his arms hotter than the fire. She jerked out of his embrace and stepped over to Father, whose coughing continued.

"Father, you must sit down."

Mother appeared from somewhere and rushed to his side.

"Oh, Frank, I was so worried about you." Her face and clothing bore telltale smudges, giving proof that she'd also been in the thick of the battle.

"Now, Mother, don't fuss." Father put an arm around her. "Have you ever known me to stand by and let others do the hard work?" As the two of them walked away, he glanced down at her dress. "Now, you, young lady, didn't mind when I said to stay back…" The rest of his words were lost in the noise of the dispersing crowd.

"That's enough fireworks for one day." Nate spoke to the people still waiting to learn whether they were needed to finish the job at hand. "Maybe we can use them during Harvest Home."

"Sounds good to me," Mayor Jones said. Many others voiced their agreement.

"A shame about your lovely frock." Garrick moved into her line of vision on the dimly lit street. "Will the soot wash out, do you think?"

The gentle concern in his voice and eyes could have swept her off her feet, had he not already implied that Tolley had started the fire. Was he truly so oblivious that he couldn't see how his question about her brother affected her? With so many people close by, she could hardly make a scene about it. Instead, she forced a smile and spoke as cheerfully as she could.

"As long as the hotel is repairable, my dress doesn't matter." She glanced at the damaged building, which his actions had saved from destruction. "You were very foolish to run into the back." Truth demanded more. "And very brave."

Now his expression turned slightly boyish. If he were a cowboy, right about now, he'd say, "Aw, shucks." Instead, he shrugged. "Ah, well. Couldn't stand by and see all of our hard work go up in flames."

"No." She couldn't think of anything more to say.

Nate gathered several men, most of them hotel workers, to shovel the smoldering rubble out onto the street, while others checked for any signs of remaining embers that could reignite the fire. Water still dripped from above, making a heavy, sticky mess of it all.

Garrick set a gentle hand on Rosamond's shoulder. "We can take care of the rest of this. Why don't you go home with your parents and get some rest?" He waved a hand down the street toward the churchyard, where they'd all been celebrating just one short hour ago.

She nodded and turned away, but he caught her arm, again with a gentleness that touched something deep in her soul.

"Please don't worry," he said. "Before you know it, we'll make everything right as rain. Let the workmen make all of the repairs before you come back. All right?"

She stifled a tiny sob trying to escape her. "All right."

But it wasn't all right and never would be. Other than her responsibilities in completing the hotel rooms, she'd have nothing more to do with this Englishman who could treat her with such refined manners while trying to destroy her vulnerable younger brother.

Garrick watched Rosamond walk away, and with her went his heart. Yes, it was true. He did love her. Tonight had confirmed his feelings. And when she'd flung herself into his arms, he'd seen in her eyes that his love was reciprocated. At that moment, he'd been overcome by a great urgency to set things right with Tolley, or at the least, find out why the younger man disliked him. Then he and Rosamond would have no barriers to their tendresse, to use the French expression his governess had been so fond of. Rosamond must have experienced the same urgency, for when he asked about Tolley, she'd turned away to look for her brother, and then been distracted by her father's coughing. Or so it seemed. Garrick prayed he'd read the events correctly.

In the meantime, despite the fire, he felt sanguine about the entire situation. Beginning tomorrow morning, he'd set to work clearing out the last of the rubble right alongside the workmen. Circumstances may have forced him to end his cowboy lessons, but surely Rosamond would appreciate his willingness to labor at the hotel with his own two hands. Even the formidable Colonel Northam hadn't been above fighting the fire, nor had Nate and Rand. Mrs. Northam also appeared to have jumped into the fray, so to speak. Garrick could do no less if he expected to be fully accepted by this family.

Oddly, Tolley hadn't fought the fire, although Garrick suspected he'd seen it. After leaving the dance upon his father's order, he'd probably ridden back toward the hotel before heading south to Four Stones Ranch. By that time, the entire town would have been hurrying to stop the conflagration.

Suspected. Without the slightest desire to do so, Garrick suspected Tolley of starting the fire. A shiver coursed down his spine. He must think this through carefully. The first time he'd seen Tolley since the shooting match was after he tripped him during the dance. They'd traded blows—Garrick touched his jaw and felt the painful, swollen reminder. Then Colonel Northam had ordered Tolley to leave, and he'd walked away in the opposite direction from the hotel. Straightaway, the young workman had burst into the party with news of the fire. If Tolley did start it, he would have done so before coming to the dance and tripping Garrick. Given the violence of the flames when Garrick raced to the hotel, was that plausible?

Yes, entirely plausible. Otherwise, why hadn't Tolley returned to help? He simply couldn't have missed the flames.

Sick at heart, Garrick worked until the last man went home before he trudged back to Mrs. Foster's house alongside Roberts.

"Good show, sir." The valet had the effrontery to slap Garrick on the back. He then gulped loudly. "I beg your pardon, sir. I fear being among these rustic Americans has dulled my sense of propriety."

"Never mind." Garrick grunted out a weary laugh. "You can make amends by saving this shirt. I rather like its color."

"Yes, yes. It's quite the thing." Roberts coughed in his nervous way. "I believe I can make the necessary repairs to both of your *cowboy* shirts."

Something in the way he said "cowboy" didn't quite match the disdain he seemed eager to convey. But Garrick was too exhausted from the day to question him. In any event, Roberts had showed himself as brave as any in combatting the flames. Such a joint effort formed a camaraderie between master and servant. Things would settle back into their proper form on the morrow.

The warmth of the summer breeze blowing in through Rosamond's window alerted her to the lateness of the hour. Her clock confirmed it: half past eleven. She'd overslept, yet she didn't feel rested. As much as her back and arms ached from carrying buckets of water to put out the fire, her heart ached even more.

Last night as Father drove the surrey home, few words

had been spoken. Then, despite his weariness, when they reached the house, he'd summoned Tolley to his office, and the two had argued into the night, their voices loud, but their words unclear. Still smarting from Garrick's insinuation that Tolley started the fire, Rosamond couldn't wait to speak to her younger brother and voice her confidence in him, perhaps bolster his spirits after Father's dressing down. What fault had Father found in Tolley this time?

She noticed that Beryl's everyday brown skirt and white shirtwaist were missing from the wardrobe, so she dressed quickly and went downstairs in search of her friend. Beryl was in the kitchen helping Mother and Rita prepare dinner.

"Good morning, sleepyhead." Mother's cheery tone sounded a bit forced, and her smile appeared strained.

"Good morning, all." Rosamond grabbed a paring knife from the utensil drawer to help Beryl peel vegetables. "Why didn't anyone wake me up?"

Beryl offered no response, and her concentration on digging the eyes out of a potato seemed a bit too focused. Rita's work at the stove also required silent, serious attention.

Mother heaved out a weary sigh. "You'll find out soon enough, my dear. Tolley's gone. He—"

"Gone?" Rosamond dropped her knife. "Gone where? Did he run away?" What a foolish question. A grown man didn't run away from home. He just...*left* when things became intolerable. "Why did he go?" She couldn't subdue her anger.

Mother's eyes reddened. "Your father..." She cleared her throat. "It was time."

Rosamond choked back a sob. The grief in Mother's voice broke her heart. After all, Tolley was her beloved son, just as Nate and Rand were. She'd miss him just as much as Rosamond would.

"Did he say where he was going?" Wherever it was, he'd manage. He would do well. At only twenty years of age, he could build a house, run a ranch, do whatever he set his mind to. Everyone who knew him could see that. Everyone except Father.

Mother seemed surprised by the question. "Why, yes. He took the morning train to go back east. To Boston. To Harvard." She spoke as if Rosamond should know this.

Stunned, however, Rosamond couldn't speak for a moment. At last, she inhaled a deep, painful breath. "Harvard? Why on earth?" Tolley loved being a rancher. He'd never wanted to go back east to school.

"Your father arranged it." Sadness permeated her whole being.

Finally stifling her indignation, Rosamond decided not to press Mother any further, but she'd speak to Father once she'd gained control of her temper. Right now she must encourage Mother.

"Well, I'll certainly miss him." She forced out a dramatic sigh. "He could've at least said goodbye to me."

Mother gave her an understanding smile. "He came into your room and kissed you on the forehead but said he didn't have the heart to wake you."

"Oh, no! I thought that was a dream." Now her tears came in earnest. "I'd have hugged him to pieces if he'd just wakened me."

Mother's chuckle came from deep within, a good sign she was dealing with Tolley's departure as well as could be expected. "Then that should give you your answer. You know how our menfolk dislike emotional scenes."

Rita and Beryl offered timid giggles, each sending Rosamond a consoling look.

She nodded her thanks. "Maybe Nate and Rand can help us finish the schoolhouse."

"It just needs painting," Beryl said. "You and I can do that."

Again, Rosamond nodded. This would give them something to do for the time being. Garrick had asked her to stay away from the hotel until he'd arranged for cleanup and repairs. Staying away from him would be easy enough. If he hadn't goaded Tolley yesterday at the shooting match, her brother might still be home instead of exiled to Boston to attend a school in which he'd never shown even the slightest interest.

The day after the fire, the resolve of the workers greatly encouraged Garrick. Or perhaps his own enthusiasm for the cleanup generated their fervor for the task. At the beginning of the project, these American men had found amusement in his use of proper English, but they'd always been respectful of him as their superior. His willingness to get his hands dirty brought a different kind of respect, which gave him a feeling of camaraderie such as he'd never known. How different from most of his Oxford classmates, who offered friendship only to those with wealth and social position. Oddly, Garrick found himself regretting that he must return to England as soon as the hotel opened for business. Perhaps Uncle would permit him to stay awhile to ensure the success of the enterprise.

As soon as the last of the debris and soot had been swept from the building, Mr. Schmidt, the carpenter, inspected the wooden studs and beams to determine which were sound and which must be replaced. He reported that, despite what appeared to be a devastating conflagration, the majority of damage was somewhat superficial. Tarpaulins and canvases had burned, along with sawdust and wood shavings, but only a few areas required studs to be replaced. To accomplish it all quickly, Garrick ordered meals from Williams's Café for the entire crew so they could work through the day. He was rewarded with their continued enthusiasm, as though they were taking pride in the hotel, not merely earning a wage.

As he worked, thoughts of Rosamond filled Garrick's mind. He longed to see her but reminded himself to be patient. Last night after retiring, he'd lain awake and considered his suspicions about Tolley. If he'd started the fire as a prank, he surely was appalled when it got out of hand. Perhaps he'd been too ashamed to return and fight the blaze. Garrick would choose to forgive him and move beyond the incident. After all, no one had been injured.

Further, he decided that once he completed the hotel, he would ask Colonel Northam's permission to court Rosamond. Upon waking, he changed his mind. He would speak to her first. Once the hotel was completed, he'd invite her to inspect it and, in the process, pour out his heart to her, explaining that while the hotel had been growing into a fine establishment, so had his love for her grown into something grand. Then, if she didn't actually reciprocate his affections, he wouldn't have the embarrassment of facing Colonel Northam in failure. But the emotion in Rosamond's eyes last night couldn't be denied. She loved him just as much as he loved her. These thoughts pleased him so thoroughly that he didn't mind getting covered in soot from head to toe for a second time in as many days. Surely Rosamond could only admire his hard work, just as these men did.

In midafternoon Garrick glanced down Main Street and saw a welcome sight. Percy and his two companions were riding into town. As they drew nearer to the hotel, Percy's cheerful expression became visible, a good sign of a fruitful quest. Garrick left Mr. Schmidt in charge of the cleanup and hurried to meet the travelers. While Percy dismounted, Garrick brushed soot from his hand and reached out to him.

"Percy, good to see you."

Percy pumped his hand. "And you, cousin." He studied Garrick from head to toe, shaking his head in dismay, then waved a hand at the piles of burned rubble being carted away by the workmen. "I say, old boy, what happened here?"

Garrick related the events of the night before, careful not to mention Tolley. He'd tell Percy everything when no one else could hear him. In the meantime, he did his best to make light of the blaze.

"You must have been devastated." Understanding filled his cousin's eyes. "A true trial by fire, so to speak."

"The Almighty was merciful. Very little damage was structural." Garrick shrugged. "It's all over now. Time to move forward and rebuild." He noticed Percy's valet and Pete, the cowboy, standing patiently beside their horses. "Enough about my little incident. How did you fare in your quest?"

"Oh, jolly good." Percy lit up with excitement. "We found our Mr. Starling."

Both stunned and delighted, Garrick stepped back and stared down Main Street. "Well, where is he?" He itched to give the man a dressing down for abandoning his wife and children.

Percy chuckled. "With his family, of course. We couldn't simply ride past Chen's laundry and not deliver him to the missus at once. We also stopped by the livery stable to tell Adam. He was beside himself with happiness and ran home straightaway."

"Ah. Of course." Happy for the lad he'd befriended, Garrick still wanted answers. He leveled a scowl on his cousin. "And just exactly what has our elusive railroad worker been doing all these months?" He tried not to imagine something too terrible, but even among his hotel workers, he'd noticed a few who didn't live exemplary lives, especially the four who'd eyed Rosamond so rudely all those weeks ago until he'd set them straight.

"The poor chap had quite a go of it. Just as we learned, he was working on the south leg of the Denver and Rio Grande Railroad. As a trusted foreman, he rode to Santa Fe to fetch the payroll, but on the way back was robbed and left for dead." Percy shuddered at the horror of his own words. "An elderly Mexican couple found him and nursed him back to health in their home. However, they don't speak English, and he doesn't speak Spanish, so they couldn't communicate. He also told us he couldn't remember his name for some time. That delayed things considerably, but eventually they brought him to the small settlement where we found him."

"Poor chap, indeed." Garrick regretted his rush to judgment about the man. "How is he now?"

"Vastly improved, although he's still healing from his injuries. We hired a wagon to bring him home." Percy included Richards and Pete with a wave of his hand. "These chaps were quite remarkable throughout the entire adventure. Couldn't do a thing without them."

"Well done, men." Garrick gave them an approving nod and then asked Percy, "Did you incur any expenses along the way?" The search was his idea, so of course he must repay Percy.

"Nothing I couldn't see to."

Garrick wouldn't press the matter now but would look for a way to repay his cousin.

Percy's blue eyes now brightened with another sort of expression. He leaned close to Garrick. "How is my Miss Eberly?"

Garrick frowned. He should have known Percy would ask about her. He stared down and chewed his lip.

"What is it?" Percy clutched Garrick's arm. "Is she well? Has anything happened to her?"

Garrick swiped a hand across his jaw. How could he discourage his good cousin from continuing his pursuit of the young lady? Yet he must if Percy was to reach his full potential and live up to his responsibilities as an Englishman.

"She is well, as far as I've seen."

Percy relaxed. "Well, then, there's nothing else for it. I must ride out to Four Stones Ranch and propose to her straightaway." He glanced down at his dusty trousers and chuckled. "After I bathe, of course." He turned to mount his horse.

"Percy." Garrick gripped his arm, scrambling to think of a reason to prevent such a disaster. "Do wait. I beg you."

Percy laughed in his jolly way. "Whatever for?"

His obvious joy unsettled Garrick. Somehow he must stop his cousin.

"I simply cannot believe Miss Eberly is prepared to emigrate to England. I've seen nothing to convince me she'd prefer to leave family, home and community for a land that is foreign to her in every way that matters." Nor did she appear to have a penchant for finer things, finer society.

Percy eyed him doubtfully. "Truly?"

"Have you ever spoken of taking her home, even for a visit?"

Percy shook his head. "Although I did tell her about the beauties of the English countryside."

"Did she show interest? Say she'd like to see it?"

Again Percy shook his head. "Perhaps she thought that would be too forward, as though she were hinting for an invitation." He snapped his fingers. "That's it! I should have told her I want to take her there." He moved toward his horse again.

Garrick ground his teeth. "What about her school? She plans to be a teacher. She's worked as hard as Rosamond to build that lovely little building over there." He pointed down the block on the opposite side of Main Street. He wouldn't think of Rosamond's dedication to the same institution. Somehow he'd convince her to leave the school to Beryl's care. "I simply cannot think she'd be happy leaving all that she knows and loves. She would languish in England, longing for the familiar things of home."

Percy gave him an uncharacteristic glare. "Did something happen while I was away? Did someone else seek her company?"

A perfect opening. Garrick took care with his next words to avoid lying. "At the dance last evening, she stood up with one particular cowboy several times. They clearly enjoyed each other's company. Her smiles resembled those I've seen her cast in your direction." Although clearly lacked the affection she felt for Percy.

Percy's wounded expression cut Garrick to the quick, yet he must forge ahead to stop this ill-advised romance. "No doubt the young man was someone with whom she grew up."

"No doubt," Percy echoed, yet his voice was filled with doubt.

"You needn't cry off your friendship entirely, but why

not step back for a while? Take Richards and go explore those mountains to the west that you admire so much. You've wanted to since we first arrived. While you're gone, I'll try to observe whether she makes her preference for her cowboy known in other ways." Garrick set his hand on his cousin's shoulder. "Buck up, old boy. I cannot bear to see you hurt."

"I can always count on you to consider my welfare, cousin." Percy's shoulders slumped as he mounted his beast and rode away.

Watching him, Garrick felt an odd mixture of satisfaction and guilt so profound that his stomach ached.

After church on Sunday, Rosamond managed to avoid Garrick by chatting with Fred Brody and then Nolan Means. She made certain neither gentleman could misunderstand and think her interest was anything other than professional. First, she asked the newspaperman to advertise the new high school. Next, she encouraged the banker to enroll his fourteen-year-old sister in her classes. Both endeavors brought her hoped-for results, although Mr. Means did ask to come calling. With all the grace she could muster, she demurred, saying she was too busy preparing the school to entertain.

As she visited with other church members, she did manage to notice that Percy gave no more than a timid wave in Beryl's direction before Garrick claimed his cousin's attention. As if causing Tolley's exile weren't enough, he still seemed determined to keep Percy and Beryl apart. In turn, Beryl wilted like a parched flower and barely spoke on the trip back to Four Stones. After dinner, she announced that she would move back home. With their lesson plans prepared and only the painting of the classrooms left to be completed, she must help her family as harvest time drew near.

Rosamond felt nothing short of bereft. After spending almost two years with Beryl, both at the academy and here at home, she felt closer to her than the other Eberly sisters, even felt as if she were her own sister. Now she was leaving, all because of Garrick.

Why had she ever found him attractive? First he had destroyed her brother's life. Now he'd ruined her dear friend's happiness. Then, that evening, when Pete mentioned Percy had borrowed horses to go exploring, it was the last straw. Garrick had sent him away so he couldn't see Beryl, and Rosamond would never speak to him again as long as she lived.

Oh, bother. Of course she'd have to speak to him, at least when she inspected the completed hotel. She could only hope he'd go back to England as soon as the building was finished.

On Monday after the Fourth of July fire, Marybeth invited Rosamond and Susanna to her house to help sew a quilt. Four-year-old Lizzy and almost two-year-old Natty kept nine-month-old Randy busy, so he didn't seem to mind another new tooth trying to break through his gums.

"This quilt's for Randy's big bed when the time comes." Marybeth distributed scraps according to color and pattern so each of them could begin their assigned part. "I know it's early to start it, but I always find it's better to work ahead."

"Oh, my, yes." Susanna gave her a dimpled smile, and her blonde curls bounced as she nodded.

"Look." Rosamond held up a square of green plaid. "Susanna, remember when we made shirts for my brothers out of this material?"

Five years ago, Susanna and her father, Mr. MacAndrews, had been guests at Four Stones after outlaws stole their horses and left the old gentleman for dead. During their stay, Susanna had made herself useful around the house while her father healed. Her sewing skill had been a special blessing to the family when she made clothes and velvet drapes for the new ballroom.

"Indeed, I do." Her blue eyes twinkled. "I also remember how adorable Nate looked when I tried the sleeve pattern on him. Who could have guessed that such a big strong cowboy could blush?"

"Just don't let him hear you call him adorable," Rosamond warned. "And don't tell anyone he blushed."

They all laughed, and Rosamond's heart warmed for the first time in many days. As she continued to chat with her kinswomen, she began to feel as if she'd found a sanctuary. As much as she missed Beryl, maybe this was the Lord's way of bringing her closer to Susanna and Marybeth. She'd have plenty of time with Beryl when they painted the classrooms over the next few weeks. At least Rosamond hoped Beryl could spare a few hours from her ranching duties.

Although Rosamond was glad to have a reason for avoiding Mr. Wakefield, whom she no longer wished to address as Garrick, she felt no little dismay over misjudging Percy. She'd been so certain he loved Beryl. Of course, with her personality changes after being shot in the bank holdup, Beryl wouldn't expect Percy to love her. The once brave cowgirl had become fearful of everything and doubtful about her own worth. Maybe Percy was just being kind to show interest in her. Either that or he truly did love her, and Mr. Wakefield had forbade the romance. What mysterious hold did he have over his cousin?

"Don't you think, Rosamond?" Marybeth asked, and Susanna looked at her expectantly.

"I'm so sorry. I was lost in thought."

The other girls traded a look and then focused on Rosamond.

"I can't imagine why." Marybeth's tone held only a hint of teasing sarcasm.

Rosamond just smiled. She wouldn't speak ill of Mr. Wakefield or Percy, wouldn't even discuss them at all, at least not with these two dear ones, in spite of their sisterly bond. In time, maybe she'd talk with Mother about her foolish misjudgment of Mr. Wakefield. While she'd always believed in giving people a second chance, in his case, her first impression of him in the Denver train station had been correct. Nothing would ever change her mind about that, and the sooner he left Esperanza, the better.

Chapter Thirteen

"There. That's the last stroke." Rosamond stood back and admired the white paint drying on the classroom wall. "What do you think?"

"Very nice." Beryl gave her a weak smile and listlessly began to clean up the mess from their work.

For the past month, Rosamond had done everything possible to cheer her friend, but nothing seemed to work. With Percy exploring the San Juan Mountains, hopes for a renewal of their romance had faded. In fact, Rosamond's own emotions constantly teetered on the edge of depression, even as the work they'd completed gave her a feeling of satisfaction. In another month, classes would begin and her dream of becoming a teacher would become a reality.

She removed the tarpaulins covering the desks and rolled them to the side where Rand could remove them tomorrow. He and Nate had hung doors and finished the roof, tasks that she and Beryl couldn't manage. How could she and Beryl have finished the school without the help of her older brothers now that Tolley was gone? Thoughts of her younger brother always brought a pang to her heart.

"There you are, Miss Northam." Adam Starling peered into the classroom, his eyes bright with interest. "Say, this is a mighty fine schoolhouse."

"Hello, Adam." Rosamond waved him into the room. "Will you be attending our classes?"

"Yes, ma'am. My pa says I can come."

"I'm so pleased to hear that. Aren't you, Miss Eberly?" Removing her paint-spattered white apron, she gave Beryl an encouraging nod.

"Yes, indeed." Beryl's perfunctory remark wasn't supported by even a hint of emotion.

To make up for it, Rosamond brightened her smile. "How is your father, Adam? Has he recovered from his injuries?"

"He's getting better every day, ma'am." Adam surveyed the room, clearly admiring it. He ran a finger over a desk in the front row, his expression filled with awe. "Is this where we'll have our history lessons?"

"Yes, it is." Rosamond felt a tiny thrill inside. What an eager scholar this boy was! Having an actual student show such interest brought her dream even closer to reality. "Miss Eberly's science and mathematics classes will be next door."

"Yes, ma'am." Adam gave Beryl a polite nod, but his preference for history was clear.

"Did you come to help?" Rosamond appreciated the young men's labors, but most were now too busy with their farm and ranch work to volunteer more time.

Adam jolted. "No, ma'am. I mean, I'll be glad to help if you have a job for me. But Mr. Wakefield sent me over to invite you to inspect the hotel. He asked me to escort you there."

Rosamond felt her jaw drop. She stared at Beryl, whose wide-eyed astonishment mirrored her own. "Has he indeed summoned me?" She tried to keep the frost from her voice. After all, Mr. Wakefield's cruel deeds weren't Adam's fault.

Adam didn't appear to be intimidated. In fact, a crooked grin teased at one edge of his lips. "No, ma'am. Not summoned. It's an invitation."

Was the hotel already finished? Rosamond had done her best for the past month to avoid the Main Street corner just one block away, and not even so much as look in that direction. For surely by now, Mr. Wakefield's horrid Palladian facade would be in place, a sight she didn't wish to see. Now she could no longer avoid it. She had a responsibility to Father and to the community to make sure the Englishman hadn't made a muck of the hotel that was supposed to bring much welcomed business to Esperanza.

"Very well, Adam. Thank you." She noticed Beryl putting on her bonnet and gathering her reticule. "You're coming, of course."

Beryl hesitated. "Well…"

"Ma'am?" Adam shifted his feet. "Um, Mr. Wakefield said to bring just you."

Rosamond turned away from the boy so he wouldn't see her anger. Did this man think he was the lord of the manor and could decide who could come or not come to the hotel? Beryl didn't need this further rejection. And if Garrick—*Mr. Wakefield*—knew where Adam would find Rosamond, he must know her dear friend was with her. Why would he so cruelly exclude her?

"You go on." Beryl dabbed Rosamond's cheek with her handkerchief. "That spot of paint doesn't match your shirtwaist." She fussed with Rosamond's hair. "If you're going into battle," she whispered, "you should look your best."

"You're right." Rosamond accepted her friend's help. "Pray for me." As she said the words, guilt crept in. She hadn't truly prayed for weeks. Not since the day after the fire, when she'd made up her mind to have nothing more to do with Garrick Wakefield. Maybe after today, that could become possible. For now, she must inspect the hotel, make the necessary suggestions and leave him to his own devices.

"There. Much better." Beryl's winsome smile broke Rosamond's heart. "Go on, now."

Rosamond squeezed her hand. "I'll see you at church on Sunday."

She donned her blue bonnet and gloves and then left the schoolhouse to walk up dusty Main Street beside Adam. As they neared the hotel, she looked toward her destination. To her astonishment, instead of a Palladian facade, the building had a charming second-floor balcony along the front adjoined to the one on the south side, with a single door on each end that would permit guests to enjoy the fresh air without going downstairs and through the lobby.

Beneath the L-shaped balcony, new boardwalks had been laid, and several of the storefront shops were already occupied, with signs proclaiming Open for Business. One glass window read Mrs. Ryan's Millinery, a shop Rosamond planned to patronize often.

She entered the hotel reluctantly, preferring to turn around and go home. Adam opened one of the double doors leading to the lobby and gave her a little bow. "Ma'am."

"Why, thank you." She gave him a nod of approval. Her future student wouldn't see her distaste over being forced into this situation.

Inside the lobby, she drew in a quick breath at the

stunning beauty of the large room. The chandelier had been moved to a central spot near the front desk, just as she'd requested, and floral relief patterns circled the exquisite crystal gaslight fixture and extended to the corners. Elegant gold-and-blue-striped wallpaper provided a charming backdrop for the blue brocade chairs and brown leather divans. Although Rosamond had helped choose the decor, seeing the reality thrilled her beyond all that she'd expected. Not a spot of dust lay on any of the furnishings, and a pleasant fragrance wafted through the air from vases holding a variety of flowers.

"This way, ma'am." Adam beckoned to her, indicating the tall, wide archway into the dining room. For the first time, she noticed that he was wearing a rather fine pair of well-fitting brown trousers, a sparkling white shirt and even a little bow tie, a far different ensemble from his usual rustic clothing worn for his job at the livery stable.

Was this Mr. Wakefield's doing? If so, how could he be so kind to Adam and yet think nothing of causing pain to vulnerable people like Tolley and Beryl?

She stepped through the archway into the large dining room, which could easily seat seventy or eighty guests at the heavy round oak tables placed randomly around the room. One table near the center was set with a lustrous white damask cloth, fine china and sparkling crystal. A tall crystal vase filled with dark red roses graced the center of the table, the scent of the flowers vying with the aroma of roast beef for preeminence in the vast hall.

On the other side of the table, Mr. Wakefield awaited her. He wore his finest black suit, a gold brocade waistcoat and white shirt, looking every bit the aristocratic Englishman he was, except for the bolo tie she'd bought for him on the Fourth of July…and a little curl that had somehow escaped his perfectly coiffed hair to lie beguilingly across his wide forehead.

As she approached him, a sweet, vulnerable expression stole over his winsome, handsome face, and his brown eyes held a hope for...what? Her approval of his work? She could grant him that, for the hotel was indeed magnificent. But she steeled herself against any attempts to renew their former, ill-advised friendship.

"Rosamond, you are a vision of loveliness, as always." He pulled out a chair. "Please join me."

She hadn't planned to sit. Hadn't planned anything at all. Of course Mr. Wakefield would think only of his own appearance. If he intended to invite her to dinner, why hadn't he considered that she might wish to wear her best, too? Wasn't that the English way? To "dress" for dinner? And here she was, dressed in an old shirtwaist, a split skirt and well-worn boots because she'd ridden to town to paint the schoolrooms. Huffing out a sigh, she removed her gloves and bonnet before sitting at the table.

"Thank you for coming." He took his place on her right. "I hope you weren't inconvenienced."

"Not at all, Mr. Wakefield." She must be polite, mustn't shame her parents.

"Mr. Wakefield?" Puzzlement crossed his face as he leaned toward her. "Why—?"

"What happened to your Palladian facade?" Even though interrupting him was rude, she refused to quibble with him over the formal way she would address him from now on.

"Oh. That." He sat back, but rather than the dismay she expected, he smiled. And her heart dipped. Why must he be so devastatingly handsome? "It seems the builders were off a bit when they laid the foundation. They didn't leave enough space for the facade."

Rosamond studied him for a moment. The facade had meant so much to him, and yet he wasn't upset about the error. "I see."

"A small loss, hardly worth mentioning." He nodded to Adam, who'd taken up a post across the room beside the kitchen. The boy disappeared through the swinging door. "I hope you won't object to my ordering dinner for us."

Rosamond drew in a breath to indeed voice her objection, but the aroma of roast beef once again teased her senses. She'd started work early this morning and now could feel genuine hunger gnawing at her stomach. She wouldn't be so foolish as to reject some much-needed sustenance before her ride home.

"Thank you. It smells wonderful." *Oh, no.* Why had she said that? She didn't want to compliment anything he'd done to set this little scene.

Adam reappeared and placed steaming plates of food in front of them, while Roberts came from the kitchen with coffee. Rosamond picked up her fork, but Mr. Wakefield gently touched her hand.

"Would you permit me to offer thanks?"

Setting down her fork, Rosamond could only nod. She'd forgotten that he was a man of faith, albeit one whose faith didn't always prevent him from being a hypocrite. He probably believed in the divine right of kings to rule other people with impunity.

He said a short prayer that sounded heartfelt, thanking the Lord for the food, for the hotel, for the present company. When he ended the prayer, Rosamond echoed his *amen*, feeling very much like a hypocrite herself.

"I do hope you enjoy the roast beef." He gave a nod toward her plate, and she realized he was waiting for her to begin eating. "In the absence of our soon-to-arrive

Chef Henri, Roberts has initiated our kitchen. He began his life in service as a boy in my uncle's kitchen and learned many skills before Uncle's butler elevated him to footman. And then, of course, he became my valet."

"Mmm." Rosamond savored the rich flavors of the tender meat and creamed potatoes. Roberts was an excellent chef. She knew he'd enjoyed working with Rita in the kitchen at Four Stones. Maybe that was his true calling. Had Uncle even asked Roberts which job he preferred? Had Mr. Wakefield demanded that he become his valet? "I'll be sure to tell him how much I enjoy his cuisine."

Mr. Wakefield spent more time talking than he did eating, although he still managed to clean his plate as well as any hard-working cowboy...of course, with better manners. But what good were superficial manners when a man's heart harbored such unkindness? Rosamond's stomach ached, but not because of the food.

"After we finish dining, I should like to take you on a tour of the guest accommodations."

"I'd like that." Not really, but she had a responsibility to inspect the hotel. Once she gave Father a report on the progress of his pet project, she could be done with it.

"I must say, Rosamond, you are a lady of few words today." Mr. Wakefield gave her a look that puzzled her, as though he were suddenly shy. "I thought perhaps, with both of us being too busy to visit each other these past weeks, that we might have many things to discuss."

To her relief, she didn't have to answer him because Roberts approached the table. "Sir, may I bring dessert?"

"Ah. Yes, of course." Mr. Wakefield turned to Rosamond. "That is, if the lady agrees."

She smiled at the valet-turned-chef. "I'd like that very

much." She wouldn't be so rude as to turn Roberts down, not when his hazel eyes exuded such enthusiasm.

"If you give me a moment to whip the cream, I shall bring it straightaway." His returned to the kitchen with a decided bounce in his step, eager to display more of his culinary skills.

Mr. Wakefield cleared his throat. "Rosamond, you must permit me to tell you how much I ardently admire you."

Rosamond stared at him, her pulse racing. What did he mean to say?

"From the moment I saw you in the Denver train station, I've been drawn to your beauty and goodness. Although I realize the disparity between our families and friends, my heart will not be denied. I am forced to admit that I love you, Rosamond. I've considered the differences in our upbringings, but you have somehow escaped the hoydenish behaviors of your friends and the hostility and tomfooleries of your younger brother. All of their flaws I will gladly overlook to win your hand. Although my income is small, I will find a position in one of my uncle's enterprises to support you in a style that will not make you ashamed. We'll have a good life, and you'll do very well among my acquaintances. They'll consider you an original, a true treasure. Please say that you have some small care for me and that my appeal to your heart is not in vain.

"Will you do me the very great honor of becoming my wife?" He slipped from his chair to kneel beside her, taking her hand in his. "I don't have a ring to offer to you today because none I've seen in this isolated wilderness are worthy of you. If you'll be patient, I shall—"

"Enough!" Rosamond pulled her hand from his grasp and jumped to her feet, knocking over her chair in the process. "More than enough. Entirely too much." She spun away from the table, vaguely aware that she should inspect the rest of the hotel before leaving. But Garrick Wakefield's outrageous proposal was beyond insulting, and she couldn't remain in his company. She stormed toward the lobby but then turned back. Why should he get away with such behavior without reprimand?

The astonishment on his face momentarily clouded her resolve. Did he truly not comprehend how he'd insulted everyone and everything she loved?

"Mr. Wakefield." She strode back to the table, righted her chair and gripped its back for support. "If you think you have honored me in some grand way by your ill-conceived proposal, you could not be more in the wrong. How dare you speak of my family and friends and community in such a disparaging way, and then expect me to fall into your arms in gratitude that you deign to love a *rustic* American girl.

"Will your friends indeed consider me an *original*? I know what that means. They'll flatter me to my face, but snicker behind their fans. They'll tell each other that I was all you could manage to get for a wife after the loss of your expectations. And you would subject me to that sort of cruelty? But then, why not? You who have been beyond cruel to my brother and to my dearest friend."

His mouth hung open, and he stared at her as if she were some strange creature. She had no trouble continuing to scold.

"I would never live in England or raise my children in any country where one's wealth or social position is more important than character or initiative, preventing both personal aspirations and one's ability to follow God's will. What arrogance! If you even lightly study the history between our two countries, you'll see that is exactly what my ancestors left behind. They were no aristocrats. They were indentured servants, some who came willingly and some who were torn from their loved ones and sentenced to a life here for some imagined offense against one of your precious kings. In spite of that, on these shores alone of any land in this world, they made their own success, their own position. That is the *American* way."

In the corner of her eye, Rosamond saw Roberts holding two cream-covered pastries, his eyes wide. Beside him, Adam wore the same horrified expression. Yet she could feel no regret for her outburst. She snatched her bonnet and gloves from a nearby chair and raised a scolding finger to add one last verbal jab.

"Furthermore—"

"*Don't* bother, Miss Northam." Mr. Wakefield stood rigid, his chin raised in a defiant pose, his brown eyes now blazing. "You've made yourself perfectly clear. I'll gladly withdraw my 'ill-conceived proposal.'"

She glared at him for three long seconds. "Good." She spun around and strode from the dining hall. To her surprise, several of the workmen stood in the lobby gawking at her. Had they heard every word she'd said to Mr. Wakefield? If so, she'd shamed him in front of those who worked for him, admired him. Yet she could feel no regret. He was the one who'd plotted to propose to her where others could hear what was said. And because he'd destroyed the happiness of her brother and friend, she'd merely given him exactly what he deserved.

Garrick watched Rosamond march away from him, and with her went his anger…and his heart. How could he have been so mistaken? How could he have failed to notice her change of feelings toward him? He'd thought her polite reserve these past weeks was merely her way of respecting his wish to give him time to finish the hotel. He'd returned the favor by not claiming her time while she completed her school. In her absence, his love had grown stronger.

How did he fail to see the anger she harbored against him? Perhaps even hatred. And with just cause. Even a cursory review of his proposal mortified him. Why had he tried to explain the complications of the life he offered her? The considerations he'd made in overlooking what always appeared to him as inferior? No wonder she was enraged. If another man addressed her thus, Garrick would call him out for a round of fisticuffs. What a blithering numbskull he was.

"Sir?" Roberts placed on a sideboard the desserts he'd been holding. "May I help you in any way?"

The compassion in his voice cut into Garrick almost as much as the anger in Rosamond's tirade. Servants should never observe their masters being humiliated. Yet his valet, his young protégé, Adam, and several of the workmen had seen everything.

"Me, too, sir." Adam approached the table, his face pale beneath his tan. "What can I do?"

Garrick cleared his throat, which, oddly, felt thick and tight. "Roberts, kindly tell the workmen I said they are to resume their labors." He took great pains to speak casually, as though this were just another ordinary day on the job. But it wasn't, and he doubted any day in his future would be ordinary again. Without question, losing Rosamond's regard utterly and profoundly eclipsed losing his place as Uncle's heir. He couldn't even care that his humiliation had happened in public. That, too, was his own fault. What arrogance had possessed him to assume she returned his affections?

Suddenly, he couldn't catch his breath. He must get out of this place. "Adam, kindly remove these dishes and help Roberts clean the kitchen when he returns."

"Yessir." The lad hastened to obey.

No matter how he longed to escape, he mustn't neglect his duty. He found Mr. Schmidt on the second floor and instructed him to continue the work as planned for the next few days.

"*Ja*, Herr Wakefield. Ve vill manage it *gut*. You go on holiday, *ja*?" The German carpenter's response was a bit too cheery. He must have seen everything, too, or at the least heard the tale from one of the other men.

Soon everyone in Esperanza would know their beloved Miss Rosamond Northam had spurned the arrogant Englishman. And most of them would probably think he deserved it.

He waited behind the hotel's glass front doors until he saw Rosamond ride south on the road to Four Stones Ranch. As he waited, Dub Staley approached him.

"Mr. Wakefield, sir?" The troubled expression on the young workman's face sent a nervous jolt through Garrick.

"Yes, Dub? Is everything all right?" What more could go wrong this day?

"Yessir. No, sir." Dub shuffled from one foot to the other. "Sir, I have to tell you something."

Impatient to leave now that Rosamond was out of sight, Garrick nonetheless gave him a nod of encouragement. "What is it?"

"Ain't no way to say it 'cept right out. My girl's been after me since the fire to fess up, so I'd best do it." His face took on a sickly look, and he twisted his porkpie hat in his hands.

A cold chill swept down Garrick's back. "Go on."

"That night, I took Sally Anne to the hotel to show off the work I done. It was dark, and I lit a candle." His face flushed red. "I set it down so's I could give her a kiss. I was planning to propose, y'see. Got so plum nervous, I knocked the candle into a pile of canvas tarpaulins. They lit up in a flash, I guess 'cause of the paint thinner on 'em." He swiped at the sweat running down his face, along with a few tears. "If'n you want to have me arrested, I'll understand. So will Sally Anne."

Garrick stared at him. Tolley hadn't set the fire at all. Yes, he'd used that lariat to trip Garrick as he danced with Rosamond—a mean trick, but not life-threatening or destructive. Garrick had earned the comeuppance for the way he'd goaded Tolley at the shooting match.

"Sir?" Dub's miserable expression mirrored the emotions churning through Garrick.

"Go on, now, Dub. Marry your Sally Anne. No one needs to know who started the fire but the three of us." He forced a smile and a wink. "And I'm prone to being forgetful."

"Thank you, sir." A large grin split the lad's face. He grabbed Garrick's hand and shook vigorously. "I won't forget this. You ask me anything, and I'll do it for you."

As he watched Dub bound happily away, Garrick felt an envious ache in his soul. At least one man would soon marry his ladylove.

Making his way to Mrs. Foster's house, he pushed his feet forward on wooden legs. With each step, he felt the eyes of the community on him, although the few people who passed him offered pleasant greetings. Reverend Thomas hailed him from a half block away, but Garrick had no wish to be tempted to bare his soul to the minister, so he merely waved and kept walking.

As he entered the boarding house, Percy met him in the hallway. "Garrick, old boy. You look terrible."

"Percy." Garrick felt a glimmer of normalcy returning to his soul. With his cousin here, he could face anything. Percy had been with him through all of his losses. He'd stand by him, support him. "When did you get back? How was your trip?"

"Just arrived an hour ago in time for Mrs. Foster's fine dinner." Percy wore a sheepish grin, as though he hid a secret. "The trip was nothing short of extraordinary. I, um, *grubstaked* an old prospector in a place called Wagon Wheel Gap, and he found a vein of silver. We made a pretty penny on it. Increased my fortune by half." He shook his head. "Whatever will I do with all that money?" He sounded as though the windfall were a dreadful burden.

His jaw slack, Garrick could only stare at Percy. Everything his cousin did added to his wealth, while Garrick suffered loss after loss. When he could finally move, he clapped Percy on the shoulder.

"Congratulations. Well done."

"I say, old boy, you look a little pale. Is everything all right? Perhaps Mrs. Foster has some of that fine stew left for you."

"I've eaten, thank you." And even though he hadn't partaken of Roberts's cream-covered pastry, he felt certain he'd gotten his just deserts. If his heart weren't breaking at this moment, he'd laugh at his own wordplay, at his own rotten circumstances. What more in this life would the Lord take away from him?

"If you're not occupied at the moment, could we have a little chat?" Percy lifted a hand toward the parlor door.

"Of course." Grateful to have someone else's concerns to divert him, Garrick preceded his cousin and settled on the settee beside Mrs. Foster's sleeping cat. He reached out to pet the black-and-white creature, but as usual when he tried to befriend the beast, Pepper roused from his sleep, stretched in his feline way and jumped to the floor to scurry out to the kitchen. Garrick's heart sank lower. Even the cat rejected him. He sighed wearily and forced his attention to Percy, who sat across from him looking rather pleased with himself.

"You must tell me about your silver prospecting."

Percy waved away the question. "If you don't mind, there's another matter I must discuss with you. Or, rather, I must tell you about."

Garrick had never seen him so resolute. "Yes, of course."

Percy cleared his throat. "I've decided to court Miss Beryl Eberly and give that cowboy some competition. He may be an old friend, but after all the time she and I spent together, I cannot believe he has entirely won her heart."

Garrick's heart sank another inch. If he couldn't succeed in his own life, at least he could prevent his cousin from ruining his. "Percy, we've discussed this. Didn't you agree that Miss Eberly wouldn't be the best choice of wife for a man with ambitions to rise in Society? With this added wealth from your silver mine, you'll be all the more attractive to well-connected young ladies in London. Think of the good works—"

"When did I ever say I harbored ambitions to rise in Society?" Percy's innocent confusion startled Garrick. "Or agree that Beryl wouldn't make the best wife for me?"

"Why, often." He searched his mind for specific incidents but could think of none.

"Dear cousin." Percy stared down at his hands and chewed his lip. Then he gave Garrick a little smile.

"While on my trip, I've come to realize that you are the one who has those ambitions for me. My ambition is to buy a farm in the English countryside and raise cattle and children with a wife who loves me for myself and whose desires are the same as mine. You've spoken of the good works I can do from a position of prominence, but why must a man be well-known in Society in order to do them? Wouldn't our Lord be more pleased with anonymous good works? The right hand not knowing what the left hand is doing and all that?" He chewed his lip again, as though uncertain how to proceed. "I know you've always meant it for my good. Can you forgive me for disappointing you?"

Forgive him? Garrick could only grant him a brief nod as another devastating reality slammed into his mind. Percy was too kind in suggesting Garrick's ambitions for him had been without a selfish motive. He'd wanted his cousin to have the place he himself lost with the birth of Uncle's eldest son. Of course, Percy couldn't have a title, but with his wealth and a well-connected wife, he could rise as high as he wished in social influence. Garrick had tried to make Percy into himself, perhaps so he could live vicariously the life that he'd lost. He'd envisioned Percy being elected as an MP to the House of Commons, with Garrick at his side to advise him. The horror of his own selfishness made Garrick ill. There was only one thing for it.

"Well, then. What's keeping you?" He could hear the false cheer in his own voice. "Go straightaway and visit Miss Eberly's father to ask for her hand."

Clearly unaware of Garrick's distress, Percy brightened. "Truly? Do you mean it? You won't refuse to receive us when we return home? That is, if she chooses me instead of her cowboy, and will live in England with me. If she won't go to England, I'll have no choice but to buy my farm right here in America. In Colorado, near her family."

Emotion once again almost choked Garrick. "I'd never refuse to see you. How can you even think I would? Don't answer. I've been a complete cad." His lifelong friendship with his good cousin demanded more. "You have no competition for Beryl's affections. That cowboy was merely a friend. I've observed him sitting with another young lady at church these past weeks." This confession was painful in the extreme. Perhaps one day he'd confess the entirety of it: that he'd come near to lying to prevent Percy from marrying Beryl.

"Aha!" Percy laughed. "And I didn't even give you the opportunity to tell me that bit of good news before I blathered on about farms and wives and cattle and all that." He jumped to his feet and strode toward the parlor door. "I shall do as you say and go straightaway to see Beryl's father." He turned back and grasped Garrick's hand. "Thank you, cousin. You've always had my best interests at heart."

Before Garrick could contradict his unfounded praise, Percy dashed out, leaving him less distressed than he expected, but entirely pensive. How could he have been so wrong? Not only about Percy's life but about Rosamond's affections for him and Tolley's involvement in the fire? What an arrogant, self-serving, contemptible blighter he'd been. The time had come for some serious soul-searching. He followed Percy out of the house and made his way toward the church, praying he'd find Reverend Thomas.

He knocked on the parsonage door and breathed a sigh of relief when the minister called out, "Come on in."

How quickly he'd become accustomed to entering a

house without a butler admitting him. How quickly he'd felt free to call this minister a friend.

Reverend Thomas greeted him at the kitchen door and invited him to share some cake one of the church ladies sent over. "They take good care of me." He chuckled. "I have to be careful not to overeat."

"I understand. Mrs. Foster has an ongoing campaign to fatten me up." Sitting at the table, Garrick once again considered the differences between here and home. Kitchens had become his favorite place to eat. Not only were they filled with the aromas of mouth-watering foods, but they were places of easy camaraderie and agreeable conversation such as he'd never enjoyed dining formally with his friends in England.

After exchanging pleasantries, the minister gazed at Garrick with pastoral concern. "How can I help you?"

He required nothing more than that simple question to throw open the floodgates. He told Reverend Thomas everything from his reluctance to come to America because he considered the country and its people inferior, to his realization that he actually admired these American ranchers and cowboys. "None of them have been held back by an accident of birth, as one is in England…and most of Europe. Here, those with ambition and energy can make their own successes." He gazed out the kitchen window at the church next door, so unlike the ancient cathedrals of Europe, yet so beautiful in its simplicity.

Inhaling a deep breath for courage, he explained how his admiration and love for Rosamond had grown, despite their early disagreements. "I found myself willing to grant her every wish for the hotel, every wish for her life."

At last he related the story of his disastrous proposal, adding his suspicions about Tolley and how wrong he'd been about that, about everything. "Somehow I've misplaced all of my former certainties. I see things differently now. But it's too late. I've destroyed every chance for happiness with the only woman I've ever loved."

Reverend Thomas sat back and regarded him pensively. "How many holidays have you taken from your labors at the hotel?"

The question surprised Garrick. Mr. Schmidt had also mentioned a holiday. "Only your Independence Day and every Sunday since I arrived. Why?"

"Everyone needs a holiday from time to time. Why don't you and I explore some of our beautiful San Luis Valley before the cold weather sets in?" He leaned forward, just as he did in the pulpit when urging his parishioners to some good deed, only this time his eyes held a hint of excitement. "I'm an experienced camper and promise not to get us lost."

Garrick had expected to be admonished, even scolded by the minister. Instead, he'd offered Garrick a respite. "That sounds grand. But what of your church services this Sunday?"

"I'll send a note out to Nate Northam. He's filled in for me before." Reverend Thomas laughed. "Even a minister needs a holiday from time to time."

"Ah, very good." Garrick would write his own note, one to Rosamond asking her forgiveness for his misjudgments about Tolley…and Beryl. He wouldn't expect an answer, but at least his heart could rest easy for having done the right thing.

Though he doubted his heart would ever truly rest easy without Rosamond.

Chapter Fourteen

On Saturday afternoon, Rosamond waited in Susanna's pretty parlor while her sister-in-law put the children down for a nap. How blessed she and Nate were. The children were well. Nate was well. All was right in their world. As happy as Rosamond was for her two older brothers and their loving families, she couldn't help but feel a tiny bit jealous. Seeing such devotion in a loved one's eyes must be wonderful.

In truth, she had seen such devotion. Mr. Wakefield obviously and very mistakenly adored her. Or he had until she'd given him what for yesterday at the hotel. She exhaled a long, painful sigh. No telling what he thought of her now. But why should she care?

"There." Susanna entered the room and sat in the rocking chair, releasing a long sigh. "The children went right to sleep, so we can visit without interruption."

"Is there anything I can help you with?" Rosamond sipped the tea she'd prepared while Susanna tended the little ones.

"No. I'm caught up enough for now." Susanna's dimples always gave her a sweet, innocent look. "It's nice just to rest awhile." As she picked up her teacup, her gaze fell on Rosamond. "You seem sad, sugar. What's the matter?"

The gentleness in her voice broke something loose in Rosamond's chest, and before she realized it, she was crying. Susanna set aside her tea and hurried to kneel beside her.

"Oh, my dear, I'm so sorry. Please tell me everything."

In a rush of words, Rosamond told her about Mr. Wakefield: how he'd been so kind and generous to Adam but had destroyed Beryl's and Tolley's lives. Then there was his outrageous, insulting proposal. By the time she'd finished her tale, she'd dried her tears and fortified herself with indignation. She looked at Susanna, expecting support.

"Oh, my, my." Susanna stood. "I'll be right back." She hurried from the room and returned with a wrinkled sheet of paper. "This is a letter from my brother. He sent it to my father shortly after you left for Boston three years ago." Her eyes glistened, and Rosamond's heart lurched.

Five years ago, when Susanna and her father, Mr. MacAndrews, had been robbed and her father left for dead, Nate had rescued them and took them to the big house to recover. There Nate and Susanna fell in love. Mr. MacAndrews had also fallen in love with the Northams' cook, Angela, and they had married once he was back on his feet. They now lived just north of Esperanza. Because they were Southerners, the old gentleman had expressed concern about how his friends and neighbors back home in Georgia would react to his marriage to a Mexican lady.

"Tell me what he said." Rosamond didn't really need to ask. Pain was written all over Susanna's sweet face. "Never mind. Just let me read it." She reached out.

"Well…" Susanna hugged the missive to her chest and sniffed back tears. "I'd let you, but his language is unfit for a lady's eyes. I'm ashamed of my brother for writing it." She choked out a little laugh. "Actually, Daddy wouldn't let me read it, but I found it crumpled in the trash at his house. I'm sure Miss Angela doesn't know what evil things he wrote. Suffice it to say Edward Jr. disowned Daddy and me. Imagine that. *Disowned* his father and sister. He sent Daddy some money to pay for his part in their business and said we were never to try to visit them, for we wouldn't be received. In fact, he planned to announce to all of our friends that he'd gotten word of our untimely deaths, for we were surely dead to him."

"Dear Susanna." Rosamond dabbed her eyes on a handkerchief. "How cruel. If only your brother could know Angela. She helped to raise me, and she's a wonderful Christian lady. I know your family suffered during the war." To his later regret, Father, as a Union officer, had been responsible for burning their plantation house and stealing some of their belongings. Yet he and Susanna's father had reconciled and had actually become friends over the years. "But how can your brother be so unforgiving?"

"That's why I'm telling you about Edward's letter." Susanna pinned her with her bright, blue-eyed stare. "Forgiveness. I know Garrick's hurt you, but I also know you fell in love with him about two seconds after you met him. Everybody could see it. Your mama, Marybeth and I agreed you'd make a fine couple." She tilted her head in her sweet way. "Why don't you forgive him, sugar? Don't give anger a place. Give Garrick another chance."

Rosamond stood and embraced her sister-in-law. "I don't know if I can. What about his interference with

Beryl and Percy's romance? His accusation that Tolley started the hotel fire? If he hadn't been so cruel to Tolley at the shooting match, Tolley wouldn't have started the fight at the dance and Father never would have sent my brother away. He never wanted to go to Boston."

"I can understand your anger." Susanna glanced down at the letter. "I have a hard time forgiving Edward Jr. But I've come to realize that letting myself become bitter will only hurt me and, ultimately, Nate and the children. I'm not saying it's easy, but it is important." She offered a tender smile. "Just think of all that our Lord Jesus has forgiven us. Our loved ones' offenses pale in comparison."

Rosamond considered Susanna's words as she rode home and turned down Four Stones Lane. As she passed the house on the way to the barn, she noticed two horses tied to the hitching post out front. One looked like Beryl's mare, a welcome sight. She quickly accepted Pete's offer to tend her horse.

"Let me take care of her, Miss Rosamond." The old cowboy was always eager to make himself useful. "Say, when's that Englishman coming back out here? He wanted me to teach him some more 'cowboy lessons,' as he called them." Pete's leathery face turned pale. "Uh-oh. I done spoke out of turn."

Rosamond approached the wiry little man. "What cowboy lessons?"

Pete ducked his head and blew out a breath, clearly put out with himself. "I wasn't supposed to tell anybody, especially you, miss. But the cat's out of the bag now, so's I might as well tell you the rest. While he was staying out here that first week, he'd get up with the chickens and come out to the barn so's I could teach him all about being a cowboy." He chuckled. "With everybody saying what a sissy he was after that cow-branding mess, I could see he was trying to impress you, so's I planned to teach him everything I know." He shook his head. "Sure did have a good time with that boy. If he ever wants to come back, tell him I'm here."

Mr. Wakefield had tried to impress her? As Rosamond made her way across the barnyard to the house, she couldn't quite reconcile Pete's story with the fussy aristocrat Mr. Wakefield had been when he arrived. But with visitors to greet, she'd have to think about it later.

As expected, she found Mother in the parlor visiting with Beryl…and Percy! Beryl dashed across the room and flung her arms around Rosamond.

"Oh, Rosamond, I have the best news. Percy and I are engaged!" She held out her hand to reveal a lovely gold-and-pearl ring.

Rosamond squeezed her friend tightly before examining the ring. "It's beautiful!" She hurried to give Percy a hug and a kiss. "I'm so happy for you." A thread of suspicion wove through her mind. What did Mr. Wakefield think of this? Had Percy finally rebelled against his cousin? "Tell me everything."

Beryl gave Percy an expectant look.

His fair, sun-burned complexion grew redder than usual. "It was Garrick who urged me to propose. He's always had my best interests at heart, even with all of his responsibilities."

"Garrick?" Unable to fully grasp the idea, Rosamond glanced at Mother, who gave her a knowing look. Susanna had said Mother approved of Mr. Wakefield. Although they hadn't discussed it, surely Mother knew about their falling out. Maybe she didn't want to interfere. "It's a good thing his responsibilities at the hotel are almost finished."

"Yes, well." Percy took Beryl's hand and led her back to the settee, where they'd been sitting. "Then of course, there's Helena."

A shocking streak of jealousy coursed through Rosamond. "Helena?" Her voice squeaked as she spoke the name. She lowered herself into a chair to receive the next bit of news. Was Mr. Wakefield already engaged?

"Yes, his sister. He feels responsible for providing her dowry. Of course, I've told him I'd be delighted to provide a dowry for my much-beloved and only female cousin, but I think his pride won't let him accept."

His pride. How like the man. And yet, relief swept through Rosamond that this Helena was the sister for whom Mr. Wakefield had bought a gift at the July Fourth fair. But why? Rosamond had no claim on him. Had, in fact, rejected her opportunity to claim him as her own. Was that a terrible mistake? No, his insults toward her loved ones still reverberated through her mind and made her heart ache. In that moment, she wished she'd never met him.

"Are you truly pleased with our engagement, Rosamond?" Beryl's blue eyes begged for approval. "What about our school? How will you do without me?"

"I'll just have to find another teacher. We were planning to hire more anyway, weren't we?" Her eyes stung as she realized her good friend would likely move to England once she and Percy married. "I've a suspicion you only took part in my plans to please me. No, don't deny it. But I've always wanted you to be happy." Indeed, from the first, she'd only wanted Beryl to heal from her wounds, both physical and emotional. Now, with the bank robbery far behind her and a future with Percy right before her, she glowed with happiness.

"We can stay until your school is well established."

Percy gripped Beryl's hand. "That is, if it's all right with you, my dear."

"Oh, yes." Beryl leaned into his shoulder. "We'll start advertising for teachers right away and won't leave until we've hired only the best."

"We owe our happiness to Garrick, of course." Percy gazed at his fiancée with devotion beaming from his blue eyes. "If he hadn't insisted I come along on this venture of his, we'd never have met."

In spite of her own pain, Rosamond had been hasty to wish she'd never met Mr. Wakefield. Seeing her friend so happy made up for her own unhappiness. It was a small sacrifice. Truly, it was.

At supper that evening, Mother regaled Father with the news of Beryl's engagement, giving a glowing account of the visit.

"Good, good." Father's eyes twinkled. "Poor George Eberly, with five daughters to marry off. Two are taken care of. Only three more to go." He gave Rosamond the teasing look she'd always loved...until now. "Mother, what must we do to get shed of our only daughter?"

"Why, I have no idea, Frank." Mother blinked innocently. "Seems you did all you could when you put her together with that handsome young Englishman." She exhaled a dramatic sigh. "I suppose she'll just be a spinster teacher after all."

Rosamond could hardly keep from storming out of the room. Her parents had no idea what had happened yesterday, nor did they know how Mr. Wakefield had hurt Beryl and Tolley. Although Beryl's situation had worked out, Tolley remained banished because of that "handsome young Englishman."

Unable to stay quiet any longer, she burst out, "Father, why did you send Tolley away?"

"What?" He sat back and regarded her, his thick dark eyebrows bent into a frown, but one more of confusion than anger. "I didn't send him 'away.' We, your mother and I, sent him to school, just as we did you." He leaned forward again, his gaze troubled. "What's this all about?"

Inhaling a deep breath for courage, Rosamond gathered her wits. She'd never challenged Father because she'd never needed to. But in this case, he was wrong, and she meant to prove it.

"From the moment Garrick Wakefield arrived here, you've favored him over your own son. Tolley's always craved your attention, yet sometimes you acted as if he weren't even here. Why? Don't you see how you've hurt him?"

Father glanced at Mother, who gave him a sympathetic nod. Didn't she see how her youngest son had been wounded?

"Daughter, I love each of my children equally. But just as I couldn't deal with all of my soldiers in the same way, your mother and I couldn't rear you and your brothers alike." He huffed out a breath that was half laugh and half exasperation. "If you think I was hard on Tolley, just ask Nate what it's like to be the oldest son on a ranch."

Rosamond had never seen her father so vulnerable, but she couldn't relent. "That doesn't explain why you sent Tolley away."

"As I said—" Father scowled. "I didn't send him away. I sent him to school."

"But he never wanted to go. He loves being a rancher."

"Well, then, he can come back in a couple of years and be a rancher." A sharp edge entered Father's voice. "If that's what he still wants." Another sigh, and his voice gentled. "Daughter, you'll just have to trust me on this. Do you remember the Fourth of July race?"

"Of course."

"You remember the watchers along the race?"

She nodded.

"One of them, I won't say who, saw Tolley strike Garrick with his crop as they rode past him."

"No!"

"Yes. Not only that, but Nate told me about that nonsense during branding. Here's a young man from a foreign country, trying to fit in, trying to help out when he wasn't obligated to, and on his first day here, Tolley deliberately made a nasty mess of him. And that business at the dance? Did you know Tolley tripped Garrick with a rope? Nearly broke his skull when he fell." Father snorted out his disgust. "That was the last straw for me. I'd always planned to send Tolley to Harvard to be a lawyer. That's what our town needs, and I believe that's a good job for him. But he's a self-centered boy, and the time's come for him to learn to think about other people. If Garrick hadn't been the target of his jealousy, someone else would have been."

Rosamond felt as if she'd been crying all day, yet she couldn't stop the tears. So Tolley wasn't as innocent as she'd always believed. Yet Mr. Wakefield—Garrick—had never accused him. He'd only defended himself. No wonder he thought so little of her brother.

As she struggled to go to sleep that night, she still believed Father could have given Tolley more attention. But now she knew there was more to the situation. And Garrick. After that first day's humiliation, he'd gone to Pete to learn how to fit in…for her sake. She was beginning to see a better picture of the man. No matter how antiquated the custom in Rosamond's thinking, he felt responsible for providing a dowry for his sister so she could make a good marriage. Then there was Adam and his family. Garrick had saved them and sent Percy to find Mr. Starling, all without boasting or even wanting others to know about his good works.

She recalled her conversation with him about the Palladian facade. He could have impressed her by saying he'd changed his mind for her sake, yet he wouldn't take credit for something that was merely a mistake.

Susanna's words came back to her with full force. Rosamond must forgive Garrick for the unkind things he'd said, especially the ones founded in truth. Tomorrow after church, she would ask *his* forgiveness for misjudging him. If he refused to speak to her, she wouldn't blame him. But she knew full well that her heart would break.

Garrick awoke to find Reverend Thomas seated on a rock by the campfire reading his Bible. In his rush to finish the hotel, Garrick hadn't taken much time for Scripture reading recently. Perhaps that had been his downfall. He certainly hadn't depended upon the Lord in regard to Rosamond. Now, on this camping excursion, he'd reclaimed his reading habits.

"Coffee?" The minister held up a tin cup.

"Yes. Thanks." Garrick sat up and yawned. "I'm still surprised that sleeping on the ground can give a man such a good night's sleep." He rolled his shoulders to work out a bit of stiffness, more from their two weeks of riding and hiking than from bedding down on the forest floor.

Reverend Thomas chuckled. "It's the mountain air."

As he took up his Bible, Garrick accepted the steaming cup of coffee and drank despite the concoction's mud-like taste. At least it woke him up. Completing his devotionals, he asked, "Where shall we go today?"

When they'd first left Esperanza, Garrick had expected the minister to preach to him about his failures. But although they enjoyed daily theological discussions, Reverend Thomas was more a tour guide than a preacher. They'd ridden beyond the foothills to the west of Esperanza and far up into the mountains, encountering vistas of breathtaking beauty. Hiking over hills and riding Gypsy across streams, Garrick couldn't remember ever feeling so alive, so energetic. More effects of the mountain air, he supposed. The minister taught him how to cook beans and cornmeal mush over the campfire, how to catch fat trout in the Rio Grande, and how to dress a rabbit and roast it over open flames.

"Would you be interested in seeing some artwork? Rock paintings left by the ancient people who lived near here?" He offered Garrick a plate of warmed-over mush with chokecherry syrup poured over it.

"Artwork?" Garrick nodded his thanks as he pictured the larger-than-life ancestral paintings in Uncle's gallery. "In this primitive land?" As soon as the words were spoken, he wished them back. Hadn't he learned his lesson about considering others inferior?

The minister tossed the last of his coffee onto the fire. "You'd be surprised."

"Then I must see them."

Yet as he ate breakfast and helped Reverend Thomas clean up the campsite, he felt pulled in another direction. "If you've no objections, perhaps we can visit the paintings another time. Oddly, I sense an urgency to go home." Home? Yes, Esperanza felt like home to him, despite his failures there. Even though he'd sent a carefully worded letter to Rosamond and entrusted it to Adam to deliver, he still must repeat those words directly to her…and more. For he hadn't only fallen in love with her, he'd fallen in love with this beautiful San Luis Valley. Whether or not he could ever live here depended entirely upon her granting him forgiveness. And returning his love.

Accompanied by her parents, Rosamond inspected each of the forty hotel rooms, making notes along the way for improvements. Some of the rooms were furnished in an elegant European style, others in a homier Western theme. As usual, Father said very little, but Mother voiced her approval enthusiastically.

"The curtains and bedding Mrs. Beal and Mrs. Starling made for the cheaper rooms are just as lovely as those we imported for the expensive suites." Mother fluffed a pillow on a bed in one of those cheaper rooms. "Rosamond, I'm so proud of you."

"Quite an accomplishment," Father added, "considering all you've done at your schoolhouse at the same time. I'm proud of you, too, daughter." His face beamed. "Too bad Wakefield's not here to see the finished product."

Hearing Garrick's name brought a familiar ache to Rosamond's heart. He'd been gone for over two weeks, and she longed to apologize to him. Even though Reverend Thomas accompanied him, she worried some mishap had overtaken them. The minister had missed two Sundays, so unlike him. Nate filled the pulpit well, but the congregation would be disappointed if their minister stayed away too long.

Not that she hadn't been busy in Garrick's absence. Her days were filled with final preparations for the hotel's grand opening next Tuesday, September 3. The seamstresses had assumed additional duties, giving some rooms more feminine touches for the ladies. Roberts, Garrick's valet, had stepped up to train the newly hired staff. Chef Henri would arrive on this morning's train to take over the kitchen.

None of these daytime distractions helped her sleep at night. Even before Adam Starling had delivered Garrick's letter, she'd admitted to herself that she loved him and wished she could take back every angry word she'd spoken.

With each remembrance of young Adam, she smiled. The boy had witnessed her tirade against poor Garrick and seemed determined to defend his own defender. He spoke respectfully, but insisted she listen while he enumerated Garrick's many fine qualities, finishing at last with, "And Mr. Wakefield gave me that ten-dollar gold piece he won at the shooting match. Said it was to tide us over until my pa is back on his feet."

Just one more reason for her to admire and love Garrick. His letter had been filled with self-condemnation, and she longed to reassure him. He also said he knew Tolley didn't start the fire, making her realize she'd had her own suspicions about her brother after Father spoke of his selfishness. Garrick's letter set her fears to rest.

Father took out his pocket watch and opened it. "Train's due in fifteen minutes. We've just enough time to get to the station." The wily glint in his eye as he strode from the hotel room bespoke more than eagerness to meet the hotel's new chef. "Come along, my dears."

Rosamond questioned Mother with raised eyebrows. Mother shrugged and shook her head. "You know how he is. No telling what's up his sleeve." They both scurried after him.

The train chugged into the station with its usual squeal of iron wheels on iron rails and explosions of gray, puffy air from beneath its massive engine. People on the platform collected loved ones or took delivery of goods. Of the six cars attached to the engine, one caught Rosamond's attention.

"Look. It's a Pullman." She indicated the third passenger car. "My, how fancy."

"Come along." Father marched toward the elegant car like a man on a mission. Just as he reached it, a finely dressed man near his own age stepped down to the platform.

"Colonel Northam!" He reached out to shake Father's hand.

"Lord Westbourne." Father responded in kind to his old friend. "Welcome to Esperanza. What do you think of our little town?"

"Very fine. Just what I expected." The gentleman offered a hand to a much younger lady disembarking the train.

"Oh, my." Mother huffed out a sigh. "I wish he'd told me guests were coming." She stepped over to join him. "Welcome, Lord Westbourne, Lady Westbourne."

Rosamond watched in amazement as her parents greeted the friends they'd met in Italy two years ago. The friends with whom they'd plotted to build the hotel. Plotted? Yes, that was exactly the right term.

"Rosamond, come meet these folks." Father beckoned to her.

Folks? Even with her mild disdain for European nobility, she knew better than to call them "folks." Yet the earl and countess didn't seem to notice.

His manners returning, Father presented her to them, as was proper. They were such an elegant couple that she almost curtsied. Almost.

"So this is the young lady you put in charge of my nephew." The earl gave her a courtly bow. "How do you do, Miss Northam."

"Very well, sir." In charge of his nephew? No, she feared she'd lost her chance even to be Garrick's friend.

"How lovely you are, my dear." The countess gave Rosamond a gracious smile and slid a knowing glance in her husband's direction. "I can well imagine our Garrick enjoyed working with you."

Rosamond returned a weak smile. "It's been my pleasure, Lady Westbourne." It truly had been, once they'd sorted everything, well, *most* things, out.

"Papa." An adorable, dark-haired little boy of perhaps six years stood in the door of the train, his tiny hand clutched by a uniformed young woman, no doubt his nursemaid. "May I get down, too?"

The earl gave an indulgent chuckle. "Yes, yes. Come along, my boy." He then introduced his eldest son, little Viscount Lord Eddington, just as he would an adult. So this was the child who'd supplanted Garrick as Lord Westbourne's heir. Rosamond could see a resemblance to Garrick in both father and son. "Left the two younger ones at home. Sea voyage was hard enough on Lady Westbourne and Miss Wilkes." He nodded toward the nursemaid.

Rosamond understood that would be their only introduction to the young woman. No such courtesy would be offered to the small army of servants disembarking from the back of the car…except for one.

"Henri." The earl called forward a tall, slender man in a black suit. "This is Chef Henri. Miss Northam, I place him in your charge."

The brown-haired Frenchman was younger than she'd expected, perhaps thirty. He gave her a bow that conveyed both self-respect and servanthood.

"Have a care, sir." One of the earl's servants, perhaps the butler, who supervised the others, spoke sharply to the train employees unloading trunks and luggage from the baggage car. "These belong to *Lord* Westbourne."

One of the workers spat to the side. "We only have one Lord around here, mister, and He ain't him." He jabbed a thumb in the earl's direction.

"Now see here—" The short, stout butler puffed up like a bantam rooster.

"Now, now, Edwards." The earl chuckled. "When in Rome." He stepped over to calm the confusion.

Mother tugged on Father's sleeve and spoke in an urgent whisper. "Frank, where on earth are we going to put all of these people?"

He patted her hand and winked. "In the hotel, of course."

While Mother breathed a sigh of relief, Rosamond's heart lurched. The hotel wasn't ready. *She* wasn't ready. And worst of all, Garrick wasn't here to receive the reward for all of his hard work on his uncle's behalf.

Chapter Fifteen

Garrick flung himself on his bed in Mrs. Foster's boarding house. The down mattress felt strange after more than two weeks of sleeping on the ground but would no doubt make for an excellent rest before supper. The bed's softness enveloped him and straightaway began to soothe away his fatigue. He didn't even care that Roberts was nowhere to be found to draw his bath. That could come later. Hot water in a brass tub made for better bathing and shaving than icy mountain rivers. Reverend Thomas had urged him to let his beard grow, but that was one concession to Western life he'd forgo. No, he must be bathed, well-dressed and clean shaven when he went to Rosamond, hat in hand, to learn whether or not she would forgive him.

With dreams of her lovely face dancing through his mind, he surrendered to sleep until a soft knock on the door roused him.

"Mr. Wakefield?" He hadn't been able to persuade Mrs. Foster to call him Garrick.

"Yes, Mrs. Foster." He rolled over and sat on the edge of the bed. His mantel clock read three twenty-four. He'd slept only half an hour.

"Young Adam is here," she said through the door. "Will you see him?"

Garrick chuckled. Adam had been dismayed at his departure. Even begged to tag along. "Yes, Mrs. Foster. Send him up." He yawned and scratched his head. Yes, a bath was in order—the sooner, the better.

Adam knocked and then opened and peered around the door. And grinned from ear to ear. "Welcome back, Mr. Wakefield." He stepped into the room. "I suppose you heard."

An odd foreboding sent a shiver up Garrick's spine. "No, actually, I haven't heard. You are my herald. Kindly announce your news."

Adam continued to grin. "Land sakes, you sure do look like him."

Another shiver. "Like whom, my lad?"

"That fancy Lord Westbourne up at the hotel. Course, he's a lot older—"

"Lord Westbourne? My uncle is here?" Garrick's heart dropped to his stomach. Now he must pay for abandoning his post for an ill-advised holiday, leaving the unfinished hotel to common workmen to complete without supervision. An involuntary groan escaped him. After a two-week reprieve, judgment would now fall upon him for his neglect.

"Yessir." Adam stared at him up and down. "You might want to clean up a mite before you go see him. They're awful fancy people."

"They?"

"Yessir. The lady and the boy." He shook his head. "And a passel of servants. Why do three people need so many servants?"

As Garrick tried to calm his racing heart, he gave

Adam a rueful smile. After tending his own needs for these past days, he wondered that himself.

"Can I help you, sir?"

"Indeed you may." He certainly wouldn't turn down that offer *or* correct the boy's grammar. "I shall be eternally grateful."

Uncle often spoke of the importance of fastidiousness, so it wouldn't do to show up at the hotel without bathing. While Garrick soaked away over two weeks' worth of soil and sweat in a lukewarm bath, he enumerated in his mind the many tasks not completed before he left. Wallpaper and drapes in the finer suites. Painting, drapes and bedding for the lower-class rooms. Wall sconces and the artwork. Completing the manager's office. Surely other tasks, but as Garrick's anxiety grew, he couldn't remember them all. This had been his one chance to prove himself capable of managing an important project, and he'd failed. He must get to Uncle straightaway and explain himself.

Yet, as he shaved and dressed, an even more important matter took preeminence and at last settled his nerves. He hadn't hurried home from holiday because of Uncle, but because of Rosamond. She must be his first priority. Instead of going to the hotel, he'd ride out to Four Stones Ranch to beg her forgiveness. The affection he'd seen in her eyes from time to time had been genuine. Perhaps he could still win her.

"Adam, my lad." Garrick fussed with his cravat, unable to fix the knot. Where was Roberts when he needed him? "Would you be so kind as to procure a horse for me? Gypsy's done enough today, and I must go to Four Stones before joining my relatives at the hotel."

"Yessir." The lad still wore that maddening grin. "But she ain't there."

Garrick glared at Adam and then chuckled as his heart leapt in his chest. "Oh? Then where is she?"

"At the hotel, of course." Adam had the audacity to wink.

Of course! Rosamond had nearly as much to gain from the hotel's success as Garrick did. She would be there to entertain Uncle.

His heart plummeted again. His comeuppance had been public, and his apology would be the same. But he wouldn't let that deter him. He gave Mrs. Foster his regrets for missing the supper she'd started preparing. Then he strode from the house, Adam following close on his heels.

Rosamond brought flowers, an extra vaseful from the hotel, to place at the front of the church for tomorrow's service. As she turned to leave, the minister entered through the side door. With his short, bushy beard and dusty clothes, he looked like a cowboy newly returned from a cattle drive. The dear man surely did need a wife.

"Hello, Reverend Thomas. Welcome back." Her heart hiccuped. Garrick would be back, too.

"Thank you, Rosamond. You look mighty pretty in that fancy gown. Are you going to a ball?" He set some papers on the lectern.

"Thank you." She walked close enough to catch a whiff of his clothes. Mercy, he needed a bath before tomorrow's service. "Not a ball, but we're having a party at the hotel for Lord and Lady Westbourne. Won't you join us? You can slip in the back door and use one of our fancy new bathrooms to clean up before you meet them."

"I'd be delighted." He studied the papers. "Good thing I planned my sermon as soon as we returned." He gave her a teasing grin. "You should tell Garrick. He's at Mrs. Foster's."

Her heart jolted again. "Good idea."

He chuckled. "See you at the hotel."

She hurried from the church. Turning down Pike Street, she had the sudden fear he wouldn't want to see her. Then she saw him striding toward her. She lifted the hem of her skirt and ran to meet him. Oh, how handsome he looked. From his wide smile and quickened pace, he seemed just as eager to see her.

Before she knew what happened, she was in his arms, and he was lifting her and swinging her around in a circle. They both laughed like school children let out for recess, her laughter mingling with tears.

"Oh, Garrick, I'm so sorry—"

"Rosamond, can you ever forgive me?"

They spoke at the same time and laughed again. She moved back a little in his arms to stare into his wonderful face.

"I understand about Tolley. You weren't to blame. And Percy and Beryl are so happy—"

"I've been an arrogant numskull. Now I see what a splendid place Esperanza is, the entire San Luis Valley, the entire United States, in fact. Wonderful people live here, many of whom I'm proud to call my friends." A shy look stole over his fine features. "I still love you, Rosamond. But I won't torment you with another brutish proposal. If you want to send me away—"

She grasped his face and stopped him with a kiss, feeling not the slightest shame that she'd instigated yet another kiss with this man. Right here on the streets of Esperanza where all of her neighbors could see them. Right here in front of Adam, soon to be one of her students.

Garrick pulled her close and returned the kiss with a depth of feeling that mirrored her own. Perhaps lengthy apologies weren't necessary. In fact, nothing mattered right now except knowing that Garrick Wakefield loved her as much as she loved him. Whatever happened in the future regarding marriage and her school, they would face it together and figure out how to make everything work.

Garrick carried his eldest cousin in his arms while Uncle conducted a tour of the hotel as though he'd built the place himself. Aunt Westbourne and Rosamond, Colonel and Mrs. Northam, and Percy arm-in-arm with Beryl, all trooped along behind them.

"You see what can be accomplished, my boy?" Uncle spoke to little Lord Eddington as he pointed to various items of interest in one of the finer rooms. "Take note. You must always find clever people to do the work." He continued on down the hall, unmindful of the cut Garrick felt to his heart.

From childhood, he'd been the receiver of Uncle's tutelage as he prepared him to inherit the title. Now that instruction went to the viscount. Yet never once in the past six years had Garrick regretted the existence of this precious boy who'd greeted him so joyfully just an hour ago, proclaiming how he and his brothers missed their dear cousin Garrick. Nor could he regret any circumstances that had brought him to Rosamond. This wasn't the life he'd expected or planned, but God's plan was proving to be far better.

"Although I believe the Palladian facade our architects originally designed would be superior to the, ahem, more modest front my nephew chose." Uncle glanced at Garrick as he addressed Colonel Northam.

A nervous sensation skittered through Garrick. He hadn't been paying attention. Behind him, however, he heard Rosamond's soft snicker and suppressed a laugh.

The facade would be their private joke. Someday he'd confess to her that when he'd come here, he'd had his own facade as ornate and well-ordered as anything Andrea Palladio had designed. Yet, in this wild, untamed land, that false front had crumbled away to reveal a better, perhaps humbler man.

Uncle had laughed off Garrick's clumsy explanation about his letter requesting permission to abandon the project and the second one saying he wanted to stay until it was finished. "I read the second letter first, so didn't bother with the first." Garrick couldn't have asked for more.

Later in the dining room, as Chef Henri served a supper befitting a king and Roberts directed the serving staff, Uncle continued his commentary, albeit with no criticisms. Aunt Westbourne must have spoken to her husband. Although half his age, the countess was a positive influence on him.

"I say, nephew." Uncle looked up from his soup. "Are you pleased about Helena's engagement?"

Garrick started. "Engagement?" He stared at Uncle. "When? Who?" And why hadn't he been consulted?

"Why, Lord Waverly, of course." Uncle chuckled. "In your absence, I granted my permission. And a suitable dowry, of course."

Garrick sputtered for a moment until he noticed Rosamond smiling across the table. Now they could marry without impediment. Another of God's blessings.

"You have my thanks, Uncle." More than thanks. If he were wearing his Stetson, he'd toss it into the air like a celebrating cowboy. "Waverly is a decent sort." And titled. "I know they'll be happy."

"Perhaps you'll be there in time for the wedding in

October," Aunt said. "We should so like to have you visit us."

The dear lady couldn't know how her words cut one last thread holding him to England. If he returned, he could only be a guest in his relatives' homes. In America, he could make his own home. Again, he looked across the table at Rosamond while answering his aunt.

"Thank you, madam. However, I plan to stay in Esperanza, so please convey my best wishes to my dear sister. You see, I've discovered I've an aptitude for teaching and thought I'd apply at the new high school."

The joy glowing on Rosamond's beautiful face suggested he'd have no trouble obtaining the position.

Epilogue

Saturday, March 28, 1884

"Sir, if you would just hold still." In the parsonage bedroom, Roberts fussed with Garrick's cravat, finally securing it with a ruby tie pin. "There." He took out his brush, whisked it over Garrick's black suit and stood back to survey his handiwork. "Now, sir, I believe you are ready to meet your bride."

"Thank you, Roberts." Garrick viewed himself in the wardrobe mirror. The jewelry was only one example of Uncle's generosity before he had returned to England the previous autumn. He'd paid Garrick handsomely for his work on the hotel. Now Garrick could bring to his marriage more than just his small inheritance. Rosamond cared for none of it, of course, but for Garrick, it was a point of self-respect. He could abandon many of his aristocratic notions, but not this one: a husband must provide for his wife, even when they planned to live with her parents until their own home was built.

On the other hand, how many aristocrats asked their valets to stand up with them for their weddings? Roberts and Richards had both expressed shock, but accepted their employers' invitations with pride. Nate and Rand had also agreed to groomsmen duties.

"I say, old man." Percy stood still while Richards inspected his appearance. "Did I not predict we'd marry our lovely brides?"

"Not at all, cousin." Garrick smirked. "You said by the end of summer, but here we've had to wait through the long cold winter."

"Ah, well, then, I suppose I must concede the point."

Nate, Rand, Reverend Thomas and the valets all chuckled, and Garrick eyed his cousin with affection. Another notion he'd abandoned was his objection to Percy's marriage. Over these past months, Percy had become considerably more assertive, with Beryl's help, and she was no longer the shy, fearful girl they'd seen on the train. Clearly, they were good for each other.

"Time to go, gentlemen." Reverend Thomas closed his watch and tucked it into his waistcoat pocket. "Let's not keep your brides waiting."

Garrick noticed a hint of loneliness in the minister's eyes. He'd no doubt conducted many weddings in the pretty little church next door. At some appropriate time, Garrick could suggest that he find a wife for himself. Or perhaps Garrick and Rosamond could play matchmaker for this godly man, just as Uncle and Colonel Northam had for them. Deny it though the older men did, the truth was evident this very day as Garrick left the parsonage and walked toward his future.

Rosamond and Beryl stood in the cloakroom at the back of the church wearing Marybeth's and Susanna's white wedding gowns respectively, and carrying white roses from Nolan Means's hothouse. Father looked very fine in his new black suit, while George Eberly twitched uncomfortably in his brown tweed. Mrs. Foster began to play "Amazing Grace," the wedding hymn the brides had agreed upon. Rosamond's two sisters-in-law and Laurie and Georgia Eberly, walked down the aisle, followed by the brides and their fathers.

Family, friends and students from Esperanza High School filled the small church to overflowing. Rosamond's brothers and the two valets stood at the front with the minister and the two grooms. But Rosamond had eyes only for Garrick. How could a man be so handsome? Her heart thrilled every time she looked at him. In just a few minutes, he'd be hers forever.

In the corner of her eye, she saw Rita, newly married to Roberts in her home church southeast of town. Today they were catering the reception at the hotel. An amusing little squabble between Roberts and Chef Henri had decided the matter, but Roberts would now be working at Four Stones Ranch, the extra help Mother needed these days now that Rosamond and Garrick would be living at the ranch and both of them would be teaching.

When they reached the front, Rosamond focused again on Garrick, barely hearing Reverend Thomas as he led the two couples through their vows. The most important words came through clearly, however, when the minister said, "I now pronounce you man and wife," to Percy and Beryl, "and man and wife," to Rosamond and Garrick. "You may kiss your brides."

The reception was also a time of departure. Beryl and Percy would leave on Monday for England, where they'd have their country farm and, hopefully, a houseful of children. Rosamond and Garrick would follow in June at the end of the school term, but only for a summer honeymoon. On their way, they'd stop in Boston to visit

Tolley. An exchange of letters with her brother gave Rosamond hope that he'd be amenable to reconciliation with Garrick. Father had been right, as always. Her younger brother needed to grow up. She prayed every day he would find his way, just as she, Nate and Rand had done.

"Penny for your thoughts." Garrick slipped an arm around Rosamond's waist.

She leaned into his shoulder. "No charge for this, Mr. Wakefield. You've made me the happiest woman in the world."

"And you've made me the happiest man, my dearest." The look in his warm brown eyes asked permission for another kiss, which she gladly granted—just one of many more to follow.

* * * * *

Dear Reader,

Thank you for choosing *Cowgirl for Keeps*, the third book in my Four Stones Ranch series. I hope you enjoyed the adventures of my heroine, Rosamond Northam, and my hero, Garrick Wakefield. For many years I have wanted to write a series of stories set in the beautiful San Luis Valley of Colorado, and now I'm doing just that.

I moved to the Valley as a teenager, graduated from Alamosa High School and attended Adams State College. Later my husband, David, and I settled in Monte Vista, where my parents owned and operated a photography business, Stanger Studios. Three of our children were born in Monte Vista, and one was born in Alamosa. Even though we moved to Florida in 1980, my heart remained attached to my former home in Colorado. Writing this series has been a sweet, nostalgic trip for me.

Those familiar with the history of this area of Colorado may recognize a little bit of Monte Vista in my fictional town, Esperanza. I could have used the real town, but then I would have shortchanged the true pioneers of Monte Vista, who deserve accolades for their courage and foresight in building such a fine community. In addition, I wanted the freedom of artistic license necessary to create an interesting story without offending the residents of my former home. Any resemblance between my characters and those who actually settled in this area is strictly coincidental.

If you enjoyed Rosamond and Garrick's story, be on the lookout for more stories set in my fictional town of Esperanza.

I love to hear from my readers, so if you have a comment, please contact me through my website: blog.louisemgouge.com.

Blessings,
Louise M. Gouge

COMING NEXT MONTH FROM
Love Inspired® Historical

Available August 4, 2015

FRONTIER ENGAGEMENT
Frontier Bachelors
by Regina Scott

After schoolteacher Alexandrina Fosgrave is stranded in the wilderness with James Wallin, he offers her his hand in marriage to protect her reputation. Both are afraid to fall in love, but could an engagement of convenience make them reconsider?

THE TEXAN'S COURTSHIP LESSONS
Bachelor List Matches
by Noelle Marchand

Since Isabelle Bradley would never marry her sister's former suitor, she offers to help Rhett Granger court himself a wife. As she warms to Rhett, a future together doesn't seem so difficult to imagine—but is she too late?

PROMISE OF A FAMILY
Matchmaking Babies
by Jo Ann Brown

After Captain Drake Nesbitt discovers a tiny boat of foundling children adrift at sea, he and Lady Susanna Trelawney begin searching for their families. What they'll discover is an unexpected love that anchors their wayward hearts.

SECOND CHANCE LOVE
by Shannon Farrington

When her fiancé dies suddenly, Elizabeth Martin believes her life is over. It's up to her betrothed's brother, David Wainwright, to help her through the pain...without falling for his brother's almost-bride.

REQUEST YOUR FREE BOOKS!

2 FREE INSPIRATIONAL NOVELS
PLUS 2 FREE MYSTERY GIFTS

Love Inspired HISTORICAL

YES! Please send me 2 FREE Love Inspired® Historical novels and my 2 FREE mystery gifts (gifts are worth about $10). After receiving them, if I don't wish to receive any more books, I can return the shipping statement marked "cancel." If I don't cancel, I will receive 4 brand-new novels every month and be billed just $4.99 per book in the U.S. or $5.49 per book in Canada. That's a saving of at least 17% off the cover price. It's quite a bargain! Shipping and handling is just 50¢ per book in the U.S. and 75¢ per book in Canada.* I understand that accepting the 2 free books and gifts places me under no obligation to buy anything. I can always return a shipment and cancel at any time. Even if I never buy another book, the two free books and gifts are mine to keep forever.

102/302 IDN GH6Z

Name		
	(PLEASE PRINT)	

Address		
		Apt. #

City	State/Prov.	Zip/Postal Code

Signature (if under 18, a parent or guardian must sign)

Mail to the **Reader Service**:
IN U.S.A.: P.O. Box 1867, Buffalo, NY 14240-1867
IN CANADA: P.O. Box 609, Fort Erie, Ontario L2A 5X3

Want to try two free books from another series?
Call 1-800-873-8635 or visit www.ReaderService.com.

* Terms and prices subject to change without notice. Prices do not include applicable taxes. Sales tax applicable in N.Y. Canadian residents will be charged applicable taxes. Offer not valid in Quebec. This offer is limited to one order per household. Not valid for current subscribers to Love Inspired Historical books. All orders subject to credit approval. Credit or debit balances in a customer's account(s) may be offset by any other outstanding balance owed by or to the customer. Please allow 4 to 6 weeks for delivery. Offer available while quantities last.

Your Privacy—The Reader Service is committed to protecting your privacy. Our Privacy Policy is available online at www.ReaderService.com or upon request from the Reader Service.

We make a portion of our mailing list available to reputable third parties that offer products we believe may interest you. If you prefer that we not exchange your name with third parties, or if you wish to clarify or modify your communication preferences, please visit us at www.ReaderService.com/consumerchoice or write to us at Reader Service Preference Service, P.O. Box 9062, Buffalo, NY 14240-9062. Include your complete name and address.

LIH15

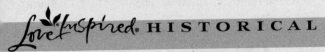
"Alexandrina," James said, guiding his magnificent horses
up a muddy, rutted trail that hardly did them justice.
"That's an unusual name. Does it run in your family?"

She couldn't tell him the fiction she'd grown up hearing,
that it had been her great-grandmother's name. "I don't
believe so. I'm not overly fond of it."

He nodded as if he accepted that. "Then why not
shorten it? You could go by Alex."

She sniffed, ducking away from an encroaching branch
on one of the towering firs that grew everywhere around
Seattle. "Certainly not. Alex is far too masculine."

The branch swept his shoulder, sending a fresh shower
of drops to darken the brown wool. "Ann, then."

She shook her head. "Too simple."

"Rina?" He glanced her way and smiled.

Yes, she definitely knew the power of that smile. She
could learn to love it. No, no, not love it. She was not here

to fall in love but to teach impressionable minds. And a smile did not make the man. She must look to character, convictions.

"Rina," she said, testing the name on her tongue. She felt a smile forming. It had a nice sound to it, short, uncompromising. It fit the way she wanted to feel—certain of herself and her future. "I like it."

He shook his head. "And you blame me for failing to warn you. You should have warned me, ma'am."

Rina—yes, she was going to think of herself that way—felt her smile slipping. "Forgive me, Mr. Wallin. What have I done that would require a warning?"

"Your smile," he said with another shake of his head. "It could make a man go all weak at the knees."

His teasing nearly had the same effect, and she was afraid that was his intention. He seemed determined to make her like him, as if afraid she'd run back to Seattle otherwise. She refused to tell him she'd accepted his offer more from desperation than a desire to know him better. And she certainly had no intention of succumbing to his charm.

Don't miss
FRONTIER ENGAGEMENT by Regina Scott,
available August 2015 wherever
Love Inspired® Historical books and ebooks are sold.

LIHEXP0715

SPECIAL EXCERPT FROM

Love Inspired®

Reuniting with her high school sweetheart is hard enough for Tessa Applewhite, but how much worse will it get when she realizes the newly returned cowboy has brought with him a baby son?

Read on for a sneak preview of **Deb Kastner**'s
THE COWBOY'S SURPRISE BABY,
the next heartwarming chapter in the series
COWBOY COUNTRY.

"So you'll be wrangling here," Tessa blurted out.

"Yep." His gaze narrowed even more.

Well, that was helpful. Tessa tried again.

"You've been discharged from the navy?"

He frowned and jammed his fists into the front pockets of his worn blue jeans. "Yep."

She was beyond frustrated at his cold reception, but she supposed she had it coming. She could hardly expect better when the last time they'd seen each other was—

Well, there was no use dwelling on the past. If Cole was going to work here with her, he would have to get over it.

So, for that matter, would she.

"Well, I won't keep you," she said, reaching back to open the office door. "I just wanted to make sure we had an understanding about how our professional relationship here at the ranch was going to go."

He scowled at the word *relationship*. "Just came as a surprise, is all," he muttered.

"I'll say," Tessa agreed.

"Didn't expect to be back in Serendipity for a few years yet. Maybe ever."

He sounded so bitter that Tessa cringed. What had happened to the boy she'd once known? Who or what had darkened the sunshine that had once shone so brilliantly in his eyes?

"Cole? Why did you come back now?"

He tipped his hat and started to walk past her without speaking, and Tessa thought she'd pushed him too far. Whatever his issues were, clearly she was the last person on earth he'd talk to about them.

He was almost out the door when he suddenly swiveled around to face her.

"Grayson." His gaze narrowed on her as if weighing the effect of his words on her.

She scrambled to put his answer in some kind of context but came up with nothing.

"Who—"

He cut off her question and ground out the rest of his answer.

"My son."

Don't miss
THE COWBOY'S SURPRISE BABY by Deb Kastner,
available August 2015 wherever
Love Inspired® books and ebooks are sold.